Whispers on the Wind

Whispers on the Wind

Kelly turned in a crouch, the knife appearing again, and as he completed the turn, just a microsecond from hurling the knife, he saw Donnelly pull his hand, empty, from under his jacket. Kelly altered his aim slightly and buried the knife in the wall, scarcely a inch from Donnelly's ear. Donnelly's head did not move; only his eyes turned sideways to look at the knife.

"Just as well you did," Kelly said, making an elaborate show of removing the knife from the wall, folding it back into his wrist sheath. "I'll be talking to ya." And with that he left the room, with Tommy Mulholland still on the floor and Josie Donnelly's mouth agape.

Whispers on the Wind

Roy French

Whispers On The Wind

Canadian Cataloguing in Publication Program
French, Roy, 1957-
    Whispers On The Wind

ISBN - 0-9680432-1-6

    1. Title.

PS8561.R443W48 1996   C813'.54   C96-900112-6
PR9199.3.F74W48 1996

 Published in Canada by
Shady Vale Publishing
527 Brunswick Avenue
Toronto, Ontario M5R 2Z6
(416) 709-1907

Mass Market:
First Edition: February 1996

Printed and bound in Canada

Acclaim For Roy French's First Novel
A Sense Of Honour

"A Creditable and contemporary Canadian terrorist thriller"
- John North, Toronto Star

"The fast-paced action is backed up by painstaking accuracy."
- Mike Beggs, Toronto Star

"201 Pages of damn-the-torpedoes adventure."
- Jim Wilson, Brampton Guardian

"A stunning twist at the end of this gripping novel."
- Des Blackadder, Ballymena Observer

"A compelling narrative"
- L. McGuire, Saskatoon Times

Dedication

This book is dedicated to my dad, "Wee" Davy French, and my cousin Noel "Leon" Featherstone, who were both taken from us far too soon.

They did not go gently into that good night: the Fighting Irish to the end.

God bless 'em both.

CHAPTER 1

Connemara

'The IRA, though ignorant of the world and many things, are, as a class, transparently sincere and single-minded, idealists, highly religious for the most part and often imbued with an almost mystical sense of duty to their country.'

Sir Henry Lawson
Lieutenant General of Ireland
1922

Mary Kelly stood at the kitchen sink, quietly shaving carrots freshly dug from her garden, staring at her reflection in the window. It was well after seven o'clock on a chill Autumn night, and darkness had fallen quickly over the coast. Beside her, on the stove, a pot full of new potatoes hissed and gurgled merrily, rattling away on the hot metal plate. She swallowed hard, feeling her eyes moisten, but she fought back the tears. There was still no sign of Sean, her husband of less than a year, and her stomach churned with nerves. She bit her bottom lip and continued to shave the carrots.

Sean was a volunteer with the IRA, fighting to drive the British out of Ireland. Since the start of the uprising a few months ago he had been on the run, and had only been able to visit three times during that period. And with each day that passed her anxiety grew like moss on the trunk of a tree. No word, no contact. She felt alone and frightened, not by the solitude, but by the constant worry that he might not come home. She worried that he was lying dead in a ditch somewhere and that she would not see him alive again.

But two days ago, when she had been to the village to sell her produce at the market, a whispered word told her Sean would be home tonight. Yet she continued to gnaw on her lip, staring out into the dark void that reflected the emptiness she felt inside.

"Jesus, Mary, and Joseph," she said aloud as a tear rolled down her cheek and her vision blurred. "Would you ever get a grip girl, standing here bawling like a child." She dropped the carrot and the knife on the drawing board and lifted her apron to wipe away the tears. She dabbed at her eyes, let the apron fall back down, and leaned close to the window to fix her hair in the reflection. "A grand sight you'll be if he shows up at the door now," she admonished herself, and started chopping up the carrots.

A shadow crossed her vision and she blinked, thinking she had imagined it. She strained her eyes, looking out into the blackness at the back of the cottage for any movement. Her heart raced; hopeful, yet still wary. She stood still, ears straining for the slightest sound. The pot rattled away on the stove, the water hissing and bubbling like a witch's cauldron.

Then there was knock, a pause, and three more in rapid succession; the pre-arranged signal. Her body trembled, frozen in time for a heartbeat, and then she was across the kitchen and dragging the door open. It was Sean. He slipped into the room, kicking the door closed behind him. She was in his arms in an instant, her lips seeking his as tears rolled down her face.

His lips were cold from the chill night air, a rough stubble on his chin. A rank odour permeated his clothes but she didn't care. He was home, and alive, and for now that was all that mattered. One hand encircled her waist, pulling her tightly against him as he kissed her hungrily. The other hand carried his machine-gun. They held the embrace for several minutes, then she broke away, smiling like a child with a new toy.

His face looked weary and he had lost weight. His clothes were ripped in several places and his hair, that wonderful mass of red curls, was damp and matted with grime. He smiled, and the room lit up.

"Miss me, did you?" he said, grinning, and set the gun beside the back door. He pulled a green satchel from over his shoulder and laid it on the ground. A loud metallic clank emanated from the bag as it hit the stone tiles.

"Just a wee bit," she replied. "Now away with you and get those clothes off; you smell something awful. I've filled the tub and I've been keeping it warm just in case you showed up. I'll boil another kettle for you now, and your supper will be ready in about twenty minutes. Then you can tell me about your adventures.

He knelt down and undid the laces on his boots, pulled them off, and padded across the room towards the stairs. He smacked her bottom on the way past, and she shrieked in mock indignation, throwing a piece of carrot at his head. He ducked the missile and ran up the stairs. She finished chopping the carrots and piled them in another pot, a sense of calm returning to her being.

Twenty minutes later Sean sat facing her across the small oak table which had been a wedding gift from his brother. Over the table, a paraffin lamp hissed quietly, its wick turned low to lessen the pungent fumes. A turf fire glowed in the hearth, casting long shadows across the room.

Mary had prepared a special meal for them; potatoes, cabbage, carrots, and bacon, washed down with a glass of stout. It was special because, in Connemara, meat of any kind on the dinner table was the exception rather than the rule. For dessert there was a freshly baked apple pie warming on the hob.

The apples came from two trees which grew at the back of the cottage. Sean was always making fun of the amount of time Mary spent fussing over the trees. "Just like an old mother hen," he would say, but each year they bore fruit, a triumph over their eternal battering from the storms sweeping in from the Atlantic.

They lived in a small cottage in Connemara, barely getting by from selling their produce at the local market. The cottage was nestled in the gently rolling hills which protected it, to a certain degree, from the fury of nature. On a summer's day the whitewashed walls of the cottage and the golden thatch would gleam, as if proud of the care and attention which they received.

It was typical of most of the cottages in the area:

two rooms, a kitchen and a bedroom upstairs. In the corner of the kitchen stood an oak dresser, polished to a brilliant lustre every day. Its shelves were empty tonight, as the good china had been laid out upon the table. It was not often that Sean was home. As a result, Mary made a special effort to make the occasion a memorable one for them both.

He was a volunteer in the Irish Republican Army, one of many who were fighting to drive the British out of Ireland. He had gone to Cork, when the fighting began, to sign up with General Tom Barry. Barry had served as an officer with the British Army during the Great War, and his training was invaluable in enabling him to instruct and shape the recruits under his control.

The IRA were a ragtag collection of men and women, poorly armed and organized, but burning with the desire to unite the Irish Nation and become, once again, masters of their own destiny.

They were led by a man called Michael Collins, 'Big Mick', who taught them the techniques of guerilla warfare. "Hit and run" was his philosophy and it worked well. There were far too many British troops for them to take on face to face, but by striking hard and fast, where they were low in numbers, this tiny force managed to keep the much larger British army engaged indefinitely. It was a new form of warfare. The British referred to it by a multitude of names, 'Ditch Murder' being the most common.

This form of warfare was later made 'respectable' by the likes of Mao Tse Tung, Tito, and others.

Connemara is one of the wildest parts of Ireland, and its people wage a continuous battle with the elements in order to endure. For centuries they have lived their lives fighting the elements, fighting each other, fighting to survive. For them, there are no half-measures, and the struggle against the British was no exception.

Sean had been fighting for over a year, and would come back to the farmhouse whenever the opportunity arose. In that time, he had been wounded twice, but always returned to the fight. He was a man of slight build, lean and hard from working on the farm. A mass of curly red hair stubbornly defied any attempts to comb it into any shape or form.

Mary was tiny and, like himself, barely into her twenties. The responsibility of looking after the farm had fallen squarely on her shoulders when Sean was away, but she managed. There was little else she could do. She loved life and possessed a mischievous disposition, one of the traits which made Sean fall head over heels for her. They met one summer at the local fair. He courted her for several months before building up the nerve to ask her, in his own awkward way, to marry him.

She lived with her younger sister on a farm in the village of Crigaun, only a few miles from Sean's home. Her father and older brother, both fishermen, had drowned at sea in one of the frequent, unpredictable Atlantic storms.

A high wind had blown up, leaving them no time to head for the safety of the shore. The huge swell and the blowing whitecaps overturned their currach, casting them into the frigid seas of the Atlantic, to their deaths. The ocean had given up her dead, but their bodies had been hammered so violently on to the rocky coast that they were unrecognizable. As was the tradition, they were identified by the distinctive weave on the Aran sweaters they wore, the unique swirls and loops showing they were fishermen from the village of Crigaun.

Mary's mother was devastated by the accident and walked the earth like a lost soul, becoming progressively weaker despite Mary's attempts to nurse her back to health. Eventually she died peacefully in her sleep. That left Mary to look after her sister, Kathleen, and run the farm, a task to which she was more than equal.

When Sean proposed to Mary, Kathleen was delighted. She and Mary could now sell the farm. Kathleen's one great ambition was to go to Dublin to train as a nurse, and with her share of the money, she could now afford to realize that dream.

That was almost two years ago. But then the fighting started and Sean had joined those fighting the British. The young couple had not spent much time together, which was why Mary tried to make his rare visits memorable.

Leaning back in the chair, Sean ran his fingers through three days' worth of stubble on his cheeks. He had decided that a beard provided some protection against the biting winds from the Atlantic. Now, he was dressed in a freshly washed, heavy cotton shirt and a pair of brown corduroy trousers. It was such a treat to be out of the filthy clothes, and to have the luxury of a warm bath and a solid meal. Life on the run was hard: never knowing when and where the next meal was coming from, never knowing if your next meal would be your last. It had been almost seven weeks since he his last visit, seven long and lonely weeks.

Sean sipped his stout and looked at his wife, trying not to think of the horrors of the past few weeks. He had killed six soldiers, in ambushes, and the images weighed heavily on his mind. As with all the attacks, he and the others rifled the bodies of the dead soldiers for money, information, and ammunition. The thing which troubled him most was that the British soldiers were often no older than he, sometimes younger. They would never experience the emotions that he felt just now, looking at his young wife.

In the flickering firelight, Mary somehow looked different. She was not her usual light-hearted self and seemed to be distracted for most of the evening.

He reached out and took her hand in his. "Mary, is something the matter? You've not been yourself this evening." That was all it took to open the flood-gates and she burst into tears, something which he had not seen her do since their wedding day. But these were not tears of joy.

"Sean, you're out fighting the British week af-ter week, coming home God only knows when. Each time you return there seems to be a new scar some-where on your body. I never know from one day to the next if you're dead or alive. I keep expecting the Black and Tans to show up here one day with your body. That'd be all the excuse they need to confiscate the farm."

She was referring to the poorly trained recruits brought across from Britain to augment the British army. They were often collectively described as a blunt, brutal instrument, renowned for their cruelty and despised, to a man, by the Irish people.

Sean was taken aback by the outburst; it was so uncharacteristic of her. "I don't know what to say, Mary. Ireland needs me, and as many others as it can find to fight the British. Big Mick Collins will lead us to victory, just wait and see. One day soon, Ireland will be a nation once again, and we can live in peace without the shackles of the British. I am tired of the fighting, but we cannot give up now."

His spirit rose, the proud heritage of his Celtic forefathers, and she could see the defiance in his eyes. That same look which was in the eyes of all those who stood up to fight for their country.

But she loved him more than life itself, and she was afraid that she was going to lose him. She had heard Sean's words many times, and usually her spirit rose to match his own, soaring like the gulls over the cliffs of Mohr. But tonight it was different; tonight it sounded just like words. They were empty for her.

"But Sean, I need you too. And your unborn child needs you here as well. You'll be no good to either of us if you're dead. And if you keep on fighting that's what will happen." She buried her face in her hands and wept.

He felt stunned. How could he be so blind? It was little wonder that his wife had been on edge all evening. He knelt beside her and gently cradled her in his arms, kissing the tears from her cheeks.

"I'm sorry, Mary," he whispered. "I didn't know. The baby changes things. We're going to have to make plans for the three of us. Some of the others are getting sick of the fighting as well, and are talking of emigrating to America. Maybe we should think of doing the same and coming back when the fighting is over. I want to live to see my child grow up."

"Oh Sean," she cried, wrapping her arms around him. She hugged him tightly. "You'd do that for me and the baby?"

"Yes Mary, I would. God knows, I've done my share and then some. I want my child to grow up in a land where he is free from oppression, out from under the heel of the British. When we win the war, then we can come back to the farm. I can get someone to run it for us while we're gone. There's enough good lads around who are looking for steady work, and my brother can check on them from time to time when he gets a break from his studies."

She smiled as she heard him unconsciously refer to the child as 'he'. He wanted a son, to follow in his footsteps. She said, "What about your brother? Have you spoken to him at all?"

A dark look crossed his face as he shook his head. "We didn't exactly part on the best of terms. He doesn't approve of what I'm doing. He thinks politicians should handle it all."

She kissed him tenderly and headed up to the bedroom to start packing. There was no time to lose. The ship left from Cork each Friday, bound for New York, and that gave them one day to get their tickets and settle their affairs. She began to sing, her spirits soaring as she lifted down the battered suitcase from the top of the wardrobe, and started to pack her clothes.

As Sean began to pile up the dishes, preparing to stack them on the draining board, there was a rap on the front door.

"Who's there?" called Mary from the bedroom.

She knew the routine.

"It's Sergeant Adams. I'd like a word with Sean Kelly," came back the gruff reply.

Mary ran down into the room and motioned for Sean to sneak out the back. She blew him a kiss and opened the latch on the front door. The old door protested as she pulled it back a fraction.

Sean picked up his Thompson sub-machine gun from beside the back door, cocked it, and peered out into the darkness. There was no movement, so he eased open the door and sprinted for the cover of the hedgerow. He had gone barely three yards when the butt of a rifle came crashing down on the back of his head.

When he came to, he was sitting on a bale of hay in his barn. His hands and feet were bound with coarse baler twine and a noose hung around his neck. He opened his eyes wide, like a frightened animal, and then closed them tightly, hoping that the vision before him was just a bad dream. The animals in their stalls were skittish, frightened by the dancing shadows cast by the flickering paraffin lamp held by one of the soldiers.

There were eight men in the barn, all British soldiers and all dressed in hybrid khaki and black uniforms. These were the colours of a popular hunt club in Limerick, known as the Black and Tans. The British had run out of their supply of khaki jackets, and had decided to use black leather jackets until regular supplies were re-established.

Mary sat between two of the men, her face buried in her hands. Every so often her body would rack with spasms of crying, much to the amusement of the soldiers. When the sergeant noticed that Sean was conscious, he walked over and punched him full in the face, splitting his upper lip. Sean shook his head, dazed by the blow. The coppery taste of blood filled his mouth.

"It's a good thing that I've got my hands tied, you British bastard," he snarled, spitting a huge gob of bloody saliva at the sergeant's face. The soldiers's face contorted with rage as he drew his revolver and pointed it at Sean's face.

"Sean Kelly, two days ago, one of our patrols was ambushed a few miles from here. Three men were shot and killed, a fourth was badly wounded, but he feigned death and survived the ambush. He recognised you and the three others who carried out the attack. He identified you as the leader of the group. One of our patrols is picking them up now. For your part in the murders of those men, I hereby sentence you to death."

Mary screamed. The sergeant nodded to his men, who quickly hauled Sean to his feet and tossed one end of the rope over the rafters.

Mary Kelly opened her mouth again to scream, but the look on her husband's face quieted her. "Don't let them see you beg, Mary," he ordered.

"They can kill me, but there will be others to take my place. Go now and keep the plans we made. God save Ireland. I ..."

His last words were cut off abruptly when the soldiers hauled on the rope and lifted him, kicking, off the ground. The soldiers on either side of Mary pinned her arms as she struggled in vain to help her husband. One of them grabbed a handful of her hair, twisting her face upwards, forcing her to watch the entire grisly spectacle. She wept, seeing her beloved's face turn from red to purple to black as the rope bit deeply into his neck, starving his lungs of precious oxygen. His legs jerked like those of a child's marionette, but in a few minutes the twitching stopped and a foul stench filled the air. The soldiers laughed.

Mary spat at them, her face suffused with blood and a black rage in her soul. The sergeant slapped his pistol against the side of her head, knocking her unconscious. The soldiers released her arms and she collapsed on the muddy floor of the barn. Then they dragged her outside like a sack of flour, and threw her on the damp grass beside the barn. One of them, almost as an afterthought, tossed the paraffin lamp back inside the barn where it shattered, igniting the dry bales of hay. It took only a few moments for the entire barn to be engulfed in flames, the animals shrieking as flames licked at their stalls.

For them, there was no escape. The fire could

be seen for miles, attracting the local priest and their neighbours to the scene. They already knew about how the bastard Tans had hanged three volunteers during the night. They had no idea yet, however, that Sean Kelly had been their fourth victim. They found Mary lying unconscious on a grassy bank outside the barn, now a black skeleton of charred oak beams. The stench of burning flesh left no doubt of what had happened to the animals. But it was not until Mary regained consciousness that they discovered Sean's fate. Sean Kelly had joined the ranks of Irish martyrs.

General Tom Barry, the C/O of Cork No. 3 Brigade and Sean's former commander, sent one of his men to see that Mary did not want for anything. His note to her spoke of what a brave man Sean had been, and how his death would serve to unite the others left behind. The words turned hollow in her heart, and she crumpled up the note and threw it into the grave beside her husband. Sean's brother, Michael, who had been urgently summoned from the seminary in Maynooth, tried to comfort her, but it was to no avail. Her eyes were as cold and hard as the legendary Connemara marble.

"They will pay for what they have done," she said.

When the ceremony was over, and Sean's body buried deep in the golden sand, she packed her bags and set off for Cork to catch the ship to America.

CHAPTER 2
Vietnam

The three choppers came in low over the trees in a tight reverse 'V' formation. Downwash from their rotors flattened the leaves at the treetops, leaving a trail like that of a mower cutting through long grass. They were several miles north of An Khe, well into enemy occupied territory, and heading for a rendezvous with a Special Forces team.

The team had been on their way back from a successful 'search and destroy' mission when they inadvertently ran into a heavily armed Vietcong patrol. A furious firefight erupted, but due to the superior numbers and firepower of the Vietcong patrol, the team were forced to cut and run. Just before they fell back, however, the radio operator put in an emergency call to Special Forces Headquarters, asking them to send choppers to pick them up.

The rendezvous, of necessity, was inside enemy territory. The Vietcong would have other units moving to cut off the team's avenue of escape. The original plan, calling for them to walk back through occupied territory, would have to be scrapped.

The two lead choppers were AH-1G Cobra's: light, highly maneuverable and armed to the teeth with a six-barrelled minigun, a grenade launcher, rocket pods, and two, 30-millimetre cannons mounted on the struts. Flying slightly behind the two was a UH-60 Blackhawk, a larger evacuation helicopter capable of carrying the team to safety. Emblazoned in white, on the sides of all three choppers, was the notorious skull and crossed sabres of the 11th Air Assault Battalion.

The chopper to the right of the Blackhawk had an additional emblem painted on the underside of the fuselage. It was a large, lime-green shamrock, put there by its pilot.

Sergeant Patrick Kelly was every bit the image of his grandfather. The Vietcong Army had put a price on the head of each and every pilot and gunner of the Air Cavalry Attack Brigade, but a special bonus was put aside for the person who could bring down the chopper with the dreaded green leaf.

He was already a Vietnam legend at the age of twenty-four. His exploits in the air and on the ground, during three tours of duty, had made him one of the most decorated pilots of the Vietnam war. The tales of his exploits were many, some true, some not so true. They were spread around mess halls and bars, elaborated a little each time they were told.

The worst culprit was Patrick Kelly himself, an instantly recognizable figure with his flaming red hair and his easy smile. His charm, combined with his rugged good looks made him an immense hit with the ladies.

Despite the numerous commendations, his military career was a little less than illustrious. His progress through the ranks was rather like that of a drunk on a Saturday night: two steps forward, one step back.

Then there were his exploits on the ground, more often than not linked to the wife of a senior officer in another battalion. He revelled in the glory of his larger-than-life persona, but was the first to admit that his stories were a 'little exaggerated, don't you know?'. He had a lilt to his voice, the result of being raised in a cloistered Irish community in Queens, New York.

His parents had died in a car crash when he was seven years old, and he had been raised by his grandmother. Young Patrick Kelly had been regaled with stories of Ireland: of Celtic kings and queens, and of his noble heritage; of the uprising against the British, and of the brave men and women who had fallen for the 'cause'. He loved his grandmother's stories, knowing them almost by heart, and would relate them to his classmates. For him, his grandfather became the equivalent of Billy the Kid, or Jesse James, or other cowboys who were the heros of the kids he called friends.

"The gift of the Blarney," his grandmother said, always astounded at the likeness to his grandfather. His favourite tale, and hers, was about the Children of Lir, an Irish legend about an evil witch who turned a young girl and her brothers into wild swans.

As the choppers approached the landing zone, Patrick Kelly could hear the reports of heavy machine-gun fire and the high-pitched whine of mortars. That meant only one thing. The Vietcong had the team pinned down. In front of him the gunner was busily arming rockets and grenades and preparing to drop smoke to cover the Blackhawk as it went in to pick up the team.

His radio squawked into life and the voice of the other pilot filled the cockpit, mimicking Kelly's Irish accent. "Well Patrick me boy, sounds like we got us a hot LZ."

Kelly laughed. "And sure isn't it a fine day for dyin'," he shouted, looking over at the other pilot.

The dense forest suddenly gave way to a clearing, and he could see the small group of men in camouflage fatigues and black and green striped faces, desperately trying to hold off the Vietcong patrol, which had them almost surrounded. None of the team were injured, as far as he could see.

"Let's even the odds a bit, you sons of bitches," he cried, banking the chopper in a tight circle to allow the gunner to get sighted on the VC positions. There was a puff of smoke from the underside of the chopper as the first set of rockets left the pods, homing in on the mortar. The Vietcong soldiers did not have time to escape as the rockets zeroed in on their position. The explosive heads detonated boxes of unfired mortar projectiles causing huge geysers of fire and earth to erupt into the air. The Vietcong tubes were literally blown to pieces. All that remained was a smoking hole in the ground.

Even before the rockets struck home, the gunner was manning the minigun, sending burst after burst into the VC positions. They scattered, knowing full well that their position was hopeless and that resistance was futile. They were no match for the heavily armed choppers. The other gunship dropped smoke bombs to cover the Special Forces team as they made their way to the Blackhawk. The two Cobra's then prowled the area like angry bees, continuing to fire grenades after the fleeing VC patrol.

The team looked on in awe as the Cobra gun-
ners picked off the stragglers with unerring accuracy, sending men spinning like tenpins before the
hail of fire. As the lead Cobra banked to return to
the Blackhawk, the team saw the Shamrock on the
bottom of the fuselage. The team's leader, a lanky
Texan, was the first to comment: "So that's Kelly."
He too had heard the stories. "Goddamn that boy's
good. I think we all owe him a few beers. Or maybe
he owes us a few. After all, we've just given him
another story to tell!"

When they landed back at Special Forces headquarters, the team spent a few minutes talking to
the pilots before heading for their debriefing, promising to meet the crew in the bar later. Beers would
be on them.

The headquarters was a collection of neat, white
buildings with concrete walks and picket fences
bordering the beginnings of a lawn. It was a far cry
from the old headquarters, no more than a collection of thatched huts which offered only a token
resistance to the fury of the frequent tropical storms.

The new buildings had an air of permanence.
There were several rows of barracks across the
street from the mess hall. Each of the barracks was
named after a special forces soldier killed in action,
his name etched on a metal sign hung over the entrance.

Further down the street, in an extension of one of the barracks, was Charlie's Club, an oasis where the men could relax and down a few beers.

The club was dimly lit, furnished with the ubiquitous formica tables and pseudo-leather couches found in low-life bars all over the world. A couple of pinball machines pinged and bleeped in the corner, interrupting the driving rhythms emanating from a brightly coloured jukebox. The Rolling Stones belted out "Honky Tonk Woman", a perennial favourite with the soldiers on the base.

At a long table at the back of the club, Kelly was holding court like King Arthur with his knights. The table was littered: beer bottles and an assortment of empty peanut, chip, and cigarette packets, junk food and beer, the usual way of unwinding after a successful mission. There were no weapons, all having been checked at the BOQ. Beer and bullets did not mix, a lesson learned the hard way.

A motley assortment of soldiers sat around Kelly, each intent on his words. It was a new story, one they had not heard before and one which they were going to relish because it involved a major's wife. It didn't matter to them which major or which battalion; the joy was in an enlisted man putting one over on the brass.

Kelly's hands were doing as much talking as his mouth, demonstrating sizes, widths and shapes of the lady's anatomy.

"So anyway," he went on, "she's lying back on the sheets shouting 'fuck me, fuck me' and I'm doing my best to oblige her. She had one of those big fans on the ceiling but it wasn't doing me any good. I could feel the sweat running down my back and she's raking me with her nails when I hear the front door slam shut. She heard it as well, and my dick was out of her like a Sidewinder out of a pod. There was nowhere for me to go so I grabbed my clothes, threw them under the bed and crawled after them. That's where the Special Forces training helps." He stopped, took a long swig of beer, looked at the faces caught up in his excitement, smiled and went on.

"In comes the major, sees the wife in bed, cheeks flushed and smelling like a forty-dollar whore, and damn it all doesn't he get a storker. He tears off his clothes and stands there for a minute, the pork sword at attention. I tell you, it's true, all those rumours about the size of officers' cocks. I once knew this navy officer who ..."

He was cut short by one of the other pilots: "C'mon Kelly, stick to one story at a time. We've got all night."

"Sorry about that Nate, I forgot how much you like to hear stories about naked white ladies," he said, grinning, and took another swig of beer. His friend Nate was black, and he was unmercifully teased by Patrick about how white ladies loved 'dark meat'. Setting the bottle back on the table he went on.

"So the major leaps on the bed, decides to skip the foreplay and rams it into her. Well, I tell you, after me it was like a pea rattling about in a jamjar. Then he wants her to call him 'Bull'. Now I have to tell you about this bed. It's about ten inches off the ground and I'm jammed in there tighter than a Cong's asshole. When the major starts pounding the old lady, this bed is taking pieces out of my back.

"So at the end of it all, with him screaming 'take it bitch' and her yelling 'fuck me Bull, fuck me', I was moaning louder than either of them. Eventually he fell asleep and I got out of there, but to this day I've still got the marks on my back."

The Special Forces team had come in about the middle of the story and were standing around, grinning like the rest of the men. They had had a luxurious hot shower, a shave, and fresh BDU's, and were now ready to party. The lanky Texan ordered several rounds of beer and then shook Patrick Kelly's hand.

"I want to thank you and your buddies for what you did today. A few minutes more and we wouldn't be standing here, enjoying this beer and listening to such 'wonderful stories'. So tell me, where did you meet my wife?"

Kelly laughed, as did all the others. "Come on

and join us," and the team found spaces around the table, settling down for an evening's drinking, where they could, at least for a little while, escape the horrors of war.

CHAPTER 3
Belfast

Major James Skinner pored eagerly through the reports on his desk, like a miner searching for a nugget of gold. He was responsible for coordinating all anti-terrorist activities in Northern Ireland, utilizing the skills of a team of Special Air Service (SAS) commandos who were well versed in the arcane art of covert operations.

Like his counterparts in other countries, he was not above sanctioning 'black' operations when it suited his purposes. The people he fought had no rules when it came to attacking the British forces, so in his mind he was fighting fire with fire.

He was a stout man, fond of his beer and his food. Early in his career he had been in perfect fighting trim, but years behind the desk had added to his girth. His full head of brown hair was greying elegantly at the temples, and his dark penetrating eyes seemed like those of a hawk: all-encompassing, all-seeing.

He moved slowly, yet his mind was sharper than it had ever been. People and events were manipulated with the skill of a grand-master at chess, his board being the map of Ireland, and each move meticulously planned and executed.

Recognised by his peers and superiors as a brilliant military tactician, he was responsible for many brilliant and daring offensives against the terrorist forces in the Province. His skills were very much in demand by security forces the world over, and many countries were starting to follow his 'modus operandi' of issuing pre-emptive strikes against terrorists.

Tossing one report aside, he flipped open another, his eyes scanning the details looking for ... he wasn't entirely sure what it was, but he was certain he would know when he found it. He poured himself a re-fill from his teapot, added a little milk and sugar and stirred the tea, never lifting his eyes from the reports. He was hoping to find some mention, however small, of the person or persons responsible for the kidnapping of his friend.

Captain Timothy White's car had been found abandoned two nights previous, several miles from Belfast, in a ditch along the coast road to Carrickfergus. From the damage to the front fender it was obvious that he had been run off the road by another vehicle. One window of the car was shattered and there were bloodstains on the driver's seat and on the road. Forensic tests on the blood samples showed that one matched Timothy White's blood group but those from the road were of a different type. There were several spent shell casings on the floor of the car, all 9-millimetre cartridges from White's Browning automatic.

Shards of glass from the side window of the car were scattered over a wide radius, suggesting that White had tried to defend himself before being overpowered. The fact that White's body had not been booby-trapped and left in the car also gave Skinner some hope that he was still alive. Terrorists seldom missed the opportunity to leave a surprise for the security forces, when the occasion arose.

When he was first notified of White's disappearance, Skinner spent hours searching for some small clue. He had put the word out to his men to check with their informants as well, but to date the search had borne no fruit. He was becoming increasingly agitated as the hours passed. In an attempt to prevent his imagination from running amok, he turned his attention to the reports on his desk, the routine business of the day.

One of the reports confirmed earlier rumours that two terrorists, possibly from the Irish National Liberation Army, were planning a trip to America. The bastards were probably off raising funds again, he thought. There was nothing like a couple of true blue gunmen at the fancy cocktail parties in New York and Boston to raise the patriotic fervour of the participants and empty overflowing wallets.

The information came from a usually reliable source, and so Skinner began the, by now, routine process of informing the appropriate security forces. Munching on a digestive biscuit, he prepared a telex to Scotland Yard, the Canadian Security and Intelligence Service (CSIS) in Toronto, and the FBI in Washington. He also pulled a copy of the mugshots of the two terrorists which would be faxed along with the memo.

The photographs would be posted at all customs offices at the points of entry to Britain, Canada, and the United States. The British authorities would probably have a copy already, as the two were high on the 'most wanted' list in Britain. It would do no harm to remind them that they were on the move.

He was putting the finishing touches to the telex when his telephone rang. There were several direct lines on the phone console, but the light winking was the number he had given his contacts to use for any information they might uncover on Timothy

White's abduction. As his hand moved towards the phone, some inner sense told him that this was the call which he was dreading. His stomach twisted and he shivered. Taking a deep breath, he picked up the instrument, preparing himself as he had done for the past two days, to hear that his friend's body had been discovered.

His hands were clammy with cold sweat, and, as he grasped the receiver, it slipped from his hand and fell over the side of his desk. "Damn," he muttered, grabbing the flex and pulling the phone up the side of his desk like a ship weighing anchor.

"Overlord," he said, using his codename for the coordination of the search for his friend.

"Overlord, this is Detail-1. We have located the missing parcel. It has been damaged beyond repair. We are situated at River Street, just south of Ormeau Road. Sir ..." There was a momentary pause in the transmission. Skinner, however, was in no mood for hesitation.

"Come on Detail-1, for Christ's sake spit it out," he shouted.

"Sir, the bastards have crucified him."

He slammed down the phone, and his heart raced as the taps opened and a stream of fire poured into his veins.

He sat for a few minutes, staring at the wall, numbed by the realization that his friend was dead. At the outset, the professional soldier in him knew that his friend was as good as dead. It would only be a matter of time before the flame would be extinguished. But, as his friend, he had kept hoping for a miracle, that somehow Timothy White had escaped. He was relieved, in a way, that the uncertainty and the waiting were over.

He rang for a car. Someone would have to make the identification, and he wanted to see his friend before the authorities carried out the obligatory autopsy. The soldier said that White had been "Crucified," military slang for badly beaten. He wanted to see just how badly beaten his friend had been so that he could repay the debt in spades.

He was soon speeding through the dark Belfast night towards the River Lagan. Lamp-posts, like silent sentinels, lined the darkened streets. They had long ceased to perform their function, their lamps shattered by bullets or stones. There was an occasional dying, defiant flicker of light from a few that had not been completely wrecked, but it was not enough to stave off the dark.

He could feel his blood pressure soar and droplets of sweat pebbled his brow. The professional soldier was in control for now, but images of his friend flashed through his mind. The photographs went back through their twenty years of service together: Timothy White and himself posing with tribesmen in the jungles of Borneo; sweating buckets in the Radfan mountains, and dressed as Arabs when they were doing undercover work in Aden City. His eyes began to water, but he forced the tears back.

There would be time for grief later.

And later still, there would be time for vengeance.

The nauseating stench from the River Lagan filled the air as he opened the car door. It was like sniffing an open sewer. He parked the car beside the river bank and climbed out, his boots making ugly sucking noises in the soft mud. His breath misted on the cold night air like the smoke from a cigarette, and he buckled up his greatcoat against the chill.

Two army Saracens were parked on the bank, their headlights burning holes in a light fog which drifted lazily atop the floating cess-pool. Two young soldiers squatted beside the front fenders, their rifles upraised, eyes staring out into the stygian night. The threat of snipers was ever-present, but the heavy fog played the role of a spoiler in reducing visibility to a few yards.

An ambulance and its attendants stood to one side, waiting for him to make his inspection. As he passed by the ambulance, he noticed a crowbar in the hands of one of the attendants. He stared at it, and the attendant, somewhat self-consciously, put it behind his back as if he had not meant for it to be seen.

He was totally unprepared for the sight which greeted him when he walked around the side of the ambulance. The young corporal who had made the call was kneeling down on one knee in front of a sheet. He was leaning heavily on his rifle, as if in prayer.

When the corporal heard Skinner approach, he stood, preparing to make his situation report. Skinner brusquely waved him aside and flung back the sheet, then recoiled in horror. Timothy White had literally been crucified, his cross tied to some oil drums and set afloat in the river.

Lagan river rats had feasted well on the body, tearing away long ribbons of skin and gnawing on fingers and toes. The eyes had been gouged out and eaten, and in some places the flesh was stripped to the bone. White's genitals had been chewed away.

As Skinner's mind recorded the grisly details, he tried to control the bile rising in his throat, but finally turned aside, spewing the contents of his stomach into the river. The corporal was beside him in an instant, grasping him firmly by the shoulders.

"It's okay, Sir. We all did the same. You've made the ID now, so we can take it from here."

Skinner inhaled deeply, filling his lungs with the cold, fetid air. It took a few minutes before he could bring himself to look at the body again. He tore the sheet completely away from the body, noting, as it fell to the ground, that it bore the bloody outline of Timothy White. He was reminded of the Turin shroud, believed to be the burial robe of Christ.

In the areas where the rats had not chewed the skin, there were several livid burn marks, probably put there by a cigar stub or a poker. The marks were too large to have been made with a cigarette. Forensics would determine the exact cause later.

The dead man's teeth were firmly embedded in the throat of a huge rat, confirming that he had still been alive before being set adrift in the river. That meant that his captors knew of the fate which lay in store for him as they cast him to his death.

There was a purplish puckered hole in the front of his right shoulder and a larger exit wound at the back. The brownish, congealed blood seemed out of place with the newer, fresher wounds, evidence that he had been wounded during the kidnapping.

The body had been nailed to the planks, the nails seemingly hammered at random into his limbs. A closer inspection of the nails revealed a small plastic flange just under the head of each one.

The corporal saw him probing at the nails. "Sir, they used a power hammer. It uses .22-millimetre cartridges to fire the nails into concrete or steel. The hammer looks like a rifle barrel and the plastic flange is used to hold the nail in position in the barrel. A regular hammer is used to detonate the ..."

"Okay corporal, I get the picture." Skinner sud-

denly realized why the ambulance attendant was
holding a crowbar. The nails would have to be pried
out of the wood before the body could be moved.
Bile rose in his throat again.

He walked around the body, counting twenty
nails in all. Six or seven would have been sufficient
to hold the body in place; the others were put there
for no better reason than to increase his friend's
suffering. What torment White must have endured.
From the signs on his body they had not been successful in extracting any information. Cooperation
usually resulted in a quick death: a bullet in the back
of the head.

He ordered the ambulance attendant to remove
one of the nails for him, a task which made the attendant's flesh crawl. In all his years as an attendant, cleaning up the remains of bomb victims, or
other poor unfortunates, he had never seen a body
so deliberately mutilated. The man was beyond suffering now, but all the same he gently extracted a
single nail out of the bruised flesh and placed it in
Skinner's hand.

An hour later, Skinner was sitting at his desk, now
devoid of the clutter of the day. A newly opened
bottle of Bushmills stood in front of him, almost
one-quarter empty. The only other object on the
desk was the blood-stained nail. It was a constant
source of amazement to him how a sick mind could

transform a useful tool, such as a power hammer, or an electric drill into an instrument of torture. Drilling holes in peoples' kneecaps, colloquially known as a 'Black and Decker job', was the IRA's favourite method of punishment: bullets were too precious to waste.

He put the glass to his lips, swallowing hard as the amber liquid burned down his throat. Then he leaned forward and picked up the nail in termbling fingers. Heaven help the bastards who did this, he swore. I'll hunt them to the ends of the earth if necessary. He took another hefty belt of whiskey, set down the glass, and, for the first time in many years, he wept.

CHAPTER 4
Flashbang

The hijacked American Airlines DC-10, recently diverted from Dulles International Airport to Fort Bragg, North Carolina, stood alone on the runway, its lights dimmed and the window shutters pulled down. Although it was well into the evening, the runway was as bright as it was during the day, the plane bathed in white light from powerful spotlights, despite the terrorists' insistence they be switched off.

The main passenger door, at the front of the plane, was closed now. It had been opened a few moments earlier by the terrorists to eject the bullet-riddled body of one of the hostages. The body, that of a young stewardess, lay sprawled at the bottom of the boarding ramp. It was a harsh statement of their intentions.

The terrorists had made on good their threat, and now were prepared to execute another hostage every hour until their demands were met. Negotiations were at a standstill, neither party prepared to concede to any demand. The powers-that-be had declared that there would be no concessions, no matter what the cost. The terrorists had crossed the line; they had shown their willingness to kill, and, after one dead body, the next would be easier. There was no alternative but to carry out a rescue attempt. The anti-terrorist team on standby were given the green light.

The lights went out, throwing the entire area into blackness. Four groups of men from the Special Emergency Response Team (SERT) glided out of the darkness like silent wraiths, the rubberized soles of their boots ensuring a quiet approach. Each SERT group consisted of four men, each man working to a carefully rehearsed schedule. They were all identically dressed in black fatigues, black mesh hoods, and CS gas respirators, the huge circular lenses of which gave them a strange insect-like appearance.

Each man wore a modified Kevlar flak jacket, which was just as effective but not as cumbersome as its traditional counterpart. Webbing criss-crossed the front of jackets, on which hung several grenades. These were stun grenades or 'flashbangs' as they were more commonly known. The grenades were constructed from mercury fulminate and exploded with an deafening roar combined with a blinding flash, which had the effect of totally disorienting anyone in their proximity.

Usually the assault team would be armed with sub-machine guns, the reliable 'Heckler'; a nickname for the Heckler and Koch MP5. However, as they were going to be in the confined space of an aircraft cabin, they had opted for their 9-millimetre Sig-Sauer pistols.

Strapped to the back of their jackets were tiny transmitter/receivers connected to earpieces to allow the teams to receive directions. On this operation they had been switched off. Each man knew exactly what he had to do to get on the plane. Inside the plane, however, was the unknown. They had no data on the location of the terrorists, the number, and, most importantly, what type of weapons they would be facing. The best intelligence they had to date was that there might be one, possibly two terrorists on board.

They had trained for countless hours on a mockup of an airplane cabin, dealing with various combinations and permutations of a hijacking scenario. Once inside the plane, they would only have seconds to evaluate the situation and take appropriate action. That action might or might not save the hostages.

The responsibility weighed heavily on the minds of the men each time they prepared to go into action. Once the preparations were done and the team committed, their minds were clear and focused. There was one goal.

Free the hostages and kill the terrorists.

Not wound - kill.

The first two groups went to one side of the plane, to the starboard wing. The other groups took the port wing. The assault would take place simultaneously from both sides of the plane. They quickly assembled light-weight, aluminium ladders and placed them against the trailing edge of the wings. Each man climbed slowly, with precise, fluid movements, and took up position on the wing, near the emergency doors.

One member of the team, on each side of the plane, waited beside the emergency door. The men cocked their weapons, hearts in mouths and waited. A horn sounded in the distance, the signal to 'Go'. The men pulled down the exterior handles, dragged open the emergency doors and tossed them on to the ground, standing aside to let the others enter.

The first man through the doors on each side hurled the 'flashbangs', with four-second fuses, and then got quickly out of the way. The remaining members stormed into the plane in the wake of the flashbangs exploding. At the front of the plane they found the terrorists, totally disoriented by the blinding flashes of light and the ear-splitting detonations.

The leading members of the team did not hesitate: each terrorist received a 'double tap', two bullets in the head and one or two shots to the body to put them down, then the men were sprinting down the aisle. Keep firing until they stop moving.

Keep their hands away from their bodies.

Keep firing, keep firing.

As suddenly as it began, it was over. The entire assault had lasted only ten seconds. The men breathed a collective sigh of relief, and went to examine their handiwork. They gathered at the front of the plane, beside the fallen, bullet-riddled bodies of the two terrorists.

As they reviewed their marksmanship, a washroom door at the back of the plane opened quietly and a third terrorist crept out. He was armed with an assault rifle. The fire-select switch was set to auto.

He rolled a mini 'stun' grenade down the aisle towards the group of SERT members who were admiring their groupings. Heads turned in his direction when they heard the noise of the grenade clattering down the aisle. A few mouths opened in disbelief, their weapons coming up too late to save them. The grenade exploded and instantly the terrorist opened up with the rifle.

The SERT member at the back of the group, Gordon Bell, a 'rookie' with only six years experience on a Tactical and Rescue team, took the full force of the burst across his back. The others were blasted in various body parts, depending on which was exposed. Great gouts of red splattered the insides of the cabin as round after round found its mark.

The hail of fire was merciless, all SERT men being hit several times. The hammer of the rifle clicked on an empty chamber and the remaining terrorist eased his finger off the trigger. He walked up the aisle to examine the bodies.

Gordon Bell moaned and put his hand to his back. It came away covered in red paint, residue from the exploding pellets fired by the 'terrorist'. The pellets had the impact of a golf ball and had caused a considerable amount of bruising across Bell's back. The SERT men who had been 'hit' in the face were pressing their fingers against the point of impact, hoping to ease the pain.

The 'terrorist', Sergeant Tony Ames of 22 SAS (Special Air Service) ripped off his mask. He was a tall, wiry man with a narrow face which had earned him the nickname of 'Bony'. He was not amused by the events which had just transpired.

"Forgot to look in the bog, didn't you? These

little beauties hurt like a bitch; I've been got once or twice myself. Anyway, one of the cardinal lessons which you have just painfully learned is that Intel is sometimes wrong and you had better be prepared to deal with such an event. Just because you were told that there were two terrorists in the plane does not mean that you relax as soon as you have got two dead bodies.

"They could have landed somewhere to pick up more members or maybe some of the passengers did not expose themselves as terrorists in light of a rescue attempt. The entire plane must be covered from front to rear to ensure that there are no surprises. Let me tell you, bullets are a hell of a lot more painful than ink pellets, but in your case it wouldn't matter too much 'cos you'd all be fuckin' dead!

"Now let's get off the plane and go over the action in the review room. You may not have noticed but the entire incident was videotaped, so we can review our mistakes."

He stared at Gordon Bell, as he emphasized the word 'mistakes'. It had been Bell's responsibility to check the washrooms, both in the centre and the rear of the plane. Bell looked away and the others stared at the floor.

Outside the plane, Captain Alain Simmonds, of the Canadian SERT, stood beside Lieutenant John

Waters of the British SAS and Major Sam Rogers of the American Delta Force. The Counter Revolutionary Wing (CRW) of the Special Air Service were putting on a training exercise for the men of Delta and had invited the SERT to join in the session.

Simmonds was a little in awe of the two men beside him because, unlike them, he had never experienced actual combat. His unit was styled along the lines of the West German Gremzschutzgruppe 9, more commonly known as GSG-9. They were a police unit, rather than a military outfit, formed in the aftermath of the Munich Olympics where a group of Palestinian gunmen had murdered several Israeli athletes.

The SERT had been drawn from members of the Royal Canadian Mounted Police, and the unit was still in its infancy. He had cringed when he saw his men file off the plane, their faces downcast and angry. When he saw the SAS man come off the plane following them, grinning from ear to ear, he knew what had happened. His men's pride had taken a beating, and the SAS men were not about to let them forget their mistake. He heard the SAS man say something to one of the others trainers about a "bunch of lumberjacks," and was about to say something when Gordon Bell came up to him.

"We fucked up, Sir. I forgot to check the toilet at the back of the plane. As luck would have it 'Bony' Tony was hiding in there with a machine gun. He raked us all, up and down. That's one mistake I won't make again. I don't think any of the others will forget it either."

"Thanks, Gordon. These SAS bastards are a bit arrogant at times, but they know their business. I think we're going to learn a lot from them. Anyway, you better get cleaned up. We're due in the review room in a few minutes."

Alain Simmonds watched Gordon Bell as he walked towards the barracks. His heart went out to the man. He could imagine how he must be feeling, but he also knew that a valuable lesson had been learned today. He was in the midst of this reverie when he heard a voice beside him.

"He won't make that mistake again," said John Waters, his face stern as he nodded at the retreating back.

"You're right. But Tony was a bit hard on them," responded Simmonds, looking at the paint-splattered backs.

"Hard my arse," spat Waters, fire in his eyes, and the others paused, startled by the outburst.

"You know as well as I do what happened at the Munich Olympics. Those snipers were well-trained. They knew how to fire. But when it came do to it, when they actually had to shoot someone, they fucking well froze. And eleven innocent people died.

"So don't talk to me about being harsh. Those little paint balls might have been real bullets, and you'd have been writing a lot of letters to a lot of widows.

"Tony did what he felt was necessary, and it's no more than he would expect if he found himself in the same situation. We're not dealing with regular criminals here in these scenarios, so your regular police rules do not apply. Most of the bastards that I've come across are totally merciless. They would shoot their own mother if they thought it would do their 'cause' some good, so if you get the chance to shoot them in the back, don't hesitate. The Geneva convention doesn't apply to terrorists. God knows they'd do exactly the same to you given half a chance.

"One of the things we will be working on over the next few days is to try to change the mindset of you and your men. We're dealing with terrorists and that means we throw away the rulebook. These people operate outside the law, and we must often revert to their tactics to get the advantage."

"But surely, by stooping to their level, we become as bad as them. We are expected to uphold the law, not operate outside it," argued Alain Simmonds.

John Waters shook his head sadly. "Alain," he said with the patience of a worldly teacher, "You're not listening to what I'm saying. In the world of international terrorism, the taking of human life or the perpetration of outrageous acts on the public at large is something to be used to make a statement. Common criminals rarely behave in such a manner.

"Until now, that is the only face of evil you and your men have known. But terrorist atrocities are proliferating, and the magnitude of the devastation has increased ten-fold. In Ireland, shooting a soldier is considered passe'. It hardly rates mention in the papers any longer. The Provos know that they need to blow up a bus full of soldiers or a hotel full of politicians to make the headlines these days.

"With the amount of terrorist activity I'm talking about, it won't be long before there is a full-scale incident in Canada."

Alain Simmonds was surprised by the statement. "Exactly what activity are you talking about? There was that bomb attack on a Litton plant a few years ago, but that was done by a bunch of extremists from the peace movement. And there has been an assassination attempt on a Turkish diplomat. Aside from those, there has been little other activity to my knowledge."

"I'm not talking about those kinds of incidents, Alain. I'm talking about fund-raising, safe-houses, secret meetings, training, and the like, all taking place on your own doorstep."

A puzzled look crossed Alain's face. John Waters caught the look and decided that he better elaborate a little.

"Alain, one of the biggest problems which we have to deal with in Northern Ireland is the influx of weapons from all points of the globe. One of the most elaborate routes which we managed to cut off was detailed in the London *Daily Mirror*. It was supervised in Canada by Jean Materot of the Quebec Liberation Front. Weapons from Czechoslovakia and East Germany were delivered to Syria and Libya, trans-shipped across the Atlantic to Montreal, and then shipped back across to the French port of Le Havre. They were then sent on to Quimper, on the French Coast, and from there by French fishing boats to Cork in the south of Ireland. The weapons were then taken from there by Irish fishing boats to some remote beach in the North for unloading and storage. Breton Separatists could see to the shipments at both ends."

Alain Simmonds was astonished. "How do you know all this?" he asked.

"The information is in our files, Interpol's for sure, and your own CSIS files. At least it should be there. We also have heard of cases where terrorists will use Canada as a jumping-off point for their operations. So if you take all of those facts into consideration, it points to the reasonable assumption that sooner or later you will have to deal with a major incident. And when that time comes you had better be prepared.

"As I said before, the West German police were not ready when the Palestinian terrorists took Israeli athletes hostage at the Olympic village, and we all know what a bloodbath that turned out to be. Their skills were tested but not their resolve.

"GSG-9 was formed soon after that incident to combat further incidents. The fact that your team has been set up shows great initiative on the part of your government. It's best to be prepared to deal with these incidents.

"Anyway, we have lots of time to talk about this over the next few days. The review is about to start so we better get over there."

CHAPTER 5
Honeytrap

T wo of the men sat behind an old, battered wooden desk whose surface was etched with count-less stains, from wet bottles and glasses, overlapping black cigarette burns. On top, a solitary sheet of paper was covered in hand-written notes.

The basement room in which they sat was small and unfurnished save for the desk and chairs, and it was permeated by the dank, damp odour of mildew. The dampness seemed to account for the strangely coloured wallpaper, puckered along its seams and peeling from the wall like the sheets folded back on a freshly made bed. Powdery cracks, lined in black mold, crissed-crossed the ceiling like an enormous spiderweb, and mildew stains appeared on the carpet like lilies floating on a pond. The structure was showing its age.

The building, a four-storey brownstone located in the heart of Queens, New York, had been constructed in the mid-1800s by immigrant Irish workers who had been forced out of their homes and homeland by the ravages of the potato famine.

It had not fared well against the ravages of time and pollution. The building was now owned by NORAID, an Irish-American organization which purported to collect funds to help those who were suffering as a result of the strife in Northern Ireland. The basement room was used as a refuge by 'Lads from the old country', a euphemism for terrorists on the run, or for secret meetings such as the one in progress.

The younger of the two men, one Joseph "Josie" Donnelly, was barely twenty-two years old, going on sixty. He wore a tweed jacket over a white denim shirt, faded jeans, and a pair of running shoes. The wear and tear of the past few years showed in the tired face and the ever-present cigarette between his nicotine-stained, trembling fingers.

An unruly shock of brown hair fell down over the right side of his face, and he was continually pushing it back out of his eyes. On occasion, he would push it back too far, exposing the ugly puckered scar running from his hairline down towards his right eyebrow. The scar had been caused by a glass shard from a premature petrol bomb explosion, a legacy from his younger days on the streets as a rioter.

The older man was Tommy Mulholland, "Tommy Gun" to his friends and enemies alike. It was a nickname earned in the early days of the 'troubles', when he had resurrected his father's Thompson sub-machine gun and, hanging out the window of a black Falls road taxi, like a Caponeera gangster, he had managed to take out several soldiers and policemen on more than one occasion.

He had since moved on to more sophisticated weapons like the Ingram MACH-11, which he now held in a shoulder harness under his green corduroy jacket. The nickname, however, still stuck to him like ivy to a brick wall.

His face could have been formed from stone by a sculptor's hands, so seldom did he betray his emotions. It was a cruel face. Even those who knew him said that it seemed as if the devil himself rode on his shoulder.

Both men were members of the Irish Freedom Fighters, an ultra-violent offshoot of the Provisional IRA who truly believed that violence was the only solution to the problems in the North of Ireland. Their credo was based on the belief that the bigger the outrage, the more the public would pressure the British government to take her troops out of Ulster.

Sitting before them, in a rickety wooden chair, wearing his customary leather flying jacket and a pair of stone-coloured chinos, was Patrick Kelly. He was wondering what the hell was going on, and why he had ever complied with his grandmother's request to meet with these men.

"Patrick, me boy," she had said. "There's a couple of brave lads come over from the old country. I'm told they're looking for someone who can fly a helicopter so I'd like you to go and see them. If you can help them in any way, then do it, for your grandfather's sake." Then she went off to the kitchen to make a cup of tea while he sat on the sofa, anxiously rubbing the almost-healed scabs on the knuckles of his right hand. He had tried to conceal them during the conversation, not wanting to get another lecture from her about brawling in bars.

When the tea was ready she poured him a cup, added milk and sugar, stirred the dark-coloured liquid, and handed it to him. She repeated the process for herself and then, satisfied with the taste, she once again told him the story, one that he knew by heart, of how his grandfather fought valiantly against the British bastards. And she wept, as she always did, when she got to the part where the Black and Tans came to her house, took him and hanged him from a rafter in the barn, making her watch as his life was choked out of him. And now she had a chance to make good on her threat.

He listened intently, as always, and when she was finished he simply asked for the address, kissed her tenderly on the cheek and left. As he closed the door behind him, he saw her heading for the mantlepiece, to the only photograph she had of her husband.

He had been sitting in the chair for a good five minutes before either of the men spoke. They had introduced themselves but there was no shaking of hands in greeting. They sat down and pulled out a pile of notes which they perused quickly, ignoring him completely. He coughed and made an elaborate show of looking at his watch to get their attention.

Tommy Mulholland spoke first. He picked up the sheet of notes, looked them over and then, still holding the sheet, looked at Patrick Kelly. "We hear you were a chopper pilot in Vietnam. Was it a combat chopper?" Mulholland asked, in his gravelly Belfast accent. It pleased Kelly somewhat that Mulholland did not use the term 'Nam', like too many people did nowadays. It implied familiarization, something which most people using it could never attain. Vietnam had suddenly become 'in vogue' and it made the hairs on the back of his neck bristle with anger.

"Yes I was," he answered. "If you've talked to my grandmother then you'll know that I flew combat, and that I fly choppers for a living. That is, if you consider flying tourists around the Statue of Liberty making a living."

"We know all about you, Patrick. We have our sources, even here in America and we know even more about your exploits during the war. Gave you a lot of medals, didn't they? And it also seems as if you've seen the inside of every jail in New York since you came home. Miss the action, do you?"

The barb hit home. Kelly fumed, on the verge of losing his patience. "None of us came out of the 'Nam the same as we went in. I still have nightmares about the place and so do many of the other vets I know. And yes, I do miss the action. But what do you want with me? You seem to be taking a lot of time getting to the point of all this."

"Patience, Patrick. Your grandmother told us you were an impulsive sort. 'Gets it from his grandfather', she said. I'm just making sure I have all my facts straight. Now, do you still keep up to date with what's going on in the army, in terms of helicopters?"

"My grandmother will have told you that I still keep in touch with my old buddies from the war, the 25th Air Cavalry. I still have a lot of friends there."

"Trying to catch me out, are you Patrick?" said

hummingbird. After that it was like a drug so I've clocked quite a few hours on the Apache. But why do you ask? Have you got one of them somewhere?"

"No Patrick, we don't. Our friend, the good Colonel, has the Russian equivalent, the Hind MI-27E, at a training camp in Benghazi. Josie here has trained as a gunner on it. I know it's not quite the same as the Apache but ..." He shrugged his shoulders as if intimating it was close enough.

"You're right there," answered Kelly. "It's nothing like the Apache. The Russian pilots have nick-named it 'the flying coffin'."

Mulholland stood up, dragged his chair out from behind the table and placed it in front of Kelly. Then he sat down, his face only inches away from Kelly's, who could smell the sour odour of stale beer on the man's breath as he spoke.

"Jesus Christ," muttered Kelly. "Don't you have lifesavers in Ireland?"

"What was that?" asked Mulholland.

"Nothing, nothing at all," replied Kelly, anxious to keep this face to face conversation to a mini-mum.

Mulholland paused for a moment as if trying to put his train of thought back on the rails. "If we were to get an Apache, Patrick, would you fly it for us? Over in Ireland I mean. We'd pay you well and it would only be for about a week. Ireland's too small a place to be making hit-and-run attacks with

Tommy Mulholland, checking his notes and allowing a tiny smile to crease his face. It was gone in an instant, the mask back in its place, leaving Kelly to wonder if he had imagined the smile.

"You were in the 23rd Air Cavalry. There was no 25th. Tell me about your friends. What do they do now?"

"Most of them stayed in the service when we came home. I opted for civilian life. I had enough of taking orders from assholes and eating rotten mess-food. The others were good pilots and the army was only too happy to keep them. Right now, most of them test choppers for the military."

"What kind of choppers do they fly, Patrick?"

There it was. The reason for the meeting and all the questions. He kept his face straight, impassive, not wanting to betray the fact that he knew. He would play this little act out.

"They test the new Apache attack helicopter down at Fort Manning. They have been spending a lot of time with them, making modifications and testing new equipment."

"Could you fly the Apache, Patrick?" Mulholland put downthe sheet and stared straight at him, as if daring him to tell a lie.

"I've already flown one. Illegally, of course. My buddy Bill took me on the base one day, and we took an Apache up for a run. It's a real dream to fly, four tons of metal darting about the sky like a come, and Kelly walked over to where Tommy Mulholland was sitting on the floor. As he reached out his hand to pull him up, he saw him give an almost imperceptible shake of his head.

Kelly turned in a crouch, the knife appearing again, and as he completed the turn, just a microsecond from hurling the knife, he saw Donnelly pull his hand, empty, from under his jacket. Kelly altered his aim slightly and buried the knife in the wall, scarcely a inch from Donnelly's ear. Donnelly's head did not move; only his eyes turned sideways to look at the knife.

"Just as well you did," Kelly said, making an elaborate show of removing the knife from the wall, folding it back into his wrist sheath. "I'll be talking to ya." And with that he left the room, with Tommy Mulholland still on the floor and Josie Donnelly's mouth agape.

"You stupid little cunt," roared Mulholland. "When will you learn to keep your fuckin' mouth shut. You could have ruined the whole fuckin' thing. I'll have to talk to his grandmother again to make sure he will still help us." He stood up, dusted himself off and left the room without another word.

*   *   *   *   *

The tiny barroom was almost empty, with the exception of a few regulars playing darts and a stranger sitting alone. According to the barman, the man was a Brit lieutenant with the Royal Greenjackets who were stationed at the local army barracks. The barracks, in the border town of Newry, only a few miles north of the Irish Republic, was a favourite target for the IRA.

The soldier's tour of duty was complete, so he was having a few drinks to celebrate his return to mainland duty.

"Good bloody riddance," said one of the darts players, and the others nodded and murmured their assent. One of the younger players pushed forward to the bar to get another round of drinks. His name was Jimmy McKeogh, renowned in the local area for his ferocious temper and his willingness to 'fight with his shadow'.

There was always some sort of cut or contusion on his face, giving him the look of a severely battered pugilist. His temper had brought him into repeated conflicts with the army and police, and he had spent more than a few days in prison on assault convictions.

When the barman finished pouring the pints of Guinness, McKeogh leaned over the bar and asked him if the Brit had taken much drink. The barman nodded as he placed the glasses on a tray. McKeogh took the tray over to the others and grinned, his mouth opening to reveal a large gap where his front teeth used to be. They had been kicked out in an altercation over two weeks ago, but it was still too soon for any reconstructive work. He said, loudly enough for the stranger to hear: "Well lads, he has got two days left over here. Who knows, he might not make it home at all!"

"I'll drink to that, Jimmy," said one of the players, raising his glass in a mock toast. Already they were mentally taking bets on who would win the scrap.

The stranger appeared totally engrossed in his drink, sipping it slowly and staring at his reflection in the bar mirror. He was, in fact, taking in every furtive glance in his direction and trying to pick up any piece of conversation. He wasn't looking at himself in the mirror either. He was watching the front door to check on anyone entering or leaving the bar.

This was not the first time he had been in such a situation, but he felt decidedly uncomfortable being unarmed, as off-duty soldiers would normally be. To pass the time he thought back to his recent trip to America - five weeks ago, yet it seemed a lifetime. If I had my way, he thought to himself, I'd rather be sitting on a beach in North Carolina, sipping a cold beer and looking at all the lovely dollies.

However, an assignment was an assignment, and the bar was reasonably warm and comfortable. He could be lying under a cold, wet meadow, somewhere near the border, manning an observation post, living in the same clothes for a week, eating cold rations and shitting in a plastic bag. He had done the OP job many times and when compared to that, this duty didn't seem so bad.

"Baiting the trap" was how Major Skinner had put it. "You're going to sit there like a big fat piece of cheese and we're going to hope that someone comes along for a nibble."

John Waters was a lieutenant, but not with the Royal Greenjackets. They were his original outfit before he joined the Special Air Service. He was now on special duty in Northern Ireland. As a specialist in all forms of unarmed combat, he and his unit had been brought into action here because of their extensive training in anti-terrorist techniques. They were part of the Counter Revolutionary Warfare group, trained at the Stirling Lines SAS base in Hereford for just such situations.

He had joined the army after leaving school at age sixteen, armed with eight 'O' levels and high hopes of following in his father's footsteps. He proved to be a model soldier, dedicated and eager to learn. He became popular with the others in his regiment because of his quick wit and pleasant disposition. The training was long and hard, but he applied himself to his tasks and became one of the regiment's top recruits. He had only one goal in mind - to join the Special Air Service.

Ever mindful that only a handful of hopefuls ever make the grade, out of hundreds of applicants, he pushed himself beyond the limits of endurance in preparation for the rigorous SAS selection process.

The thorough medical was passed with ease, and running one and a half miles, in army boots, was accomplished in eleven minutes, one minute under the allotted time. Next came the forced marches over the Brecon Beacons in Wales: some of the most windswept, desolate wilderness in Britain. Again, the training he had done in preparation for the test saw him through.

The next group of tests had to be done solo. In this set, he was required to use a map and compass to navigate his way across mountains, performing a series of tasks: laying charges at certain key points or carrying out covert surveillance of a specific area. After, he was to required to give a report to a group of seasoned SAS veterans.

They would debrief him with the thoroughness of an interrogator. To a man, the veterans liked the spunky youngster in front of them and passed their feelings on to the selection officer. The final task, and the most difficult, was the endurance march. Forty-five miles across country, carrying a fifty pound pack, a belt-pack weighing twelve pounds, and an eighteen-pound rifle which had to be carried by hand, as it did not have a sling. The march was to be completed in twenty hours. Success would bring the much-sought-after temporary status with the regiment.

To the surprise of his instructors, he completed the journey in just under nineteen hours, collapsing to his knees after crossing the 'finishing line', almost totally exhausted.

The instructor then applied the sickener factor, designed to select those who could reach within themselves for one last effort. It could be applied at any stage of the selection process, and its use was totally at the discretion of the instructor.

As Waters rose to his feet, the strain clearly showing on his face, the instructor smiled and said, "Okay Johnny, now you've got to go all the way back. Good luck." Waters cursed the instructor under his breath, composed himself, smiled at the man and set off back to the starting point. Two miles down the road, the instructor was waiting in a truck to take him back to the base. He had made it.

Now came three years of specialist training in demolitions, communications, and marksmanship. At the end of those three years he spent another year in specialist study as a close-quarter-battle-marksman with the Counter Revolutionary Warfare Wing. Then he was ready to put those deadly skills into practice.

His unit had been posted to Northern Ireland

when terrorist attacks took an alarming upswing, especially around the border. Working in their traditional two- and four-man teams, his team had been assigned to the area to prevent terrorists from crossing into the North, carrying out their attacks, and then fleeing to the comparative safety of the Irish Republic.

The regular army did not have the necessary skills to counter these raids, and were incurring significant casualties. Waters's team had managed to reduce the number of terrorist incursions into the North.

Right now, however, he was acting as "bait" for the major in an attempt to stem the number of attacks on off-duty soldiers. Of late, several young soldiers had been lured from local pubs by bright-eyed Irish girls who promised a good time and a nightcap back at their place. The good time meant getting laid and then getting a .38 slug in the head as they lay sleeping. The ambush was generally referred to as a 'honey-trap', and despite frequent warnings, off-duty soldiers were still being killed.

Since none of the soldiers survived, there were no witnesses. It was also practically impossible to trace the soldiers' last movements because of the ability of the local population to develop instant amnesia.

Waters and his team had been selected by the major to pose as soldiers going home at the end of

their tours. Their instructions were explicit: get rid
of these bitches by whatever means necessary. So
they visited different towns each week, drinking in
the local bars, like off-duty soldiers.

This was the third bar so far that Waters had visited, but he had not been approached by any girls.
He hadn't even seen girls in any of the bars. He
positioned himself in front of the mirror so that he
had a good view of the regulars in the corner and
also of the door behind him. So far, the only person
to come in and out was the young loudmouth playing darts in the corner. The cigarette machine had
run out of his favourite brand, so he had gone to
the local store, returning a few minutes later.

Waters was sipping the last of his drink when
the front door opened and two girls walked in. He
did not lift his head but watched them in the mirror
as they came over and sat down at the bar. They
were both in their late teens or early twenties, casually dressed in faded jeans and sweatshirts proclaim-
ing that they had 'done it' in Majorca.

Wrapped around their handbags were green
coveralls, so he presumed they were from the local
spinning mill, dropping in for a drink after their shift.

Both girls had shoulder-length, curly brown hair,
and from the similarity of their features, he guessed
that they were somehow related. They were also
extremely attractive, something which he did not

need in his present state. It reminded him that he had not been on leave for several weeks and had not been near a woman in all that time. He pushed the thought to the back of his mind and concentrated on eavesdropping. The barman approached them, and from his greeting appeared to know them quite well.

"Evening girls. Just finished your shift then? How did it go today?"

The older of the two girls answered.

"That Mary Martin is a real slave driver. She never let up on us all day, the bitch. We thought we'd come in for a drink before we go home. I know I need one."

"You'll have the usual then? Gin and tonics?" he asked.

"Sure we will. Might as well make them doubles."

The girls continued talking as the barman went off to mix their drinks. Their conversation centred around fashions and music and who was dating whom, verbally abusing their supervisor whom they felt had never been on the receiving end of a good screw, and then they went on to discuss a dance which was to be held at the local hall on the weekend.

Waters let them talk for a few minutes and then turned his head round to face them. "Good evening ladies," he said in his poshest British accent. "I couldn't help overhearing you had a bad day. Could I possibly buy you a drink?" Both heads turned in his direction. He had their attention.

"I'm going home in a couple of days and this is my last chance to have a few drinks on the town. It would be nice to have some company." He deliberately slurred a few of the words to give the impression that he had been drinking a lot.

"That would be nice of you," answered the older girl, who had spoken to the barman. "My name's Maureen Ryan and this is my cousin Margaret." They picked up their overalls and came down the bar to where he was sitting to shake his hand. A waft of delicious perfume assaulted his senses.

"My name's John Simpson, and I must say I am delighted to meet you." As he introduced himself he tried desperately hard not to stare at Maureen, as her sweatshirt was doing a poor job of hiding some very appetizing curves. "I thought my last evening here was going to be boring. Instead I get a chance to spend it with two charming ladies." He paid for their drinks and ordered another for himself.

"I take it you both work in the Mill," he said, pointing to the overalls.

"You're right there," answered Maureen. "The work's not very interesting but it's better than being on the dole. And the money's not too bad either. If we could just get a better supervisor it would be perfect. The one we have is a proper bitch. I think she's frustrated."

"Perhaps I could introduce her to my captain," he offered, smiling. "They sound as if they were made for each other. He's a real bastard. I wouldn't shed too many tears if the Provos got him, I tell you. They'd be doing the entire British Army a favour.

"Anyway, I don't want the thoughts of him to ruin my evening. Tell me, do you live around here?"

"I do," replied Maureen. "But Margaret lives just outside the town. We stop in most nights for a quiet drink on the way to the bus stop. It doesn't come for about twenty minutes - the bus that is, not Margaret."

Waters laughed heartily as Margaret punched her cousin in the ribs, her face flushing with embarrassment.

"I take it Margaret is the quiet one in the family," he said, and they all laughed.

"I'm only quiet until you get to know me," she said, poking him playfully in the ribs. "Anyway, it's hard to get a word in sideways when Maureen here gets started. I think her mother kissed the Blarney stone too many times."

"Not to worry. I'm only too glad to have the company."

"Well it won't be for long," said Margaret. "The last bus leaves in a few minutes and I want to catch it. If I don't then I'll have to walk all of eight miles to get home. I'm sorry I can't stay longer."

He turned to Maureen. "Do you have to go as well?" he asked, a sorrowful look on his face.

"I don't have far to go," she replied, "but I'm not sure that I want to spend the evening drinking."

"I'd really like you to stay if you could. You don't have to drink. Some company would be nice on its own."

She hesitated for a few moments, as if not sure of what to do. She looked to her cousin for advice, but Margaret simply winked and nodded at Waters. "I'd stay if I could," she said, emphasising the 'I'.

Maureen shrugged her shoulders. "Okay, I'll stay. I wasn't planning to do anything serious this evening anyway. The laundry can wait for another day." She smiled at him, showing off her pearly white teeth, and his pulse began racing. Margaret left a few minutes later, apologizing profusely for having to go, leaving them to chatter on aimlessly about everything and nothing.

They talked about music and their favourite television programs. He told her about his childhood in Yorkshire, all the while mentally undressing her. She asked questions about London, a place she had never been but would love to visit. He told her about the West End, where all the hit plays were performed, about Trafalgar Square where the pigeons were so tame they would eat out of your hand. He described the red-light district of Soho and Picadilly Circus where the junkies hung out. Hung out what, she asked, and was embarrassed when he explained.

She listened, enthraled by his stories and then told him what it was like for her to grow up during the bad times with all the bombings and shootings. Her eyes misted over at times when she talked about friends who had been killed by the 'troubles', victims of the constant sectarian violence in the province. He tried to trip her up in subtle ways but could not and then felt guilty about trying to do so. He began to wonder if she could be a terrorist, capable of murdering young soldiers in cold blood, or if he was just very lucky guy to be spending an evening with a beautiful young woman. Or maybe he was just becoming jaded by the whole affair, thinking that everyone he met was a terrorist, or had some links to terrorism which would pose a threat to his existence.

"Can I get you another drink?" he asked, pointing to her empty glass. "It's almost closing time."

"No thanks, John. You've bought me enough drinks tonight already, and I do have to get up for work in the morning. You know some of us have to work for a living. We can't all ride around in jeeps all day long, doing spot checks on old ladies."

"What do you mean?" he asked, feigning indignance. "Those old ladies really like getting frisked. It's the most fun they've had in years."

"Oh, I see," she laughed. "You like frisking older women."

"Well, just some of the time," he replied. "If I can't find any attractive young ladies." Her eyes twinkled mischievously.

He said, "Do you really have to go? These last few hours must be the most pleasant I've spent since I came to the Province. Apart from frisking the old ladies, of course." She laughed and tossed back the remains of her drink. He made a long face and looked into her eyes. What he wanted to see was some indication that things might be going the way she had planned, if in fact she was a terrorist. There was none.

"You can come back to my place for a while, if you like. The barman's going to be throwing us out of here in a few minutes. It's not too far from here."

The alarm bells which had been clanging in his head a few moments ago were now silent. He was going to spend a couple of hours in the company of a very attractive girl. There was no way the major was going to hear about this episode.

The few drinks had mellowed them both and she seemed really at ease. As they left the bar, he put his arm around her waist and was pleasantly surprised when she did the same to him. She turned her face up to look at him and he felt that old familiar stirring in his groin. He brought his lips slowly down to meet hers. They were warm and moist, offering no resistance, and it was a few seconds before he pulled away.

"Mmmm, nice," he said, and she smiled at the compliment.

Her flat was only a few minutes walk from the bar, as she had said. When they came to the front door, she put her hand through the letter-box and pulled out a piece of string with the front door key attached.

"Just in case Margaret wants to get in when I'm not here," she explained, seeing the surprised look on his face. She opened the door and let them both into the flat, pulling the key back through the letter-box when they were both inside. On the floor were several letters, all mailed to Margaret Ryan. He began to relax.

The flat was small, but cosy, with a few pieces of furniture seemingly scattered at random across the floor. No two pieces matched, and she explained that it was furnished by the landlord, hence the decor. The living room seemed to be the main area as all of the other rooms lead into it. There was a bedroom, a dinette, and a washroom, all visible from the living room.

Out of instinct he scanned the room, looking for any item which might seem out of place. A basket of dirty clothes sat on one of the chairs and she hurriedly picked it up and put it under the table. A small television sat atop a wooden dresser. Beside it were several empty glasses, a half empty bottle of gin, and a full bottle of whiskey.

She took off her coat and held out her arm for his. He draped it over her arm and she wandered off into the bedroom to hang them in the closet. He followed her, not wanting to let her out of his sight. His guard was down, but not all the way. She took two wire hangars out of the closet, put the coats on them and hung them back up. She turned to go back into the living room and walked straight into his arms.

His arms encircled her gently and once more his lips sought hers. He encountered no resistance and began to feel the gentle pressure of her body against his. As he ran his hands up the back of her sweatshirt, she slipped her tongue between his lips and began a gentle duel with his. He could taste the alcohol on her tongue. Her skin was silky smooth and he moved his hands up to gently massage her shoulders. Much to his delight, he discovered that she was not wearing a bra, and so he moved his hands around to cup her full, firm breasts. Her nipples were hard with desire and she pulled away and moaned as he softly stroked them with his fingers. The sweatshirt had ridden up her body and he stooped down and took one of her nipples into his mouth, tugging it gently between his teeth. He could stand it no longer.

"Let's get rid of these clothes," he whispered, barely able to recognize his own voice. "They're only getting in the way."

She did not reply but stepped back and pulled the sweatshirt over her head in one fluid movement. He gasped involuntarily at the beautiful sight. She reached over and switched off the lamp, leaving the room in semi-darkness. The bed creaked as she lay back, kicked off her shoes and pulled off her jeans, then she was tugging at his shirt as he fumbled with his trousers.

He dragged off his boots and piled his trousers and underwear on top of them at the side of the bed. He then pulled back the sheets and slid into bed beside her. Her arms were around him in an instant, pulling him down towards her. She let his hands roam over her body, touching and probing, eliciting soft moans of pleasure each time he touched a sensitive spot. She kissed him hungrily, moulding her body to his. He was still in control of his emotions, still afraid to let himself get caught up in her passion. He felt like a spectator rather than a participant.

She seemed to sense he was holding back, so she took his hand and guided it across her flat stomach to the soft patch of fur between her legs. His fingers began to probe the wetness between her thighs as she moaned and thrust herself against his hand, his well-lubricated fingers sliding in and out of her effortlessly. At the same time she grasped his rigid cock firmly, stroking it gently. He gasped. It was a long, long time since he had been with a woman, and if she continued he was going to come, and much quicker than she expected.

He slid down the bed, forcing her to let go of him as he licked her stomach in lazy circles, his slick fingers caressing the gentle curves of her breasts. She knew what was coming and grasped his head firmly, pushing his face against her lips and grinding her hips against him. He needed no direction and ran his tongue up and down the moist entrance, savouring the musky aroma and her sweet juices.

Dipping his tongue in and out of her, he slipped a finger into her and began to thrust it back and forth as he licked the tiny nub of flesh which was now engorged with blood. She panted loudly, her cries urging him on and he could feel tiny muscle spasms grasping his finger.

"Now, John, now," she cried. "Please now."

She lifted her legs and pulled him up, opening the way for him. He raised himself on top of her as she took him in her hand and guided him inside her. He cried out, penetrating deep into the velvety warmth. As he entered her, she sank her teeth into his shoulder and locked her legs around his back. It was like being caught in a vice. She pushed her hips up to meet his, matching his rhythm, thrust for thrust, until at last she screamed, the veins in her neck cording against her skin. Her body shuddered as she reached orgasm, and moments later he ejaculated, thrusting violently again and again until he collapsed on top of her, exhausted and spent.

"That's what I call a going-away present," he whispered. "I feel totally knackered. I thought I was going to have the 'brewer's droop' after all those drinks. But you certainly brought out the best in me."

He brought up his hand to stifle a yawn, and Maureen grinned at him as she began to yawn as well. She said, "It's always good to get that first one out of the way. Then we can get down to some serious business. Anyway, I though you army types were fit for anything. I bet your Captain wouldn't like to hear that you're no match for a woman."

He laughed, and she eased herself out from under him and climbed out of the bed. She stood there for a moment, allowing him to savour the sight as the faint glow from the streetlights illuminated her curves.

"I'm going to clean up a little bit," she said, walking over to the washroom.

"Well don't be too long or else I'll be asleep," he replied, yawning again loudly to emphasize the point.

She went into the washroom, pulled on the light, and closed the door gently. She turned on both taps to allow the water to heat up a little before damping a facecloth to wipe her face and hands. When she was finished, she towelled herself dry and then reached over to flush the toilet. As it was gurgling loudly, she lifted the top of the cistern and pulled out a plastic bag which was lying on the bottom. The bag contained a silenced, 9-millimetre Beretta with a nine-round clip of hollowpoints. It was her favourite weapon and one which she had used many times.

She removed the gun from the waterproof bag, pulled back the slide to chamber a round and then draped the towel over it. The gun had been checked earlier in the day, but her training forced her to check and re-check it as if her life depended on it, which it did. She reached out and switched off the light, then pushed open the door with her foot.

Filtered light from the streetlamps outside the bedroom window shone on the bed, showing the outline of the sleeping figure.

"Good bye Brit," she whispered, and squeezed off three rounds in rapid succession into the prone outline. The discharge was no more than a quiet cough and the bullets impacted in a small cluster. One would have been sufficient but her instructor always emphasized to her to make sure of the kill by using one or two more. She stepped forward to inspect her handiwork, the smoking gun still trained on the body.

Suddenly, a garotte went around her throat. She dropped the gun and tried to struggle, but it was to no avail. The pressure of the garotte was increasing and her lungs began to scream for air. Then she heard his voice. It was cold and hard.

"How will Margaret know you've done your dirty work?"

When she had climbed out of bed, Waters had taken the garotte from his boot and arranged the pillows under the sheets to look like a sleeping figure. He was fairly sure she did not pose a threat but he was not taking any chances. If she was a terrorist then now would be the moment for her to make a move. He went over to the washroom door, praying he was wrong in his suspicions. He felt a momentary sadness when he heard the lifting of the toilet lid behind the sound of the toilet flushing, and the familiar click of the first round being eased into the chamber of a pistol. Then his reflexes and the adrenaline took over.

The garotte loosened a little to allow her to speak.

"I'm to hang the key out the door and Margaret will know the job's over." Her voice was a hoarse rasp.

He released the wire and she inhaled deeply and with relief, filling her oxygen-starved lungs. Then, suddenly, he pulled the handles together with all his might, his arms trembling with the effort. The wire bit deeply into her throat, like a cheese-cutter, almost decapitating her. There were great spurts of blood and loud gurgling noises as the wire cut through her windpipe and into her jugular vein. He then released the handles and let her fall. She was dead before she hit the ground.

When he had finished washing the blood off his hands, he left the taps gurgling loudly and went back into the bedroom to dress. Maureen's sightless eyes stared at him as the dark blood began to form a dark halo on the carpet around her head. Some fucking angel, he thought.

He dressed quickly, went to the front door and hung out the key, and took cover behind one of the armchairs to wait. It did not take long before he heard the key being inserted in the lock. The door opened and closed quickly.

"Maureen, did you get the bastard?"

He recognized Margaret's voice immediately. In the dim light he could see her turning towards the washroom where the taps were gurgling loudly. She had a silenced pistol in her hand. As she reached out to turn on the living room light, he stood up. She blinked when golden light filled the living room.

He said, "Hello Margaret, remember me?"

She opened her mouth to scream. The pistol in his hand coughed once, the bullet striking her in the forehead, knocking her sprawling against the wall.

It exited at the back of her head, covering the walls behind her with gore and pieces of scalp. An expression of surprise persisted on her face as she slid down the wall, leaving a broad red trail like that of snail. He kicked away her gun and shot her once more in the head. Then he walked over to the phone and, using a piece of cloth, dialled a pre-arranged number. When a voice said 'Mousetrap', he replied 'full' and gave the number and address of the flat.

Major Skinner put down the phone and smiled, pleased that the operation had produced some results at last. The clean-up could begin and John Waters could at last go home for some well-deserved leave.

On the local news the following morning it was reported that at approximately 3:30 a.m., an explosion occurred in a flat in James Gate. The flat and two neighbouring stores had been completely destroyed. Partial remains of two bodies were discovered in the flat but no positive identification could as yet be made. Combing the devastation, the police were hard-pressed to find a finger, let alone a fingerprint. Often, in cases where the victims were in close proximity to the explosion, their extremities were literally vaporised. Police forensic experts were certain, however, from their preliminary tests, that the flat was being used to store explosives as quantities of prima-cord, detonators, Memo-Park timers, and other bomb-making equipment were found in the rubble. It was presumed that something had gone awry during the making of a bomb.

Margaret and Maureen Leary joined their brother John in the ranks of Irish martyrs and were buried with full military honours. He had been shot dead a few months earlier while trying to ambush an army patrol.

CHAPTER 6
Apache

The hastily constructed platform groaned under the combined weight of the assembled politicians and military brass. Given it was a Saturday morning, and on a long week-end, it was surprising to see how many politicians had shown up. They were there ostensibly to see a demonstration of the McDonnell Douglas Helicopter's AH64A-Apache, but most of them had come for the free drinks and lunch that followed the exhibition.

The Apache was the anti-tank helicopter favoured by the U.S. military, and Canada's Ministry of Defense, about to spend several million dollars on a modernization plan, decided that the Apache should be considered.

The review came about after several months of well-planned, intense lobbying by senior management of McDonnell Douglas Canada (MDCAN). Their proposal to build parts of the Apache at their plant in Toronto, creating several hundred jobs there and many more in spin-offs from sub-contract work, would be a feather in the current government's hat. Hence the number of politicians.

The demonstration for the military was taking place at the Canadian Forces Base in Downsview, a suburb of Toronto, so the Apache could be flown easily to the MDCAN plant in Malton and serviced there each evening. A second demonstration, scheduled for the following morning was for MDCAN executives only. Two American pilots had flown the Apache up from the United States especially for the demonstration. As it was an anti-tank helicopter, they had requested a few out-of-service tanks for the demonstration, so that the politicians could witness first-hand the awesome power of the Hellfire missiles. Red-faced officials had to explain that they did not have any tanks available. They did have a number of out-of-date tanks, but they were still in service.

The American pilots sensed the acute embarrassment over such an admission and suggested that some vans or trucks from a scrapyard could be used as substitutes. Their suggestion was heartily welcomed and so it came to be that several old, battered trucks sat on waste ground a few hundred yards from the front of the platform.

A public-address system had also been set up, and from here the marketing director from McDonnell Douglas Helicopters was delivering his sales pitch, the well-rehearsed dialogue rolling off his tongue as smooth as his expensive Armani suit, silk tie, and black, wing-tip shoes. He had worked the crowd like a presidential candidate before election night. He glanced down at his watch, mindful that the chopper would be arriving at any moment. Just like comedy, he thought; timing is everything. Over the top of the platform he could see the tiny speck in the distance, approaching at 192 miles-per-hour, its maximum operational speed.

It was time.

With a flourish which would have made a ringmaster proud, he announced, "Gentlemen, I give you the finest anti-tank chopper in the world, the AH-64A Apache."

The chopper roared in over the top over the platform, its two 1693 shp, T700-GE-701 turboshafts screaming and leaving more than a few feathers ruffled. Anyone who had dozed off during the presentation was now fully awake.

The pilot made one circuit around the platform and then disappeared into the distance. The co-pilot/gunner was using the fire-control system in a heads-up mode, relying on the visual display from the FOV (field of vision) cameras installed in the nose of the Apache, to acquire his targets.

The images were relayed through an optical relay tube to the small monitor on the gunner's console. Immediately above the monitor were the two FOV eyepieces which relayed the infra-red images from the TADS (Target Acquisition and Designation sight), also installed in the front of the Apache.

These were primarily used for night operations and for combat under reduced visibility. None of these were required today as the sun was beating down through a cloudless sky.

The gunner quickly acquired the targets and, using the RF/IR (Radio Frequency/Infra-red) seeker configuration, went into launch mode. He was using the LOBL (lock-on-before-launch) method to perform the demonstration. He then thumbed the fire button on the handgrip at the right-hand side of the fire-control console.

A small puff of smoke preceded the launching of the first set of Hellfire missiles. Then the trucks disintegrated as the 44.8 kilogram projectiles simultaneously impacted and exploded in a huge swirling fireball. Four hardpoints on the tiny stub wings of the Apache carried sixteen of the deadly missiles, one of which was sufficient to destroy any tank.

Firing two Hellfire missiles at an old, dilapidated truck was a bit of a waste, but then politicians were usually impressed with a bit of overkill. There were more than a few gasps of surprise when the Apache destroyed six trucks in a single pass, leaving only smoking craters and scattered pieces of metal as a testament to their existence. The missiles had been appropriately named.

The salesman smiled like a proud parent. The next pass of the chopper brought the remote-controlled gun into action. Several oil-drums had been set up as targets to demonstrate this function. The gunner used the monitor again, and, as he moved the fire control column, the camera in the nose panned across the terrain until the cross-hairs settled on the first of the oil-drums. Then he depressed the Fire button on the console. Immediately the XM230E1 chain gun, situated in the under-fuselage turret, began to spit its 30-millimetre load, the bullets pounding through the drums and spending themselves in the ground beyond. It was as if the earth itself was exploding in great gouts of soil and metal.

He then moved the gun back and forth, demolishing each drum in the same manner. When the pass was complete the pilot brought the chopper gently to earth, a suitable distance from the platform. It would not be appropriate to have the military brass scrambling after their hats were blown off by the chopper's downwash.

As the whine of the engines began to subside, the salesman continued his pitch. "Well Gentlemen, that is the Apache, and I don't mind saying it, the finest goddamned chopper in the world today. If you'll just step over you can take a look around her. And don't be afraid to ask questions of the pilots. Those boys are both Vietnam vets, and are well accustomed to flying attack helicopters. The one feature that they will explain to you is the exhaust system. The Ruskies have a chopper just like this one, called the MI-27 HIND E, and have used it extensively in Afghanistan against the Mujahideen guerillas.

"The big difference between theirs and ours is the specially-designed exhaust system. This bird is not susceptible to heat-seeking missiles because of the passive, engine exhaust, infra-red suppressor; whereas the Ruskie version can easily be brought down with SAM missiles. That's why the Russian pilots nicknamed it the 'flying coffin'.

"One of the key points of this chopper is its survivability.

The pilots will elaborate on the Pilot Night Vision System when you inspect the chopper, but I'd like to take a moment to cover survivability.

"As you can see, this chopper is designed to operate in a hostile environment, and to do so it must be extremely durable. It has many features to protect it in enemy terrain but I will just deal with the key features. First, it can withstand 7.62-milli-metre machine-gun fire and 23-millimetre cannon fire. Its transmission and gearboxes are designed to function without lubrication for one hour and, and, this is a biggie, it can withstand a vertical impact of up to thirty-five miles per hour.

"We have taken a lot of time to incorporate elaborate defensive mechanisms in the chopper, such as a passive radar warning system, an infra-red jammer, a radar jammer, and a laser detector. In other words, we can get to the bad guys before they realize we're there.

"You might have seen some of the images of the Apache on television, as this baby was in the first wave of the attack on Iraq. And you can't get a more hostile environment than that!"

He stepped down from the podium and led the way over to the chopper, where the pilots, resplend-ent in their blue Air Cavalry flying suits, stood wait-ing to answer questions. The military brass stood back and viewed the chopper with a professional, detached air, asking questions which served to ex-aggerate their own self-importance. The politicians scrambled around, trying to find some of the hot, spent, shell casings, "Souvenirs for the kids."

The salesman took the defense minister's arm and led him to one side. "Well, what do you think?"

The minister smiled. "All in all, that was quite a

show you put on for us. I'd say this will satisfy our requirements, pending a further review by the military, but I think you can count on their support. We can talk some more about it during lunch. By the way, where are you keeping the chopper? Someone said that it's not staying here at the base."

"That's right, minister. We're storing it over at the MDCAN plant in Malton so that we can service it each evening. There's one more demo tomorrow and then we're going home. We took the precaution of hiring extra security guards for the duration."

"That's good" replied the minister. "I wouldn't like to see this machine fall into the wrong hands."

The salesman laughed. "I hardly think so. Who in Canada would want to steal an anti-tank helicopter? And what would they do with it anyway?"

*   *   *   *   *

The drive to the Canadian border was long and boring but Patrick Kelly didn't mind. He enjoyed driving. He had never been up this way before so he wanted peace to appreciate the scenery without any distractions.

Conversation was sporadic at best, consisting of a few 'What's that?' or 'Where are we now?' questions from Tommy Mulholland.

Josie Donnelly lay sprawled across the back seat

of the car, totally uncommunicative. Except for a brief lapse, he had not uttered a word since leaving New York.

From time to time Kelly would look back in the rear-view mirror to see a pair of black, angry eyes staring at him. He gave an involuntary shudder each time, his spine tingling, warning him to be careful. He had seen that look in Vietnam, on the faces of those who had crossed the edge and for whom killing had become a pleasure. They became consumed by their bloodlust, driven by inner forces which, when released, could only be stopped by another bullet. He had come close to the edge a few times in the pursuit of revenge, but mercifully had been able to veer away, guided by veterans who recognised the signs.

Following the disastrous meeting, Kelly had upped his price and they reluctantly agreed, knowing he had them over a barrel. He explained what had happened to his grandmother, but that he would still go through with the operation as a favour to her. She had kissed him on the cheek and then promised to give Mulholland a 'piece of her mind'.

Kelly had picked them up at their hotel shortly after leaving his grandmother's house. The parting with her had been a tearful episode: she had clung to his shoulders, almost afraid to let him leave.

"You make sure and come back now," she ordered, releasing her surprisingly strong grip on his shoulders. "And be careful of that Joseph Donnelly. I heard what happened at the meeting. I have the feeling that he may try to get his own back on you, so be warned."

"Don't worry grandmother," he said reassuringly. "I grew an extra set of eyes when I was in 'Nam. I'll be careful." He bent over and kissed her softly on the cheek.

"May God go with you, Patrick, and bring you safely home to us."

As he left the room, he saw she was staring at the grainy, black and white photograph of her husband which sat on top of the mantelpiece. Its gold frame, a present from Patrick many years ago, gleamed and sparkled from its daily polishing. He closed the door quietly behind him.

They drove along interstate ninety-five, the scenic route up through the Catskills mountains. The silence in the car was interrupted when he drove past a sign for a little town called Antrim, nestled snugly in the hills. The two terrorists seemed enervated by the sign, the discussion prompted by the fact that the two had blown up the Deerpark hotel in the town of Antrim on the outskirts of Belfast. Kelly filed the information away for future reference.

Following that short outburst, they both returned to silence, each content to stare out the window looking at the scenery. Pine trees, like sentinels, lined the road just like their counterparts in the Glens of Antrim. The scent of pine filled the car, almost eliminating the overpowering smell of the terrorists' aftershave.

The journey continued without event, and they were soon entering the outskirts of Niagara Falls. They had decided to attempt the crossing into Canada at the Queenston-Lewiston bridge, as security was a little less stringent than at Niagara. At one of the ubiquitous donut shop littering the town, Kelly went over his plan to get them across the border.

As the pair had entered the United States illegally, using false passports, they would pose as American citizens going to visit Toronto. They had obtained fake driver's licenses in New York, which would pass a cursory examination by the border guards. The licenses were considered second-level proof of citizenship, primary proof being a birth certificate. Getting fake birth certificates took a great deal of time, a luxury they could not afford.

The decision not to use the false Irish passports was made by Tommy Mulholland. Suspicious border guards could result in a visit to the immigration office, which would effectively put an end to their plans, and an Irish passport would have the undesired effect of putting the guards on alert.

The border officials were still smarting over a recent incident. Joe Cahill, the former commander of the Provisional IRA's Belfast Brigade and current finance officer of the IRA Army council, was making an incognito visit to New York. Alerted to the fact the FBI were on his trail, he fled, not bothering to return to his Bronx apartment, and headed for the Canadian border.

Using a fake Irish passport, he passed across without incident. This was despite the fact that his photograph was on an FBI 'Most Wanted' poster, adorning the walls of the border office.

Kelly had insisted that they change their clothes for the trip. The ill-fitting suits which he wanted them to wear made them a little conspicuous, even in cosmopolitan New York. He had gone out and purchased brightly coloured shorts and shirts for them both, as well as some sneakers. When Mulholland had first put them on, his white skin gave Kelly the impression of a cadaver. He told Mulholland that he had seen better looking corpses and was answered by a gruff 'Fuck off'.

After finishing their coffee, they made one final stop at the duty-free shop close to the bridge. Kelly told them that no one in their right mind would cross the border into Canada without taking some duty-free booze. The prices in Canadian bars were exorbitant, so they would be expected to bring some bottles.

After paying for the duty-free liquor, he drove towards the bridge and the booth where he had spotted a pretty female guard.

While sitting in the lineup however, he began to wonder if the two men would be able to pass muster. They had sat in the sun for two days prior to the trip in an almost futile attempt to get a tan. Right now they both looked like medium-done lobsters.

Joanne Ryan was having a bad day. She and some of her friends had been partying the previous evening at the Library, a popular nightspot in Buffalo, and she had woken up with an unrelenting headache. That, combined with the fact that several of the drivers coming into Canada had given her a hard time, had put her into a foul mood. More than a few had been unceremoniously directed over to the customs booth to be searched for contraband. At least she only had another twenty minutes to go in her one-hour rotation, before moving to the second line, the immigration office.

A car had just pulled up to her booth and without looking she snapped the question, "Nationality?"

"Well now, isn't that a fine way to greet anyone, and on such a beautiful day," came the reply. She was just about to let loose a tirade starting with, "Answer the bloody question and quit the bullshit," when she turned and found herself looking into a disarming smile. The bright eyes, well-tanned skin, and red curly hair framing the driver's face sent a ripple through her body.

Patrick Kelly was well aware of the effect he had on women, and used it to his advantage whenever possible. She tried hard to keep her face straight, but failed miserably and smiled back in return, the black mood dissipating like an early morning mist.

"I'm sorry," she started. "I've had a really bad day and I was wrong to take it out on you."

"That's quite alright," he replied. "I've had days like that myself. As a matter of fact, we're off up to Toronto for a wild week-end of wine, women, song, and more women. You wouldn't by any chance know any good spots in Toronto? You look like a lady who likes to party."

She blushed, remembering her antics at the Library the previous evening. She had taken a solemn oath that very morning never to drink shooters again. At some point during that outing, a point which she could not remember, her friends had told her she was dancing on top of the bar and singing. Given the fact that she couldn't carry a tune in a bucket she was doubly embarrassed.

She said, "There's a disco called Sparkles in the CN Tower; it's not too bad. There's another couple nearby called Brandys and Scotland Yard. They're all usually packed on the weekend and they are pretty well known. You won't have any trouble getting directions.

"But why go all the way to Toronto? There are lots of good bars in Niagara Falls and lots of available women."

"For example?" he asked.

"Bars or women?" she joked.

"Well let's start with the bars. Then we'll get down to the serious stuff."

"The Library is a really popular spot", she said, emphasizing the word 'Library'.

"I take it you go there a lot," he replied, leaning on the word 'you'.

"Most evenings. A bunch of us go after work and sometimes close the place. It's a good crowd and the prices are reasonable. And, of course there are plenty of single women."

"Do you think you could find dates for my friends here?" he asked, nodding at the others. She barely looked at them; she was too entranced with Patrick Kelly.

"Oh, I don't think that will be a problem."

"Okay, then. We'll be coming back this way on Sunday evening about six or seven, so we'll be sure to call into the Library. My name's Patrick. What's yours?"

"I'm Joanne. You better get a move on. There's quite a line-up behind you. I'll see you on Sunday night. Bye now."

He drove past the booth without looking behind. As the car passed her, she saw his friend in the back seat pushing back his hair. She caught a fleeting glimpse of what looked like a scar on his forehead.

The next car pulled up and she began the customary routine. It was only when she heard the answers coming from the driver that she realised she had not spoken to the other two men in Patrick's car.

Mulholland and Donnelly both breathed a large sigh of relief when Kelly stopped to toss a couple of coins into the toll basket before driving towards the Queen Elizabeth highway for Toronto.

"We're in Canada now," he said.

It was a few minutes before Mulholland spoke. "By God, you certainly do have a way with the women. Anyone'd think you had kissed the Blarney stone."

Kelly laughed. "That's what my grandmother always says. It's a pity we're not coming back on Sunday, though. Joanne looks like a lady who can handle herself."

CHAPTER 7
Hijack

Patrick Kelly parked the car in the lot of the Red Lobster, a sea-food restaurant situated directly across the road from McDonnell Douglas Canada. It was Sunday, a few minutes from midday, and the lot was beginning to fill up with the after-church crowd and lunch-time regulars.

After checking into their hotel the previous day, Mulholland suggested meeting in his room after supper. That would give them some time to rest and freshen up. Two others had shown up at the hotel when they first checked in, and Mulholland had introduced them as Peter Farrell and Sean McNally, the logistics part of the operation, as he described them. Two more unsavoury characters, thought Kelly as they sized each other up.

Shortly after showering and enjoying a well-cooked steak from room service, Kelly made his way to the meeting. Donnelly let him into the room and he took a seat at a long table which had been set with seven chairs. "Expecting company?" asked Kelly, pointing to the extra chairs.

Mulholland looked over but said nothing, continuing to read the paper. Mulholland took a beer from the bar fridge, and was about to pop the lid when Mulholland said harshly, "No drinking until we're done."

Donnelly stared at him, pulled the tab defiantly, and took a long swig before setting the can down. Kelly was reminded of a child trying to establish its authority with a parent. He sensed hostility between the two. They were staring at each other when a knock came to the door. Donnelly looked out through the peephole, opened the door, and allowed Farrell and McNally into the room.

Seconds later there was another knock. Donnelly looked through the peephole again, opened the door, and two extremely attractive females walked into the room. Kelly ignored the two men, and instead focused his attention on the women. They were both dark-skinned, that olive colouring peculiar to people of middle-eastern origin, and both wore their hair cut short. Not a bad idea, he thought as he ran his fingers through his damp curly mop. One looked slightly older than the other, and both had similar features which lead Kelly to think they might be related. They wore tight, faded denims and white skimpy T-shirts which revealed that they were bra-less. He noticed that fact right away and commented as much to Mulholland.

Mulholland laughed, almost a first for him, and shook his head. "You're right, Patrick, they are sisters of a sort, friends of ours from Libya, courtesy of the good Colonel. So I wouldn't bother trying it on with either of them. They'd cut your balls off and eat them for breakfast."

"I do like a challenge," replied Kelly, prompting a chuckle from Donnelly. "We'll see what happens later. I presume they are coming to Ireland with us."

Mulholland hesitated for a moment, obviously choosing his words carefully. "That they are, Patrick. The Colonel wants to get a first-hand account of how his money and weapons are being used. These two are part of his elite bodyguard. They have been extensively trained by the KGB so he thought they might be of some help during the operation. And they're sort of checking up on us, you know."

They sat down at the table as Farrell unfolded a large map of the facility where the demonstrations of the Apache were being held. For the next three hours Mulholland reviewed the plan, going over the timings, responsibilities, and contingencies, until they could perform their roles blindfolded. Kelly was impressed with the thoroughness of Mulholland's planning. When he was satisfied, Mulholland rummaged in his bag and pulled out a bottle of Bushmills whisky. "Time for a quick drink then it's off to bed with you," he said.

"Do I get to choose?" whispered Kelly, a gleam in his eye. "Or can I have both?"

"Fuck off," replied Mulholland, but he was smiling.

Tommy Mulholland sat in the passenger seat, checking his watch periodically while scanning the carpark.

"What are we waiting for?" asked Kelly. It was a hot, humid day, typical Canadian summer weather, and they had been sitting in the car for almost fifteen minutes. The air-conditioning unit was broken and the car windows were open, but there was no breeze. Sweat stains began to appear on their shirts and perspiration dotted their foreheads.

A brown Ford LTD turned into the parking lot and pulled up beside them. It was followed by a green mustang Cobra, whose occupants, the women from last evening, nodded to Tommy Mulholland, climbed out of their car, and made their way across the road towards the factory. Farrell and McNally were in the Ford. They came up to where Kelly was parked and nodded in greeting. "Howareye Tommy, Josie," said Farrell, leaning down and peering into the car. "Hot enough for ye?"

"You might have got us a fuckin' car with air-conditioning," snorted Mulholland, beads of sweat trickling down his face.

"You know what they say about beggars not being choosers," retorted Farrell. "Anyway, I take it we're on our way. Is the flyboy ready?"

"Everything is on schedule as planned," answered Mulholland.

"Grand. Sean is putting the gear in the back of your car now."

As Kelly watched, the two women made their way across the road and up to the factory's main guardhouse. The previous Friday had been a bank holiday, and most of the plant's employees had taken off for the weekend. The first shift was not scheduled to start until 4:30 that afternoon, so only a skeleton shift of guards would be on duty.

The women opened the door of the guardhouse and walked inside. The interior of the hut reeked of stale sweat and leftover fast food. Empty pizza boxes gaped from the garbage bin in the corner. There were two guards: one sat on a rickety wooden chair reading a book, the other leaned on a countertop which ran the length of the hut. Both wore blue cotton shirts with their names on the breast below an embroidered crest which read 'Security'.

Brian Peters was in a foul mood because he had to work on the long weekend, the air-conditioning wasn't working properly, and he was on duty with a jerk who had swallowed the rule book. When he saw the two women walking across the parking lot towards the hut, he had watched their breasts jiggling tantalizingly under their thin T-shirts. When they walked through the door, he pulled himself up from the counter and tried to exude an air of authority. The sweat rings under the arms of his shirt won out.

"Hi there, ladies," he said, smiling, his eyes never leaving the erotic feast before him. "What can we do for you?"

They both smiled, revealing pearly white teeth which triggered off another explosion of fantasies. The women leaned on the counter, exposing enough cleavage to drive him almost to distraction. He felt himself grow hard as he gazed at their breasts. The older of the two women fumbled beneath the counter, as if trying to get something out of her holdall. He was about to offer his assistance when she produced a very evil looking weapon. Being a fan of action movies, he thought it might be an UZI or a MACH-10, very small and very lethal. He knew that the squat metal tube on the front of the gun was a silencer. His erection faltered and died. A shiver raced down his spine, an involuntary action.

"For a start you could move away from the counter," she ordered, motioning him back with the muzzle of the gun. "And keep your hands where we can see them." The other woman now produced an identical weapon and was covering the rule-book fiend who had just noticed what was happening.

"What do you want?" he asked in a tremulous voice, finding it difficult to comprehend the events which were unfolding. Then he made the connection. The thought must have registered on his face because the woman nodded and smiled again. There was no warmth in the smile.

"I see that you have just realized what we are after. However, you will come to no harm if you do exactly as we say."

"Yes, yes," he stammered, totally mesmerized by the gun, the barrel of which was pointing in the general area of his crotch.

"How many guards are on duty, and how many are guarding the helicopter?"

He opened his mouth to answer, but was cut off by the other guard, the rule-book freak.

"Don't tell them anything," he shouted. "I'm not afraid of their guns. Let them find out for themselves."

Brian Peters could not believe his ears. As he turned to tell the jerk to shut his mouth, there was a quiet 'phutt', and a hole appeared in the jerk's fore-head.

Everything seemed to take place in freeze-frame motion. The back of the man's head came away in a splash of gore, just as it did in the movies. Except this was not the movies. The hole in his forehead was no bigger than a dime, and the guard was rolling his eyes upwards to look. The bullet slammed him back against the wall, and his knees buckled. He hung there for a moment as if deciding whether to stand or fall, and then pitched face down across the floor.

A pool of blood began to radiate from the guard's shattered head, inching its way towards the frightened man's shoes. He could see right into the skull cavity, a mess of blood and bone splinters and grey matter. He shuffled back, like a child trying to avoid the waves at the seashore, until he hit the wall. The movement had the effect of both pistols being trained on him and two knuckles whitening on separate triggers.

"I don't have time to play games with you," one snarled, smoke from the barrel curling up around her face like a scarf. "Tell me what I want."

He began to whimper when his bladder voided itself into his trousers. He looked down in shame at the spreading stain, and the smell of hot urine filling his nostrils. "Okay, okay, I'll tell you what you want to know. Promise me you won't kill me."

"I am rapidly losing patience."

"There are four regular guards on duty today. The other two are out making their rounds. They should be returning in a few minutes. There are two armed men from an external security firm guarding the chopper. They asked us to call them on the radio if anyone from the base shows up. That's all I know."

"What sort of weapons do the guards have?"

"I don't know," he pleaded. "I didn't recognize them."

"Well did they have rifles or did they just have side-arms, pistols?"

"They were carrying rifles of some sort," he replied. "And I think they were wearing holsters as well."

"That confirms what we have been told," and she nodded to her partner, who gently squeezed the trigger and fired a short, muffled burst into Brian Peters's chest.

His mouth opened and closed, as if to protest the unfairness of life, and a bloody froth came to his lips. He put his hands up to his chest and felt the warmth of his own blood trickling over his fingers. Everything started to go black. The spark of life vanished, and he collapsed in a heap on the floor beside the other guard.

The two women slipped into the back room of the hut to await the arrival of the other guards. A few moments passed and then they heard voices approaching. The guards entered, totally oblivious to their fate, and were dispatched quietly and efficiently with short controlled bursts of fire.

The women had their orders: no witnesses. Those orders came directly from Mulholland, outside of the meeting where Kelly was present. The older of the two went outside and waved to Mulholland. The other picked up the expended, brass shell casings. Ten rounds had been fired; she had to account for all shells. Leave no evidence, no clues. The words echoed in her mind from her early specialist-training days in the camps.

Mulholland turned to Kelly and said, "Stay with Josie until we take care of the men guarding the helicopter. The others are going to take over at the guard house. When you get the signal, drive up to the gate and Peter will let you through. Follow the directions to the main warehouse. We'll be waiting for you there."

"What happens if you can't take care of the guards?" asked Kelly innocently.

Mulholland shot him a look full of venom, but kept silent. He slammed the door, much harder than was necessary, and went around to the trunk of the car. He took out a bag that made a clanking sound, and then walked across the road with Farrell and McNally.

The men now carried holdalls like most of the regular factory workers did, and which a casual observer would assume to contain their lunch and perhaps some tools. The bags did contain the tools of their trade: a silenced Ingram MACH-11 machine pistol and several extra clips of ammunition for each. Farrell and McNally had provided all the ordnance in advance, each weapon having been test-fired on a deserted farmhouse north of the city. It was all they could get, given the short notice.

When they entered the guardhouse, Mulholland surveyed the carnage with the detached eye of a professional killer, his nose twitching at the smell of death. These women know their job, he thought. I could do with a few like them at home. He looked up as Farrell came out of the back of the hut buttoning up one of the guard's shirts over his white t-shirt.

"Found a spare one in a bag," he offered. "Just as well I did, 'cos those others are in a bit of a state." He nodded towards the back room of the hut, where the dead guards lay in a communal pool of blood, their blue cotton shirts saturated. He picked up one of the guards' caps and tried it on for size. It was a little big, but for the length of time he would be wearing it, there was no point in searching for another.

"You look like a regular little soldier," commented Mulholland, and then realized his mistake when he saw the cloud pass over Farrell's face.

The older of the two women checked her watch. "We must deal with the other guards quickly and quietly. They are armed, but they will not be expecting us."

Mulholland pulled a scrap of paper from his pocket and oriented himself with the buildings in front of him. "Follow me," he said. Farrell took up his position behind the counter, and he watched the three disappear into the bowels of the factory. His machine pistol rested on a shelf below the counter amid a pile of temporary badges and gate passes.

McNally had closed the door into the back room; the stench was nauseating. In a tiny washroom he had found a can of air-freshener and had liberally applied it to the inside of the reception area.

This would be a bad day for anyone who decided to come to work early, he thought, leafing through a copy of the Toronto Sun, taking a few moments to admire their "Sunshine Girl." His instructions were the same as the women's: no witnesses.

Lieutenant Bill Mossley, the pilot in charge of the helicopter demonstrations was furious with himself. During the morning's exhibition his wallet must have slipped out of his flying suit and fallen on the floor of the cockpit. He did not notice the wallet was missing until he went to pay for his lunch at the officer's mess. Fortunately, one of the Canadian pilots was in line with him and graciously paid for them both, sparing him the embarrassment of having to explain to the girl at the cash register that he had no money.

This was not the first time that his wallet had slipped out. The pockets in the flying suits were not deep enough, and during some of the more acrobatic manoeuvres, gravity had allowed it to fall out of his pocket. He knew exactly where it would be.

After lunch, he managed to borrow a car to make the trip back to McDonnell Douglas, and so, armed with a set of directions, he set off to the factory.

The trip across the 401 was uneventful, except for the unwanted delays due to road works, and he was soon driving up Airport Road towards the plant. At the main gate, he waved at the guard through the car window, assuming that the air force decals would be sufficient to get him through. He was correct, and drove through the barrier, noticing as he did so that it was a different guard than the one who had been on duty when he left.

He didn't give it another thought. If he had looked in his rear-view mirror, he would have seen Peter Farrell staring in his direction and talking frantically into a two-way radio.

Tommy Mulholland and the two women ran quickly through the plant, past hulking machines, their footsteps virtually soundless on the rubberized floors. Today the machines were silent, immobile, awaiting the arrival of their human masters to feed them the material they required to perform their tasks. Eventually the machines would be completely integrated in the manufacturing process, eliminating as much human intervention as possible. It was no wonder that the unions were running scared from such technology.

The heavy smell of machine oil hung in the air as the trio ran past barrels filled with gleaming spirals of waste metal. At each turn, Mulholland carefully checked a crude, hand-drawn map to ensure they were proceeding in the right direction. The plant, he had been warned, was a labyrinth of corridors and tunnels, and newcomers often went astray trying to get from one location to another.

He breathed a sigh of relief when he saw the sign for the cafeteria: they were almost at their destination. The warehouse was just on the other side of the cafeteria. Before they reached the doors, they passed huge, rectangular tanks of acid, open to the air, awaiting the constant dipping of pieces of metal. They seemed quite innocuous, yet the lethal acid was strong enough to disintegrate a human body in minutes.

Mulholland balled the map in his hand and tossed

it into one of the tanks. The surface of the acid boiled, briefly sending concentric circles across the tank. By the time the first tiny wave touched the side of the tank, the centre was again calm, like the eye of a hurricane.

They approached the warehouse from the rear, away from the end where the guards were standing watch. The element of surprise was important. Unlike the security guards, these men were armed. Mulholland opened the door slightly and peered inside.

"No problem," he muttered over his shoulder, and slipped through the door. The two guards were obviously unconcerned about security; they were standing together with their weapons propped against some storage drums. They were having a heated debate about the performance of the Blue Jays versus the Boston Red Sox. When the women were within range, they stood up, immediately catching the attention of the soldiers. The men, caught completely unawares, died where they stood, stitched across the middle by well-timed bursts of fire. They fell to the concrete floor, their heels beating out a brief but macabre staccato rhythm. Then they were silent.

The two women busied themselves dragging the bodies out of sight while Mulholland pulled open the warehouse doors. Suddenly, his radio crackled into life. He released his grip on the doors and pulled the two-way radio from his belt.

"Tommy, Tommy it's Peter. An air-force car with one person inside just came through the gate. It's heading in your direction and should be there in a couple of minutes. Over."

"Okay, Peter. We'll take care of him," he replied, and ran to where the girls were picking up spent shell casings. He quickly explained the situation, and all three took cover behind some packing cases near the hangar entrance. They could hear the car approaching.

Bill Mossley pulled the car up to the hangar doors and switched off the ignition. He was surprised to see that the doors were partially open. He immediately became suspicious when he was not challenged - where were the guards?

He opened the car door and put a foot out; but some inner sense, the same that had saved his life many times in Vietnam, warned him, and he promptly slammed the door shut and switched on the ignition. The engine turned over but did not start; a typical government vehicle. He cursed, noticing as he did so a blur of movement from inside the warehouse.

One of the women sprinted from her hiding place and fired two bursts through the side of the car. The first burst cut through the car door, the thin panels having little effect on the bullets. The full force of the burst hit his stomach, knocking him back across the seat. A second burst shattered the window beside the driver's seat, exactly where his head would have been. Instinctively he clasped his hands across his gut, but he could not staunch the flow of blood from his ruptured intestines. Blood welled up through his fingers like water bubbling from a spring. He closed his eyes, waiting for his attacker to come and fire that final bullet into his skull. The merciful release did not come, and waves of pain pounded on the shores of his senses. He was dying.

He had seen enough men die in Vietnam to know that he was finished. It was a strange way to end it all, after surviving three tours of duty in Vietnam, in the most hostile environment that anyone could imagine. And here he was, in Toronto of all places, gutshot and bleeding to death. He coughed, spitting bloody phlegm down his arm.

Another car pulled up across from the hangar door and two doors slammed shut. Heavy footsteps echoed from the warehouse. Bill Mossley listened intently, the momentary distraction taking his mind away from the pain. Already the rapid pulse of blood was beginning to ebb. Darkness would come soon. "Come, come, sweet death." The words echoed in his mind from a book he had once read about soldiers in the French Foreign Legion. Now he understood how a man could welcome death.

Using up his rapidly dwindling reserves of strength, he pulled himself up to where he could just peer out of the car's shattered window. His eyes welled up with tears as the pain became nigh to unbearable, but more so because he had just seen his good friend Patrick Kelly climbing into the cockpit of the chopper, the chopper which he had shown Patrick, against all the rules, how to fly. The treacherous bastard obviously had some other agenda in mind when he asked for some flight time in the Apache. He knew Patrick had fallen down on his luck after leaving the army, but he had no idea just how far. Now he knew.

Another man was busily loading the ordnance from crates on the ground, and two women stood on guard nearby, their weapons in plain sight. He presumed one of them had done the shooting.

The scene before him began to slip in and out of focus. He knew his time was drawing close. With his final breaths, he began to scrawl a message on the inside of the car, using his blood as ink. He never finished the message.

Patrick Kelly was in his element. He sat at the controls, quickly familiarizing himself with the switches before firing up the engines. The rotors began to turn, slowly at first, then increasing to a steady throb. He leaned forward and patted Josie on the helmet, a superfluous exercise as the helmets had built-in two-way microphones. He gave him the thumbs-up sign and lifted the four tons of metal up into the air and off northwards towards Brampton. He activated the passive radar jammer, so that they could not be tracked. All he had to do was follow the flight plan Mulholland had given him and they would be home safe.

Mulholland and the women took Kelly's car and drove out to the front gate to where the others were waiting. As they passed, Mulholland gave the 'thumb's up' sign. The trio were booked on a flight to Prague. From there they would fly to Havana and then on to Shannon in the south of Ireland. Once they got to Shannon, there were hundreds of ways to get across the border to the North, to meet up with the chopper. It was a long, boring trip, but it ensured they could get into Ireland incognito.

Farrell grinned, removed the guard's shirt, and ran across the road with McNally to their car. Then they set off down to the airport. They were unknown to the authorities, and were booked on a flight directly into Belfast, a charter run by Maple Leaf tours. Their flight was scheduled to leave just two hours after the others. They would all meet at Rathlin Island, just off the Northern coast of Ireland, for the second phase of the mission.

CHAPTER 8
Rendezvous

Joanne Ryan arrived early for work. It was Sunday, and a long week-end in Canada, so traffic coming into the country again today was expected to be heavy. She changed into her uniform in the locker room, put on some make-up, and made her way out to her booth.

In the hallway, she performed the daily ritual of checking the bulletin board where the FBI regularly posted photographs of known felons or suspected terrorists. It was an exaggerated act, done deliberately in case her supervisor was watching. There were no new faces, but she scanned those existing ones, just to refresh her memory.

The day passed slowly, the line of cars like a column of ants. With the long wait, up to two hours in the broiling sun, many of the drivers were short-tempered when they reached her booth, as if she caused the delay. Those foolish enough to voice their discontent found themselves pulled over to the office, thoroughly searched, and their car ransacked, delaying their journey even more, and making them wish that they had kept their mouths shut.

Eventually, the leaden arm of the clock made it to five o'clock, and she thankfully returned to the locker room to get out of her uniform. She felt more human when she put on her regular clothes and then she headed out to her car. The 'gang' were all going to the Library for the night, and she was looking forward to an enjoyable evening.

When she thought of the Library, she remembered the guy from yesterday, and wondered if he would show up as he promised. The memory of his face was still vivid. As she passed the bulletin board, which normally she ignored until the start of her next shift, her subconscious registered the fact that something had changed.

She stopped, retraced a few steps, and looked. There were some new mug shots. More out of curiosity than anything else, she carefully looked at each photograph, and then her stomach sank as she recognized one of the men. Actually, it was the scar across the forehead she recognized, similar to the one which she had glimpsed on the passenger in the back seat of Patrick Kelly's car.

She debated whether or not to say anything; she had not spoken to the two other men in the car. Her superiors would hardly accept getting chatted up as a valid excuse for not doing her job properly. Yet upon reading the descriptions below the photographs, she felt compelled to confess what she knew. It was not necessary to tell the whole truth.

Two hours later, she was beginning to wonder if she had made the right choice. She was sitting in the local RCMP office, relating the story, minus a few details, to two officers. They kept going over her story, with no sign of letting up. Now and again a strange face would appear and she would have to repeat her story. The arm of the clock seemed to have increased its speed, and she could see the evening disappearing.

Eventually, they told her that she could go, and they thanked her for her trouble. She mumbled something about duty and left. The two officers felt she was keeping something back, but they were both convinced that she had seen Joseph Donnelly and Tommy Mulholland, and that they were now in Canada.

The senior officer picked up the phone and called his contact at the Canadian Security and Intelligence Service (CSIS), relayed the information about the two terrorists and then hung up the phone. His responsibility for the incident was now ended. CSIS would handle the matter.

*   *   *   *   *

Kelly followed the flight plan given to him by Tommy Mulholland. Flying over land was fine, but he was extremely uncomfortable about flying out to sea to rendezvous with a freighter, especially at night. They did not have sufficient fuel to return to the coast, so if the freighter was not where it was supposed to be, they would have to ditch in the ocean.

He was using the night vision system to fly in the darkness. The outside world appeared tinged with green on the helmet- mounted display which sat against one eye. The real-time, passive thermal image of the outside world was generated by the forward- looking infra-red sensor located in the PNVS turret. It was like watching a tiny television with one eye.

Periodically he would turn his head from side to side. The turret-mounted infra-red camera would then follow the movements of his head.

The high resolution FLIR imagery allowed him to execute low-level nap-of-the-earth flight, which enabled him to avoid detection. It did, however, have a profound effect on Josie Donnelly. In the camp in Libya, where Donnelly had trained on the HIND MI-27, the pilot had not performed any of the manoeuvres which Kelly was using. He was relieved when they started flying out over the sea, because the flight had levelled out. Until then it had been like riding a roller-coaster blindfolded. It was all he could do to prevent himself from throwing up in the cockpit.

Kelly smiled to himself as he heard Donnelly curse each time he put the helicopter into a dive. As a result, he did it more often than was really necessary. When reached the open sea, he had to turn his attention to other matters. The freighter could easily be missed, especially if it had drifted from its coordinates.

Landing the chopper on the deck of the freighter was also going to be a problem. Tricky enough during the day, at night it was going to be almost impossible. He voiced these opinions to Donnelly, who did not seem concerned in the slightest.

"The freighter will be where I told you. The captain is an old friend and gets very well paid for his help. Besides, he knows what would happen to him and his family if he betrayed us."

"I hope you can swim then, because we're almost out of fuel," replied Kelly drily. "This chopper weighs about four tons and does not do 'boat' impressions."

"Relax, Patrick. Have a little faith. We'll be there soon, you'll see."

Kelly could not resist poking fun at him. "Your voice sounds a little strange, Josie. You're not feeling sick by any chance?"

"Fuck you, Yank."

The freighter SS Connaught, en route from Montreal to Glasgow with a cargo of lumber, rode the tide a few miles off the coast of Maine. It was late evening, the sky was clear and the sea calm, all ideal conditions for a rendezvous.

The ship's captain, Colm Brady, stood on the deck, looking towards the coast. Around his neck hung a pair of high-powered night-vision binoculars. Periodically he would put them to his eyes, and scan the horizon. He regularly checked the ship's position to ensure that it had not drifted too far from the designated coordinates. If corrective action was necessary, he would issue the necessary commands to bring the ship back to its original position.

A glance at his watch showed him that the chopper was a few minutes overdue. He looked down towards the deck, where his men had put the specially constructed landing pad over one of the holds. The chopper weighed over four tons, he had been told, but he had constructed a pad which could safely carry in excess of ten tons. He preferred to err on the side of caution.

His ears pricked up as he heard, or thought he heard, the sound of chopper blades beating the air. He put the glasses to his eyes and directed them once more towards the coast. On the first pass, he missed the tiny light in the sky, but on the second it came into focus, heading directly towards him. He picked up the microphone and barked some orders for the deck crew, and then dark shapes moved about on the deck, preparing the landing pad and the camouflage netting for the chopper.

Kelly was the first to spot the ship. He pointed it out to Josie Donnelly who immediately breathed a sigh of relief, despite his earlier optimistic comments.

"Boy, am I glad to see that," said Kelly, as they neared the ship.

"What did I tell you, Patrick?" asked Donnelly. "I said he'd be there."

"I wish he'd put on some lights other than those in the cabins. I'd prefer to land this bird using regular lights rather than this night scope." As though in answer to his question the deck lights came on, flooding the landing pad with their beams.

Deckhands stood around the sides of the pad, ropes in hand to secure the chopper once it landed.

Kelly brought the chopper alongside the freighter, parallel to the landing pad. He moved the chopper sidewards until he was over the platform and then, with a silent prayer, eased it down. The structure groaned as the chopper settled.

The deckhands were around the chopper, like ants on a scrap of bread, fastening ropes even before he had switched off the engines. When the rotors started to slow, he opened the cabin door and climbed out on to the deck, closely followed by Donnelly. The deckhands paid furtive attention to them; they were well aware of Donnelly by his reputation. These were individuals who were not to be messed with, under any circumstances.

Colm Brady stepped forward to greet them.

"Hello, Josie. Nice to see you again." There was no warmth in the greeting, Kelly noted, and it was obvious the captain would rather shake hands with the devil. "I'll take you to your cabins. I've had the cook keep something aside for us for supper, so once you stow your gear we can eat."

Donnelly made no attempt to introduce Kelly, nor did Colm Brady ask. The less he knew, the better off he was. They went down below deck, farther than Kelly liked, to where the crew's living quarters were located. The tiny rooms were extremely cramped, and Kelly didn't like the fact he had to bunk together with Donnelly. From the expression on Donnelly's face the feeling was entirely mutual. They put the bags away in the metal lockers at one side of the room and then followed the captain to the mess-deck.

The ship started to roll gently as the freighter got under way. Kelly, a self-confessed poor sailor, began to feel queasy. Judging from the look on Donnelly's face, he was not alone. He had been hungry when he first sat down and had wolfed a huge helping of meat and potatoes. Now he was beginning to regret that action. He suspected that his dinner would be reappearing during the evening.

Colm Brady laughed as he saw Kelly's face turn a little pale, but an icy stare from Donnelly put an end to the humour. The captain got up from the table, went into the kitchen, and reappeared a few minutes later with a bottle of anti-nausea tablets.

"I don't think much of your dessert," groaned Kelly, holding his stomach.

Brady laughed again, but when a glance from Donnelly silenced him, he stood up from the table.

"I've got to tend to the ship. We have breakfast at 6:00 a.m., served in the mess. If you're not feeling up to it, I'll have some tea sent to your cabins. You'll find flasks of water there already: one of the dangers of sea-sickness is dehydration. I'll see you later."

Donnelly's eyes followed the captain's back when he left the room. "Fuckin' prick," he said, to no one in particular.

CHAPTER 9
Pandemonium

Peter Farrell parked the car on the fifth floor of the airport carpark. It had been stolen the previous evening from a parking lot in Hamilton, but would eventually be identified by the attendants during their periodic inspections.

The machine pistols were left in the trunk of the car; there was no way to get them into the airport undetected. Ever since the Air India disaster, security at the airport had increased significantly, even with passengers on internal flights now being searched. For Farrell, it was a shame to waste weapons that could be put to good use back at home.

It was not necessary to wipe the car for finger-prints; they had both worn rubber gloves, which would be disposed of in trash cans inside the terminal.

Farrell was suspicious by nature, which was one of the main reasons that security forces had never managed to get their hands on him.

In his late thirties, he had been a member of the IFF for over four years, a major accomplishment considering that most of his contemporaries were either dead or rotting in jail. His father, now in his seventies, was an ardent IRA supporter, and had been responsible for many of the war-time attacks on British factories.

It was only natural that when his son was old enough, he would join the ranks of those fighting the British, and that time came when Peter Farrell turned sixteen. His birthday present from his father had been a .38 calibre Smith and Wesson revolver and enrolment into the IRA. Different than the rest of the 'volunteers', his shadowy leaders wanted him to continue at school and go on to university, seeing he had the aptitude and the potential.

They had big plans for him: students could travel at home and abroad virtually unnoticed. So young Peter Farrell became a courier, taking documents and money between Ireland and Europe. As he matured, he was given more and more responsibility, and was soon negotiating arms deals with black marketeers in Switzerland and Germany.

But he grew bored, longing for the action which his father had described to him from his childhood. To mollify him, the leaders had agreed to send him to the training camps in South Yemen. They felt that a few weeks of gruelling training under a burning sun would soon have him pleading for the soft, easy life.

They could not have been more wrong. He far outstripped the others, surprising his instructors, but most of all the old men back at home. When his training was finished, and many friendships forged with other like-minded individuals from the Baader-Meinhof and Red Brigade, he made it clear that he wanted to make use of the training.

His bosses reluctantly promised that the next big operation outside of Ireland would be his chance. But Farrell had too much information that could harm the movement, if he was caught. If the operation went awry, Mulholland was instructed that Farrell should not be left alive for his captors.

Sean McNally had their tickets in his inside pocket. They were booked on Canadian Airlines flight CP806, which departed Toronto at 6:00 p.m., bound for Belfast.

It was well-known however, that Irish charter flights changed destinations, depending on the disposition of the pilot. A direct flight to Belfast often became a direct flight to Dublin and then on to Belfast, or vice-versa. Either destination was fine for the two men. They could cross the border with ease in either direction.

Both men were members of the Irish Freedom Fighters, but had never been arrested or detained, and as a result, were able to move freely between Ulster and other countries, posing as tourists. There was no reason for the authorities to be suspicious of them.

They took the elevator to the departures floor and made their way to check their luggage, which contained enough clothes for a one-week visit, to augment their cover. They had carried some travel guides around for a few days to give them a well-used look, and had packed a few souvenirs under their clothes.

The check-in counter was thronged with tourists, visitors from the North and South of Ireland telling each other about what a wonderful time they had and how the weather was great and how sad they were to be going home. They were strangers, brought together by a common bond - they came to see Canada, to visit relatives, who, like the Irish during the potato famine, had left hoping for a better life. Here, there were no Protestants or Catholics, no lines of demarkation or confrontation, just simple people enjoying a breath of freedom from the 'troubles'. And among them walked Peter Farrell and Sean McNally.

One of the biggest problems facing the security forces in Ireland, and those in other countries, is that terrorists blend in with their surroundings. They dress the same, talk the same, and do most of the day-to-day chores that common, ordinary folk do with one notable exception. They use their basic anonymity to kill and slip away, unnoticed.

This was the first time however, that McNally had carried out an operation in a foreign country, and he was nervous. His eyes darted anxiously from side to side any time a security officer from the terminal walked past. Farrell noticed and leaned over to whisper in his ear.

"For God's sake, Sean, would you relax? As soon as we get these bags checked in we'll go and get a drink. You look like you need one."

"Yeah, alright. I don't know why but I get the feeling we're being watched."

"We're not being watched, you eejit, but if you keep jumping every time one of those guards walks past, someone may get suspicious. So just smile and talk to those nice people in front of you. Ask them where they went during their holidays or something."

Stuart Meredith stood with his hands clasped behind his back, looking out over the check-in counters through a two-way mirror. He scanned the sea of faces, as he had done for the past twenty years,

looking for something. The 'something' was difficult to explain, if he had to define just what had
alerted him to a pickpocket or a thief. It was like
trying to hold smoke in your hand.

He was well suited for his job as chief security
officer, and he could best be described by an on-
looker as being 'average'. 'Nondescript' was how
he put it himself: it was one of the factors he attrib-
uted to his success at apprehending criminals. He
could blend in with any group of travellers like a
chameleon, offering himself as a mark for some unfortunate pickpocket.

Over the years, he had catalogued a library of
expressions from the faces of people leaving on a
journey or arriving home: tired expressions, on the
faces of well-worn travellers; happy, excited expressions on the faces of those who did not fly often
and for whom getting on an airplane was an adventure; and apprehensive looks on those who were
afraid to fly but had no other choice. It was the
irregularities that he looked for, deviations from the
norm that would signal a possible felon. He was
receiving such signals now from the man waiting at
the Canadian Airlines check-in counter. The man
was nervous about something, that was for sure,
but he did not fit Meredith's profile of a nervous
traveller. Something else was making him uneasy.

He picked up the flight manifest and his finger
stopped at Counter 17, which was boarding pas-

sengers for a Maple Leaf charter flight to Belfast.
Hmmm, he thought to himself, rubbing his chin
thoughtfully. Immediately he became more interested in the traveller.

One of the covert security checks that may be
applied to an unsuspecting air traveller is what is
known as 'profiling'. It is extremely clever in con-
struction, easy to apply, and the unsuspecting passenger is oblivious to its application.

Stuart Meredith applied the profile to the young
man, hesitated a few moments while he pondered
the situation, then he picked up the phone and dialled the check-in counter.

*   *   *   *   *

The first workers to return to the McDonnell Douglas plant for the afternoon shift passed through the
guardhouse and commented on the absence of
guards, who were usually there in droves to check
badges. It was a small blessing that they were not
around: they were widely regarded as a bunch of
arrogant assholes.

At 4:30 p.m., the vice-president of manufacturing drove up to the guardhouse and waited for
one of the guards to open the barrier to allow him
to drive into the executive parking lot. Ever a patient man, he waited for all of thirty seconds before
blaring his horn. When this failed to produce any

result, he took umbrage at the perceived insult and climbed out of his car, preparing to give some poor unfortunate a tongue-lashing. He ducked under the security barrier, glared at some workers who were coming in late, and strode over to the back door of the guardhouse. With a curse forming on his lips, he pushed his way into the back room.

The stench was overpowering, and the sight of the bodies, lying in pools of blood, glassy eyes staring up at him, made him retch violently. He threw up several times over the floor and the nearest body, as his legs turned to lead and held him immobilized.

Outside, some late workers turned to see the VP kneeling on the floor, throwing up for all he was worth, and beyond him, the reason for the nausea. Two of them grabbed him and dragged him outside into the air. A third man ran across the road to the police sub-station and informed them about the bodies.

Two officers arrived on the scene within seconds. The elder of the two, a grizzled veteran of the Korean War, entered the back of the hut to check for any signs of life. It was a futile exercise but rules were rules. It had been a long time since he had seen such violence and he was not unaffected by it, but he pulled the door closed behind him to spare the others. It was not a sight which ordinary people could deal with. He called to his young partner, who was on the ground beside the incoherent VP.

"Jim, get the Coroners' office on the radio. Tell them there are four bodies in there. And call in homicide and the forensic guys as well."

He looked up as another worker came racing across the yard to the guardhouse. The man's breathing was ragged, and he inhaled deeply to fill his lungs with air.

"Calm down, sir," said the older officer. "Just relax and let it out. What is the problem?"

"There ... There are three dead men in the warehouse. Shot to pieces. And the Apache's gone."

"Good Christ," blurted the younger officer. "I better get the RCMP over here as well."

"And some backup too," ordered the sergeant. "The press are going to be here like flies on hot shit once this hits the air.

Call for backup first so we can seal off the area. Don't give out any details over the air just yet, in case the frequencies are being monitored." He sighed and shook his head. "Going to be a long night."

*   *   *   *   *

The attractive lady at the check-in counter took the proffered tickets from Peter Farrell and began the standard routine of checking them against the passenger manifest, flight numbers and destinations. Farrell's appeared to be in order and she was in the process of checking Sean McNally's ticket when her phone rang. She reached out and picked it up, cradling it on her shoulder as she continued her inspection.

"Canadian Airlines, Michele speaking. How may I help you?" she asked.

"Hi Michele, Stuart Meredith here. I was just watching the two men in front of you. Are their papers in order?"

She recognised the voice immediately, and glanced involuntarily up at the two-way mirror on the wall, behind which she knew Stuart Meredith was standing.

"Yes, everything's fine," she replied. "No problems at all."

"Okay," he answered. "Just wanted to check. Thanks, Michele."

The phone went dead, and she replaced it on the hook. At the same time she looked up at Sean McNally, her fingers poised above the terminal.

"And you, would you like smoking or no-smoking?"

"I don't think I could go for eight hours without a fag," laughed McNally.

"A window or aisle seat?"

"I want to sit at the window," stated McNally. "I like to look out when we're taking off."

She punched in the data and when the computer had printed out their boarding passes, she put them inside their tickets and handed them back.

"Your flight is boarding in thirty minutes from Gate M. Have a nice flight."

The glance by the reservations clerk did not go unnoticed by Farrell. Casually turning to Sean McNally, his eyes had angled upwards, but the only thing he could see was a huge mirror covering the entire wall.

"Is there a problem with our tickets?" he asked, nodding at the phone, wishing that he had brought one of the guns into the terminal.

"Oh no," she replied, smiling disarmingly. "I'm supposed to meet someone after work for dinner and I wasn't sure if I could make it or not. Two of the other girls called in sick and we're really swamped, so our boss said we might have to work overtime."

"That would be too bad," he commented. "Especially for the fellow who is taking you out."

At the duty free shop, they ordered their one-litre bottles of whiskey and cartons of cigarettes. Next on the list was a quick drink at the airport bar. Then they set off to the departure lounge. Farrell was amused by the security check proceedings and turned to Sean McNally, a huge grin on his face.

"Makes you feel right at home, eh Sean? At least they're a little bit more gentle than the Brits," he commented, looking at the female security officer who was doing scan.

"I might even get one of these for the wife," he added, and the security officer laughed as well, finding it impossible to maintain her composure. "Well now," he said. "That's much better. Laughter is good for the soul. Sean, I think you should come over and get scanned by this lady. She's got a gentle touch."

The security officer blushed as the two men picked up their wallets, keys, and loose change. They followed the circular corridor until they found their departure lounge, which was packed with other passengers waiting to board. Opposite the departure lounge was a tiny bar.

"Order us a couple of beers, Sean," said Farrell. "I'm off to the toilet."

He took the end stall, as instructed, and proceeded to remove the wall plate using the screwdriver blade on his Swiss Army knife. In the recess, which was used to gain access to some electrical boxes, was taped a padded envelope, put there by a local sympathiser who worked as a janitor. He removed the packet and cut through the duct tape used to seal it. Reaching inside, he felt the butt of a revolver.

There were two in the envelope, plus a box of bullets. He popped open one gun's cylinder to ensure it was loaded, and then did the same for the other. Satisfied, he emptied half of the box of bullets into his pocket and kept the remaining half for Sean. He then sat back to wait.

McNally ordered two beers as he watched Farrell go into the washroom. When they arrived, he paid the barman the exorbitant prices, took a long sip and waited for a few minutes to allow Farrell to get the guns. He then walked to the washroom and took the cubicle beside the one at the end. He rapped on the side of the occupied cubicle and Farrell passed the envelope through to him under the metal wall.

McNally went through the same process as Farrell, checking the gun and emptying the box of bullets into his pocket. When he was finished, he opened the door and deposited the envelope in the garbage. Both men went back to the bar, each feeling more comfortable with the familiar weight in their inside pockets.

Stuart Meredith could not get rid of the nagging feeling in the back of his head. He stood and watched the ebb and flow of passengers in front of him, his eyes unfocused as his subconscious replayed the images of the two men waiting at the check-in counter. Suddenly he realised what had made him suspicious. The younger of the men had become jittery whenever the security officer passed by on his regular rounds.

He reached down and picked up the phone that connected him with the officers on the floor.

"ALPHA-1, this is control. Please respond. ALPHA-1, please respond," he said, hoping that his friend Joe Dimorro was not on his break. Dimorro's voice crackled through the speaker.

"Control, this is ALPHA-1. What can I do you for?"

"Joe, we have a couple of suspicious characters in the boarding area at Gate M. I want to ask them a few questions. I'll meet you at Gate L and point them out to you. Then you can bring them over to security."

"Okay Control. See you over there."

The two uniformed officers were waiting at Gate L when Meredith arrived. At the window adjoining Gate M, he peered through. The departures area was crowded with passengers, milling around like cattle, but he saw the two men, sitting in a corner of the bar.

He pointed them out to Dimorro and his partner and then went back to the security area.

Farrell was the first to notice the officers making their way through the crowd. Although they did not seem to have any particular destination in mind, they were headed directly towards them.

"Sean," he hissed. "Looks like trouble. Relax

and follow my lead. Let's see what they want."

The officers stopped directly in front of them, hands resting near their newly issued GLOCK-17 pistols. "Excuse me, gents," one asked politely. "Could I trouble you to come with us to security? There appears to be a problem with your tickets."

"But the girl said ..." McNally was silenced by a stony stare from Farrell.

"Okay officers. Where do we go?" asked Farrell, downing the remains of his beer.

"Down the corridor to the entrance to the departure lounge. Take the first door on your right and go up the stairs. We'll be right behind you."

The milling passengers parted like the Red Sea as the quartet exited, the officers flanking the two men. Farrell put his hand inside his jacket, letting his fingers curl around the familiar shape. McNally did the same and on a nod from Farrell, they turned on the two officers, guns cocked and aimed directly at their heads.

Joe Dimorro's face dropped as the two men spun around, and he began to raise his hands. His younger partner did not have the sense to do the same. Instead, he leapt at McNally as soon as he spotted the gun.

Dimorro screamed "No," but it was drowned out by the report of the pistol. His partner's leap was abruptly halted by the force of the bullet slamming into his head. It exited the back of his skull, showering Joe and nearby passengers with blood. The moment froze, and then pandemonium ensued. Passengers pushed and shoved each other to get out of the way. Children screamed when the man's body slumped to the ground, pumping blood over marbled tiles.

McNally turned his pistol on Dimorro, who put his hands up in a vain attempt to ward off the bullet. It passed through the palm of his hand, striking a bone, and entered his eye at an angle, tearing through his brain and erupting from the side of his head in a spray of blood, hair, scalp, and bone.

Farrell was already running towards the boarding gate as the security man's lifeless body hit the floor. McNally followed, a few feet behind Farrell, who pushed open the doors and headed towards the aircraft. Farrell caught up with a stewardess, fleeing from the melee, just as she was nearing the door of the plane. He pushed her into the cabin, where she slammed into the wall and fell in a heap on the floor. He pointed his gun at the remaining cabin staff who were standing, mouths agape, looking at the pistol.

McNally pulled open the cockpit door, levelling his gun at the flight crew, who were busy carrying out their pre-flight checks. The captain turned to see what the problem was and blanched when he saw the barrel of a gun.

"Don't do anything stupid," ordered McNally.

"We are members of the Irish Freedom Fighters. Two security guards are both dead now, just like you're going to be if you don't do exactly as we say."

Simon Maynard, the captain, had attended seminars on aircraft hijacking and now tried to recall the instructions. He was a leading member of the Air Line Pilots Association (ALPA), and was an outspoken advocate of the Association's demands to increase the level of pre-board screening of passengers. This was the pilots' response to the ever increasing attacks on commercial aircraft. Once on board, there was little a pilot could do to deal with a terrorist, so the pilots wanted to prevent the terrorists from doing just that.

He was also part of the committee which decided to make it a requirement that all pilots of commercial aircraft attend courses dealing with the aspects of terrorism pertaining to aircraft. As a result, most pilots, as well as having to carry out their regular training, now had to learn how to recognize and handle explosive devices in flight, and also learn about hijack management and criminal psychology.

Cooperation was the main thrust of the lecture; the avoidance of confrontations, trying to get them to talk. It was obvious that this was not a planned hijacking but an action which the terrorists had been backed into. As such, he hoped that it could all be settled quickly and without violence.

The safety of the crew was his responsibility and it was up to him to ensure that they were not harmed. He swallowed hard, then spoke quietly, hoping that the fear he felt would not show in his voice.

"All right. What do you want me to do?" he asked.

"That's good," smiled McNally. "I want you to get this plane out on to the runway, away from the ramp. Now!"

"Okay, okay," replied Maynard, and turned to the controls, the professional pilot now in command. In executing his preparations, he reached out to the console and surreptitiously removed a fuse from a bank of switches. The movement was incorporated so smoothly in his start-up routine that even if the terrorists had been watching they would not have taken the movement as something untoward.

The bank of switches which he had just disabled contained warning lights and buzzers for the plane's emergency exits. If any of them were opened while on the ground or in flight, a buzzer would sound, and the warning light for whichever door was opened would flash.

In most hijackings of commercial aircraft, where the authorities had decided to storm the plane, the entry of the assault team was through the emergency doors above the wings. If the negotiators could not find common ground with the terrorists and decided to storm the aircraft, he did not want to place any of the flight crew in jeopardy. He was well aware of the strident tones of the buzzers. And if they did sound, the terrorists might think that he or one of the others in the flight crew was responsible.

In 1977, the captain of a hijacked Lufthansa jet, on landing at Aden, was murdered by the hijackers when they suspected that he was secretly communicating with security forces. Maynard did not want a repeat of that incident, and the buzzer going off might just have that result. As well, removing the fuse could give the assault team precious seconds to get on the plane undetected, if it came down to an assault.

McNally spoke over his shoulder to Farrell. "We're moving out to the runway now. Someone will be contacting us shortly, I should imagine. You can deal with them."

Farrell nodded and then turned his attention to the cabin crew who had not moved since his dramatic entrance. There were seven stewards - five women and two men - scattered the length of the plane.

"All right," he called,. "I want somebody to close the cabin door, and then I want you all to come up front, men take the window seats, and the ladies, the seats beside them. And put on your seatbelts as well."

The cabin crew quietly obeyed and moved to the front of the plane, into the seats. They too had been trained in what to do in case of a hijacking, and so tried to avoid direct eye contact with the hijackers.

At the back of the plane, Diane Thornton sat in the toilet, her face buried in her hands. She had spent the previous evening at Pat and Mario's on the airport strip, having one drink too many and dancing the night away. Now she had a mother of a hangover and felt nauseous. She had not looked forward to playing wet-nurse to a bunch of drunken Irishmen for seven hours.

She heard the commotion at the front of the plane and through the mist realized the plane was being hijacked. She heard the others moving up to the front of the plane, but instead of joining them, she slipped the lock open while holding the door closed. The 'occupied' light went off and the tiny washroom was enveloped in darkness. She prayed that the men would not check too closely.

The plane rocked gently as Simon Maynard moved it slowly back from the ramp and onto the runway. As it began to move, there was frantic activity among the ground crew, who were unaware of the events inside the terminal. They scrambled out of the way, and the plane moved to a position about one hundred yards away from the ramp.

"Is that far enough for you?" Maynard asked, and the plane stopped with a shudder.

"That's grand," replied McNally. "Now we wait."

CHAPTER 10
Negotiations

Stuart Meredith realized something was terribly wrong when he saw passengers spilling out of the departure area and into the main terminal. People were screaming hysterically, pushing and shoving one another. He saw one woman fall and get trampled by others. "Holy God," he moaned. "Somebody get those people under control before more get injured."

He picked up the phone and called Joe Dimorro, but all he received back was an ominous static hiss. He grabbed one of the portable two-way radios, ran down into the terminal and collared a guard, a young man whom he had recently hired.

"What the fuck's going on?" he asked, a desperate fear growing inside.

"There's been a shooting at Gate M," replied the guard, his face edging towards panic. "Apparently two of our guys are down and out. Two men shot them and ran on to the plane. I've just heard that it's been moved on to the runway, but its baggage doors are still open. One of the ground crew was almost run over."

Meredith looked over to the departures area, where the tide of passengers were still flowing out, now in increasing numbers. As the passengers from Gate M had rushed to escape the gunfire, passengers in other departure lounges panicked, and ran like frightened animals to escape the assumed threat as well.

"Come on," he said, seizing the guard's arm and propelling him in the direction of the stairs. "There's no way we can make it through these crowds. We'll get into Gate M from outside. We need to see if either of the guards are still alive." He pushed the transmit button on his radio.

"Attention all guards," he ordered. "I need two men - Taylor and Sumner - to meet us at Gate M. The rest I want in the general area to look after this mess."

He phoned to let the remaining staff know what was happening, then he and the guard ran down the stairs to the outside of the building, where they made their way along the outer wall of the terminal to Gate M.

Using his security card to gain access through the alarmed doors, he found the departure lounge deserted, with the exception of the two bodies lying on the floor. Meredith's stomach roiled at the sight of the pools of blood which encircled the guards' heads like red halos and seemed to be everywhere over the chairs and seats nearby.

Joe Dimorro and he went back a long way, and he felt a huge sadness as he looked down at the lifeless body of his friend. He made a mental note to call Rosa, Joe's wife, to let her know what had happened. She was a diminutive, Italian woman, totally devoted to her husband and he knew that the news would devastate her. He then decided to call her son Al, a homicide detective assigned to 23rd Division. It would be better for Al to break the news to his mother.

At the same time, realizing the press would be getting into the act, he depressed the transmit button on the radio.

"Karen, this is Stuart. Call my wife and let her know that I'm safe."

"Sure thing, boss," came the reply. "Anything else?"

"Yes. Go to my card file and get the number for Alfred Dimorro. I'll be up there in a few minutes.

Oh, and pull the video tape from the surveillance cameras and stick in a fresh one. The police will want to get a look at those guys."

He took a moment to stare out the window at the jet, knowing the men responsible for his friend's death were on board. There was a hard look in his eyes, and he clenched his fists until his knuckles hurt, a fierce hatred for those men growing inside him. He wanted to hurt them for destroying a good man, but he knew it was a futile request. There were others on the jet, and their safety was his prime concern.

He looked at the security guard who had come with him. The young man's face had turned ashen, his lips trembled, and he blinked his eyes furiously. He was close to tears. Meredith knew what was going through the man's mind. This was supposed to be an easy job: nicking the occasional purse-snatcher or out-of-control drunken passenger. No-one was supposed to be confronting armed terror-ists.

Meredith touched the man on the arm, making him look away from the shattered bodies, and said, "I'm going back to the office to set up communica-tions with the jet. I also want to get some compos-ite pictures of those bastards while their faces are still fresh in my mind. You wait for Sumner and Taylor and stay here until the coroner arrives. No-one goes in or out until then. Understand?"

"No problem," replied the guard, putting on a weak show of bravado. "I'll come up to the office after that. I want to call my wife to let her know I'm okay."

"Fair enough. I'll see you up there."

In the crisis centre, a special room that had been set up for just such an event, Meredith was surrounded by RCMP officers and police. The hostage negotiator, Detective-Sergeant Ross Parker of the Peel Regional Police Force, was almost ready to open communications with the plane. Parker, a veteran, was one of several senior officers who dealt with the serious hostage negotiations in the Toronto area.

He was tall, well over six feet, with broad shoulders and muscled arms, a testament to his daily work-outs. He looked uncomfortable in the small chair, as if his body had been levered into position. On more than one occasion, a suspect had felt as if he were going to be torn apart by those huge limbs if the necessary information was not forthcoming, but a threat could also dissipate with a twinkle of his eyes.

Hostage negotiators had to be patient, strong-willed individuals with a capacity for understanding aberrant behaviour. An extensive knowledge of psychology was also required. Self-doubt, depression, or joy at the successes all made for a roller-coaster ride of emotions.

He, with several other members of the force, had trained at the FBI Academy in Quantico, Virginia. That team was now his 'support group', who would walk through any incident with him in a bar or hotel room immediately following the conclusion of the hostage incident.

At the academy he learned of the techniques first pioneered by Harvey Schlossberg and Frank Bolz of the NYPD hostage negotiating team. The two men had the honour of being legends in their own lifetimes for their success rate in hostage negotiations.

The FBI had merely taken those techniques and refined them into what was currently recognized as one of the best courses available in hostage negotiations. The old axiom 'never play cards with a man called Doc' was now jokingly extended to cover anyone who had taken the negotiating course.

After taking a sip of water, Parker depressed the 'Record' button on the large reel-to-reel tape recorder, and then spoke into the microphone. His voice was crisp and clear, without a trace of hesitation.

"This is Detective-Sergeant Ross Parker of Peel Regional Police. Can anyone hear me? Please acknowledge."

A hush fell over the room, with everyone staring at the speaker on the wall, as if willing it to come to life. Unconsciously, as with the others in the room, he was holding his breath.

"Well hello there, Detective-Sergeant Ross Parker. This is Peter Farrell of the Irish Freedom Fighters. My comrade, Sean McNally and I, have been forced to take control of this plane." The voice was steady, the gravelly accent unmistakably Northern Irish.

"Our demands are quite simple. We want the plane fuelled and then we want the captain to fly us to Havana. That's all, so it shouldn't take you long to decide on what to do. It's almost eight minutes past five right now. You have until six o'clock to finish fuelling this plane or I will execute one of the hostages."

The assembly groaned when they heard the threat. Parker put his hand over the microphone and glared at the others. He was not easily flustered. He had heard threats like this before from jealous boyfriends or estranged husbands who had taken their wives or girlfriends hostage.

"Peter. Let's not talk about harming the hostages. Alright? I'm not in any position to say yes or no to your demands. Let me discuss your requests with my superiors and see what we can do for you. It's going to take a little while to do that - you know what these superiors are like. Do you understand?"

"First of all," came the reply, "You're not my friend so don't call me Peter. It's Mister Farrell to you. And second of all, I don't give a fuck about

your superiors. You have until six o'clock, otherwise one of these nice people gets it. And then another, one hour after that. Do you understand, Mister Detective-Sergeant Ross Parker?"

"Okay, Mister Farrell, whatever you say. We'll
be in touch before six o'clock."

Parker leaned back in his chair, smoothed his
tie, and sighed deeply. He had been dreading the
day that this might happen. Dealing with domestic
disputes was one thing but this was a different
ballgame. Most terrorists were totally unpredictable, often quite willing to die for whatever they
felt was their 'cause'. That meant they were also
prepared to execute hostages.

"Has anyone managed to get hold of the Chief
yet?" he asked.

"Not yet," came the answer. "They think he
might be out in a boat fishing. We're trying to contact the special branch officers assigned to him."

"Keep trying. Also, find out if we have anything on the Irish Freedom Fighters. If not, call CSIS
and then the FBI. They usually keep up to date on
terrorist organizations and splinter groups. I've
never heard of this bunch, but I'll bet dollars to
donuts there is some connection with the Provisional IRA."

The mayor of Mississauga, Nora McCallister,
had just arrived and was sitting beside Stuart
Meredith watching the events unfold. A grey-haired

lady in her late fifties, she was a second-generation Irish immigrant and a hard-nosed politician with all the charm of a pit-bull terrier. She was, as ever, elegantly dressed in a light-blue linen suit over a yellow silk blouse. A single strand of pearls adorned her neck. She ran her city as if it were her own business, and as a result the municipality was one of the best run in Canada. Parker often thought she would have made a great prime minister.

As the playback of the conversation finished, she turned to Parker. "So what are we going to do until six o'clock, Ross? Are we going to sit and hope that somebody can find the Chief before the deadline? Is there no-one else who can make these decisions?"

Parker was accustomed to the mayor's tirades.

"Mayor, we should have no difficulty in contacting the Chief within the hour. But you know the PM has been extremely outspoken in his condemnation of governments who yield to terrorist threats, and recommended they all take a harder line.

"To that end, I have been in contact with the solicitor general and outlined the scenario. He will take the matter to the prime minister but he has already given permission for the Special Emergency Response Team (SERT) to be put on full alert. Twelve of them are now on their way.

"However, the final decision lies with the Chief."

"Is it possible the Chief might let the plane go?"

she asked, a strange look on her face.

Ross Parker thought for a moment, feeling that he was being manoeuvred into a corner. "Yes, it is possible that the plane may be allowed to take off. The safety of the hostages is paramount, and if he feels that their lives are in danger he will allow the plane to leave."

"What?" The mayor almost leapt out of her chair. "Do you mean to tell me that you'd consider letting the plane go, especially after those bastards have just murdered two security guards in cold blood. Are they just going to walk away scott free?"

Parker bit his tongue. The outrage was sincere and mirrored his own feelings. It was well known the mayor was not one for double-dealing and so the show of emotion was not for his benefit. He had to choose his words carefully.

"Mayor, Joe Dimoro was one of the guards who was shot and killed. He has been my friend for the past twenty years so you can only imagine how I feel. I'd like to go in there and tear the bastards limb from limb. However, I am a professional and I must put those feelings on hold when dealing with a scenario such as this.

"We have to separate the two incidents completely. The killing of the guards and the hostage-taking are two issues. Right now, we are dealing with the hostage incident only."

The mayor nodded, easing back into her chair.

"Do you think SERT will have to storm the plane?"

"I couldn't honestly say," he replied. "It depends on a lot of factors. Deadly force will be our last option, I assure you. I have a call in to the Belfast police to see if they can give us any information on these two terrorists. We need to get some reading on how likely they are to carry out their threat. We should be hearing back from them shortly."

The phone rang and one of the officers pointed to Ross Parker. He picked up the extension.

"Ross Parker here." The mayor watched as his brow furrowed at the news he was receiving. The conversation was punctuated with okay's and alright's from his side. When he eventually put the phone down, his face was pale.

"More bad news, I'm afraid," he said. "Six security guards and an American pilot have been shot to death up the road at McDonnell Douglas. The Apache attack helicopter which was being demonstrated to the government has been stolen." He shook his head. "What a fiasco!"

"Do you think these two incidents are connected?" asked the mayor.

"I'd say it's more than coincidence," he replied. "It was probably a well-planned operation that was screwed up when Meredith became suspicious. They went through the standard security checks, but somehow managed to get weapons in the departure area. That takes planning."

*   *   *   *   *

Major Skinner shrugged his arms into his greatcoat, picked up his briefcase, and was about to leave his office when the phone rang. He cursed under his breath: his day had not been particularly pleasant. There was not so much as a whisper about Timothy White's death, despite his efforts to turn up leads, and no organization had claimed responsibility, which was in itself unusual. The factions were normally falling over each other to claim responsibility for killing a high-ranking British soldier.

He decided to answer the phone: he would probably be tracked down at his quarters anyway. The call was from his old friend Colin Soames, chief constable of the Royal Ulster Constabulary. "Hello major, you're working late tonight."

"You know what they say Colin," he laughed. "No rest for the wicked, and if they can't rest then neither can I. What can I do for you?"

"No beating around the bush, eh major? I've just received a call from the police in Toronto. Two terrorists have shot and killed two RCMP officers at the airport and have taken over a plane. They have about nine or ten hostages on the plane with them. They claim to be members of the Irish Freedom Fighters and have given their names freely to the negotiators.

"We don't have anything on them, but they could be using false names. The people in Toronto don't seem to think so, though. Could you take a look and see if you have anything on your files? "Oh, and one other thing. They say they will execute a hostage every hour unless the Canadians agree to their demands. They want to be flown to Havana."

"Ah, the old escape route courtesy of Mr Castro," exclaimed Skinner. "I'm surprised though, about the hostages."

"That's correct, major. This is the first time that alleged Irish terrorists have hijacked an aircraft. The people in Toronto want to know how likely they are to carry out their threats."

"It's hard to predict what they might do. Anyway, stay on the line and I'll check them out for you. What are their names?"

"Peter Farrell and Sean McNally."

Soames could hear the tap, tap, tap of the keys as the major signed on to the system.

When the first menu screen appeared, Skinner picked up his other phone and dialled the computer centre at Lisburn. When one of the computer operators answered, Skinner identified himself and said he would be accessing the system. He replaced the phone and commenced the regular signon procedure. The computer operator would now see him on the master console, but as he had received the requisite phone call, no action would be taken.

Skinner had put in place an intricate plan, so that when the operator saw an unauthorized access to the system, no phone call for verification, a series of steps were to be followed.

First, the userid which had tried to access the system would be made inactive for a few moments while a program was run to switch certain indicators in the prime database. Second, a message would be sent to the user telling them that the system was slow due to backups being run and would speed up in a few moments. Lastly, when the program to set the indicators had run successfully, the operator would reactivate the illegal userid and monitor the transactions which that id was trying to access.

Each online inquiry now pointed to a file of fictitious data. These were files which showed that certain high-ranking terrorists were passing information to police, and had foreign bank accounts padded with funds which should have been for the 'movement'. This was one of Skinner's ways of passing disinformation to 'the enemy'.

Using the two-finger method, he diligently entered Peter Farrell's name, surname first, ensuring that the spelling was correct. After the program scoured the database trying to find a match, it finally responded with the message:

'** NO DATA ON FILE FOR THIS NAME **'.

He then keyed in FAR, to ensure to cover spelling variations, but there was no Peter Farrell.

When he keyed in Sean McNally's name, the system responded with the same answer. He frowned. Strange there was no mention of either of the two men. The system had information on most known terrorist members, since they were few in numbers - unless they were using fake passports.

"Sorry Colin, we don't have anything. Either they were travelling on false papers or we have two new unknowns. I'll put the word out, to see what we can find about these two. If I hear anything, I'll be in touch. Goodnight, Colin."

"Thanks major," he replied, "I owe you one. I'll pass the information on to Toronto."

CHAPTER 11
Deadline

Sixteen members from the 'on-call' team of the Special Emergency Task Force (SERT) sat aboard a Canadian Forces Lear jet, en route from Ottawa to Toronto. The plane had been provided through an arrangement with the Canadian military, in which distant deployment transportation would be made available to the team on request.

When the message to put the team on standby in Toronto came through to SERT headquarters, the men thought it was just another exercise and were treating it such. It took the base commander all of five seconds to dispel that notion. The camp was soon abuzz with the news.

Excitement coursed through the plane like an almost palpable entity. In the cabin, the men mentally and physically prepared themselves for the possibility of putting their training into practice.

Lieutenant Alain Simmonds, leader of the team, sat at the front of the plane, examining a diagram of a DC-10's interior. He was dressed, as were the other fifteen members, in lightweight black fatigues, rubber-soled boots and Kevlar bullet-proof vests. At the front of the vest hung two stun grenades, commonly known as flashbangs, and two CS gas grenades. At both sides of the vest were rappelling harness hooks. A holster strapped to his leg held a Sig Sauer automatic pistol. On the floor beside him sat his Heckler and Koch MP5SD sub-machine gun with an aiming-point projector, and his gas respirator. Folded inside the gas mask was a black, flame-retardant hood.

His second-in-command, Sergeant Murray Walters was marking escape routes on the diagram with a pencil. He then referred to the hastily scribbled notes on his notepad and drew some 'X's to show the alleged positions of the hostages. Putting the tiny pencil in his mouth, he unconsciously began to chew the end.

"Looks like we'll have to go in along the wings," he offered.

Simmonds looked over at his sergeant's outline of the DC-10. "The SITREP indicates the hijackers are at the front of the plane. So are the hostages. Two terrorists have been identified and confirmed, but we can't rule out the possibility there may be others. We'll have to go in as near to the front as possible, with two teams, one for each wing entrance. What do you think, Walt?"

The sergeant was known to everyone on the base as 'Walt', the origin which remained a mystery to him. When two instructors from the British Special Air Service came to carry out their training, they had delighted in calling him 'Walt'. It seemed that just about everyone in the SAS required a nickname, even visiting military personnel from other forces. One of their main functions, it seemed, was to give everyone, including senior officers, the most unflattering soubriquet possible.

Gordon Bell, who had failed to check the plane's washroom during the Fort Bragg mock hijacking, had been dubbed 'Tinker' - after Tinkerbell, the clumsy cow in a children's nursery story. Following his discovery of its origins, when in proximity to the SAS trainers, he could be heard muttering under his breath.

The two instructors had spent several evenings in the bar with the men, regaling them with stories about the SAS and its origins. One of the stories which Walt liked best was about Colonel Charlie

Beckwith, the driving force behind the American DELTA force, who had gone to Britain to train with the SAS. It seemed his feet were too tender for the habitual SAS route marches, and as a result he earned the uncomplimentary nickname of 'Blisters'.

"I agree," said Walt, moving the pencil to the other side of his mouth. "The problem is that the jet is sitting out on the runway, in broad daylight, and does not have a ramp up to the door. Timing is going to be critical.

"Also, the baggage doors are still open. The terrorists had the plane moved before the porters had finished loading. We might be able to go up through the bottom of the baggage hold."

Simmonds nodded. "Yes, I agree. Call the crisis centre in Toronto and find out if there has been any more contact with the plane, if the hostages have been moved, and how much fuel the ground crew managed to get into the tanks? Make sure you stress the importance of that fuel estimate!"

In their early training, several 'volunteer' hostages had pointed out that they could feel the plane rock as the rescue team ran across the wings. As it was a test aircraft, the wing tanks were empty, and so the plane was more prone to reflect any movement.

Simmonds looked over his shoulder to the other men in the team. They, like himself, had been recruited from Emergency Response Teams from all over Canada, following a gruelling, intensive nine-day selection process which focused on physical and mental fitness.

He scanned their faces looking for signs of uncertainty or unease, but there were none. These men were all veterans, each having served a minimum of eight years, most of which was spent on the Emergency Response Teams of their respective areas.

Some were checking their weapons and harnesses. Others, their inspection complete, stared out the windows, each immersed in his own private thoughts. They were all 'loners': they could work on their own initiative or with a minimum of supervision. However, they functioned best working in small groups of four, a 'brick', where the capability of the team far exceeded the output of four individuals.

Some of them were family men, and sat scribbling notes to their wives and children. The men were realists - they knew that if they were sent into action any one of a hundred things could go wrong and they might not survive. The few words might ease the blow to loved ones if they did not make it through the assault. If they did survive, the notes would be shredded.

He turned his attention back to the layout of the DC-10, and began making various notes and diagrams around the doors. A plan was beginning to take shape in his mind, and he pencilled in the names of the team members at the various strategic points. It was a simple plan, though difficult to execute and would depend on many factors, some of which as yet unknown.

He saw a note on the chart informing the user that the rear windows of the cockpit could be removed from inside the plane, an escape hatch for the captain and crew in case of an emergency.

The deadline was due to expire in five minutes, and Ross Parker was becoming worried. His tie was now loosened, the top button of his shirt wide open, and a few errant hairs pushed through. On the table before him was a miniature pyramid of empty coffee-cups. Christ, I need a cigarette, he said to himself. He held his hand out and watched it tremble slightly. He had given up smoking at his wife's insistence several years ago, but the cravings were still as strong.

There was still no word from the chief of police, and to make matters worse, the air traffic controller had not completed details of the flight path to Havana.

He picked up the telex from Belfast and reread it one more time. It stated simply that the two terrorists were unknown to the authorities. It was possible they were 'sleepers', extremist sympathizers who had emigrated to Canada or England in the early days of the 'troubles'. Some had set up a cover, so that they might be used in a time of crisis or during a routine mission.

There was a brief outline of the Balcombe street siege in London, where four IRA terrorists took a man and his wife hostage. Minutes after the BBC announced on the radio that the SAS were on the scene, the terrorists promptly surrendered.

After a moment's hesitation, Parker picked up the microphone, the sudden movement surprising everyone in the room.

"Mr Farrell, can you hear me?" he asked.

"Yes, I can hear you. It's two minutes to six."

"We have not yet been able to contact the chief of police," he answered, "but should be hearing from him shortly. The air traffic controller is trying to arrange a flight path directly to Havana. It is a complex process and very time-consuming. We need more time. In the meantime I can send over some coffee. Or tea perhaps. My grandmother always maintained that the Irish love their tea. Personally speaking, the stuff she drank was more like tar. You could stand a spoon up in the stuff. Barry's tea I think it was. My grandfather ..."

"Fuck your grandfather," came the interruption. "You're stalling." The voice was full of venom. The transmission ended and a hush fell over the room like a snowfall on a winter's night.

"Mr Farrell, Mr Farrell," called Parker, anxiously trying to re-establish contact. There was no reply.

All faces in the crisis centre now turned to the clock. It was two minutes past 6:00, then three, then four. Parker inhaled a deep breath of air like a swimmer surfacing from a dive.

"I think they're giving us more time," he said, taking several more deep breaths to calm his racing pulse. He shivered, an involuntary motion. "Jesus," he whispered. "Someone just walked over my grave."

At 6:10, Peter Farrell came out of the cockpit and walked up to the hostages. None of them attempted to make eye contact with him, one of the fundamental rules in surviving a hijacking. He smiled, knowing the rules as well.

"Look at me," he commanded. "The police want to know that no one has been harmed, so one of you will open the door and wave out. You can shout and tell them that everyone is okay. They have special microphones and cameras to pick it up. Have any of you got children at home?"

McNally stared at Farrell, a blank look on his face, then turned away to guard the pilots.

"I have," offered one of the hostesses. "I'd like them to know that everything's all right. They will probably be worried."

"Okay, you'll do fine," answered Farrell. "Just

open the door, wave out for a couple of minutes, tell them you're alright and close the door. Then maybe we can get this settled."

"Something's happening."

All eyes in the crisis centre turned to the monitor. The cabin door at the front of the plane opened and one of the stewardesses appeared, waving her arms and shouting.

"Zoom in on her face," ordered Parker, a puzzled look furrowing his brow, "and turn the mike on her. Find out what she's saying."

The camera zoomed in closer until her face filled the screen. Then the sound was fed through the crisis monitors.

"Annie, Sheila, it's mom. I'm okay and so are all the others. Tell daddy not to worry. I'll be home later."

Parker looked at the Mayor. His brow was lined with furrows.

She asked, "What's going on, Ross?"

He shrugged his shoulders but he had an uneasy feeling. They wouldn't, he said to himself, again and again like chanting a mantra, but his mouth went dry.

The stewardess repeated her message, waving frantically in the direction of the terminal as if she could see the people inside. Suddenly, the front of her face tore away from her skull in an eruption of blood and brains. For one awful second, the camera showed her head, a great gaping hole where the right side of her face used to be, and then she disappeared from view as her body fell to the runway. The camera had a momentary glimpse of Peter Farrell as he closed the cabin door.

The sound of retching echoed around the room. A gut-wrenching wail emanated from the mayor, and Parker fought back the bile rising in his throat like mercury in a thermometer on a hot day. The intercom crackled into life and Farrell's voice filled the room.

"One more hour, one more hostage. Don't fuck around with us any more."

The room was silent once again, everyone stunned by what they had just witnessed. The Mayor sobbed uncontrollably into her handkerchief for a moment and then ran to the washroom to be sick. Parker shook his head in disbelief. Today, his worst fears had been realized.

The mayor came back out of the washroom, wiping her mouth with a tissue. "Animals," she said between clenched teeth, barely able to suppress her anger. "Fucking animals."

Parker said, "I'll inform the Solicitor General and recommend we send in the SERT. I don't think we'll get any argument from him."

The phone's ringing startled him. He pulled back his hand as if the phone was electrified. It rang one more time before he picked it up. "Parker here."

"Sir, the SERT have just landed. They should be here in a few minutes."

"Thanks," he replied and put down the phone. He turned to see the police chief, dressed in army fatigues, walk into the command room. The chief did not take kindly to having his weekends interrupted. His face was white with anger, having just witnessed the execution of the stewardess through the window of the tower.

He pulled the baseball cap from his head and tossed it in a corner. Crows feet glowed at the side of his eyes, a testament to the constant squinting into the sun over the past few days on the lake. He ran a hand through his wiry white hair, a wasted attempt to pat it into place, and sat down on a chair beside Parker.

The two men were of similar build, the Chief a little less muscular than Ross. In his early days on the force, he was a formidable athlete, specializing in cross-country running. In the photographs on his desk and in his den at home, he had that gaunt, emaciated look peculiar to long distance runners. His wife had made the comment on several occasions that he used to look like a greyhound.

Now, a few years on, his frame had filled out as he was no longer able to maintain the exacting workouts of his early days. He still ran several miles each week, a habit which had carried over from his younger days. But now the miles were on the decline as the years crept up on him. He was just a few months away from his fifty-fourth birthday.

"Okay Ross, bring me up to date."

Parker took a swig of coffee to moisten his mouth. "Two terrorists have taken over a Canadian Airlines charter flight to Belfast and are holding the crew hostage. They have demanded to be flown to Havana or they will execute the hostages, one every hour. We were still trying to set up the flight path to Havana when the deadline expired. I told them that it was going to take longer than we anticipated but they went ahead and executed one of the hostages as you witnessed. The SERT team has just arrived. That's it in a nutshell."

The chief then began a volley of questions. Parker answered them as best he could, always impressed with the man's incisive reading of any situation. The chief, well respected on the force, was known as policeman's policeman, more concerned about getting the job done than with political ambitions. As a result, he was frequently at loggerheads with the Mayor.

"How many hostages?"

"Ten, including the pilot, co-pilot and radio officer."

"Are we sure about the number of terrorists aboard?"

"All we know for sure is that two men shot and

killed the security guards and ran on to the plane. In the confusion it's possible that there might have been more. The one who calls himself Peter Farrell identified himself and Sean McNally. But that's not to say that there couldn't be more."

"They identified themselves?"

"Yes, Farrell said that they are members of the Irish Freedom Fighters. Our people have never heard of them. Neither has Belfast. They think that it could be some offshoot of the Provisional IRA."

"I'm surprised they identified themselves," said the chief. "The IRA get a lot of their funding from Canadians and Americans so they are particularly careful about avoiding any bad publicity here. Seems strange." He scratched the stubble on his chin.

The phone beside the chief rang. He picked it up and passed the receiver to Parker who listened intently for a few moments before replacing the receiver.

"The prime minister has been contacted. We have been given permission to storm the plane. Let's hope our boys are up to it."

The SERT members spilt up into their customary groups of four. One team, designated Echo-1, would storm the main door of the plane, teams two and three, Echo-2 and -3 would go in along the wings, and team four, Echo-4, would handle the cockpit area.

Using extendable, lightweight aluminium ladders bolted together in fours, the men from Echo-2 and -3 climbed on to the top of the wings. They had learned that the fuel tanks were almost full, so the plane would not rock when the men ran along the wings. The terrorists had shut the window blinds to avoid surveillance, but even if they had been open, Farrell and McNally would not be able to see the men pressed against the side of the plane like barnacles on a boat.

At the front of the plane, the ladders had been positioned under the main door to give easy access to the emergency handle. The huge door opened hydraulically, and was slow, so the men positioned themselves where they could get a line on the terrorists as soon as it cracked open. All they needed was a two or three inch gap.

The first man on each team crept across the wing to the emergency door, all the while listening in their earpieces for a warning from ground surveillance. They took care to step on the rows of rivets, where the aircraft skin was joined to the ribs, for firm footing.

Members of Echo-1 and Echo-4 crept under the plane towards the main cabin door, located above the body of the dead stewardess. The lifeless, crumpled body was a stark reminder that this was not a drill. Two more aluminium ladders were placed against the front of the plane leading up to the cockpit's emergency exits; the removable windows.

Just above the men, the leading members of Echo-2 and Echo-3 were ready to hurl their 'flashbangs' into the cabin. The men had to act quickly, because a buzzer would sound as soon as the emergency doors were opened from the outside, thus alerting the terrorists. The flashbangs, an SAS colloquialism for the special stun grenades, exploded with an ear-splitting bang and blinding flashes. They had been developed by weapons experts in the SAS for just such a purpose as storming a plane, or clearing a room.

In the control room, silence had fallen. Those inside stared at the speaker, waiting. Parker chewed on the ragged edge of a fingernail, looking at the monitor at the black-clad figures pressed tightly against the side of the plane.

"Echo one ready."

"Echo two ready."

"Echo three ready.

There was a brief pause, then came the final "Echo four ready."

Alain Simmonds, standing under the plane, touched his chest to activate his transmitter and spoke into his throat microphone.

"We go in three. Three, two, one." He pressed the detonator in his hand and a fuel-tanker, placed about a hundred yards in front of the plane exploded in a blinding flash of orange and black flames. The klieg lights illuminating the plane were abruptly shut off.

A fraction of a second later, two men pulled down the emergency handles and pushed the folding doors back into the plane. In their first attempts at storming a plane, one of the lessons learned was that the man who entered from the port wing had to be left-handed. Their first attempts used a right-hander, who had to re-orient himself in order to throw his grenade down the passageway. That re-orientation took vital seconds and cost the lives of two of the 'dummy' hostages.

Simultaneously, at the front of the plane, the protective cover of the main door handle had been cracked open and released, and the cockpit windows smashed, the two SERT men there tracking their guns into the cockpit.

The SERT men who entered the plane through the emergency exits had to throw their grenades through the air to hit the front bulkheads where the terrorists were standing. The purpose of the throw was to have the grenades hit the soft inner walls and drop to the floor near the feet of the terrorists. All attempts at rolling the grenades had proven unsuccessful in their mock assaults.

The SERT member bursting through the port-wing door was jokingly called 'Steibie', after the famous left-handed pitcher of the Toronto Blue Jays. In practice, his throw was unerringly accurate - and fast. So much so, he was in great demand as a pitcher for the SERT's baseball team. Today's throw was no exception. The two men tossed their stun grenades towards the front of the plane and then scrambled out of the way, drawing their weapons.

The next two men on either side ran into the plane, their silenced Heckler and Koch MP5 pistols at the ready, just as the grenades exploded.

"Police - get down," they yelled and stepped into the aisle, their weapons tracking on the terrorists, fingers tightening on the triggers as they assessed the situation. Behind them on the wing, the other men from Echo-2 were clambering through the emergency doors, weapons up and ready. They entered the cabin at the same time as their counterparts in Echo-3 on the other side of the plane.

Peter Farrell and Sean McNally were standing beside the cockpit door, looking out at the gasoline fireball when the lights went out. Then the grenades slammed into the bulkhead wall and landed at their feet, just as the main door hissed and started to open. The three-second fuses gave the two men time to turn, but no time to react. The great ear-splitting thunderclaps disoriented them, and then the blinding flashes from the magnesium-based powder blinded them.

While Farrell and McNally rubbed their eyes furiously, trying desperately to regain their lost vision, the lead team members tracked the red dots from their sights on the two terrorists and fired at their heads.

Simultaneously, the members of Echo-1 started firing through the gap at the main door, continuing to fire into the bodies of the terrorists until they stopped moving.

Blood and bits of grey matter decorated the cabin door, as the terrorists' heads split open like overripe tomatoes. The hail of bullets, specially designed 'Ranger' rounds, ripped through flesh and bone, tearing away chunks of flesh, leaving a bloody pulp where their faces used to be.

The SERT members from Echo-2 and -3 had reached the front of the plane, covering the fallen terrorists. The men from Echo-1 were just coming through the main door which now gaped open. The man from Echo-1, whose call-sign was 'Six', looked around at the remaining hostages, cowering in fear in their seats. They were all unharmed. Flicking the safety catch on his MP5, he spoke aloud, the combined transmitter/receiver in his ear picking up the relief in his voice.

"Six to sixteen. We have two cold badgers and nine hot doves."

Below, Alain Simmonds, call-sign 'Sixteen' grimaced. The two known terrorists were dead and nine hostages safe, but there was one hostage missing. He was afraid now that there might be a 'warm'

- wounded hostage or perhaps another 'cold' - dead hostage. He pressed the transmitter switch again. "Sixteen. We have one missing dove." Now he waited for the call from the other parts of the plane where his men were checking for any remaining terrorists.

After sprinting down the aisle towards the back of the plane, quickly checking each row, Gordon Bell was in the lead, kicking in the doors of the toilets and the galley, prepared to obliterate any terrorist found lurking inside. The incident at Fort Bragg was etched firmly in his mind. There would be no mistake this time.

Diane Thornton heard the explosions and the pistol shots. She thought the terrorists were executing the other hostages. Her heart was beating like a jack-hammer as she heard the sound of boots and splintering doors. She stuck her hands in her mouth, biting down hard in an attempt to prevent herself from careening over the edge of hysteria.

Bell kicked in the door of the toilet, his MP5 tracking on the interior. In the darkness, Diane stood up, screaming. Catching a blur of motion in the dark interior, Bell squeezed down on the trigger of his MP5.

The red-dot from his laser sight appeared on the figure's forehead, but a momentary glimpse of a stewardess's uniform instantly signalled his finger to ease back on the trigger. He grabbed one of the flailing limbs and dragged her out of the toilet. She was screaming hysterically.

He flipped the safety catch on his machine-pistol to 'on', swung it to one side, and then grabbed both her hands. Pinning her arms to her sides, he said, quietly and firmly, "It's alright, it's alright. I'm one of the good guys. Tom Bell. RCMP."

She went limp in his arms; the strain had been too much and her body sought the only logical reaction. He manoeuvred her over to one of the seats and eased her down gently. Two other members of the team gathered around as he touched his chest-switch and called for a doctor through his radio.

"Good job, Tinker" said one of the others. "That was a close call."

"You got that right," said Bell, under his breath as he walked back towards the cockpit.

At the front, other team members were helping the dazed cabin crew and the flight crew from their seats. Ambulances were waiting outside the plane to take them to nearby hospitals for observation.

The entire assault had lasted only ten seconds.

CHAPTER 12
Conflict

The train moved off in plumes of steam and smoke, leaving the solitary figure alone on the platform. It was a few minutes past 6:00 a.m. when John Waters stepped on to the deserted platform. He was home. The small town of Haversham nestled deep in the English countryside amidst rolling hills beside the dark waters of the river Wye.

Cocks were beginning to crow the dawn chorus, announcing the first golden rays of sunlight.

He picked up his case and walked through the station, down the steps to familiar cobbled streets, and then on out through the end of the town towards his father's house.

The town itself was beginning to stir, like a child rising and stretching from a peaceful night's sleep. A silent-running electric cart from the dairy glided along the street, bottles of milk rattling in their crates. The driver touched a finger to his brow in greeting.

As he walked, he inhaled the fresh country air, thinking of the early mornings in the small back roads of South Armagh. But here, there would be no Provo ambushes, or booby traps, or culvert bombs, or people whose feral hatred assaulted your senses. Here there was peace.

His eyes roved back and forth over the hedgerows and fields, an instinct drilled into him during his training in Hereford. It had saved his life more than once. The terrorists would often plant booby traps to be triggered by a trip-wire, a virtually invisible, thin piece of nylon filament. However, in the early dawn, dew would cling to the filament as if it were a spider-web, catching light for a short time.

As he walked, the tranquility of his surroundings began to ease the tension from his body. It was like putting on an old, familiar sweater.

Here were the hedgerows he explored as a child for the treasures among their leaves. When he was seven years old, his father had taken him out along the narrow lanes to search for nests, and they had returned home with several small eggs - the pure white of the robin, the speckled blue of a songthrush, and the larger dark grey of a blackbird - neatly cocooned in tiny wads of cotton wool.

He had watched in awe as his father made a tiny pin-prick at each end of the eggs, and then was almost ill when his father put the eggs to his lips, thinking his dad was going to suck the yolk into his mouth. The expression on his face brought a great guffaw of laughter.

Instead, his dad blew hard into the tiny openings, forcing the yolk and albumen out the bottom. When it was empty, he placed each shell gently in an empty biscuit tin which he had filled with sawdust. So started Waters's collection of birds' eggs. That tin of eggs and several others still sat in his bedroom, their precious contents intact, still retaining their bright hues.

Tempted now to stop and pry beneath the leaves, he laughed out loud at the thought, surprising himself and several cows who were grazing in the field beside the road.

He had soon covered the mile home and was strolling down the narrow, tree-lined driveway to the house. Loose gravel crunched under his feet, raising tiny eddies of dust as he walked. A thin snake of smoke from the chimney meant Mrs McClean, his father's housekeeper, was up and working in the kitchen. She had come to live with them shortly after his mother died. Five years old at the time, he had not understood the meaning of cancer. Many years later he came to comprehend the agony his mother had endured.

Mrs McClean was a rotund, jovial woman of indeterminate age, and treated John and his father like the family she had hoped for but never had. Her husband had been killed during the war, and she had not been able to find anyone else to fill that emptiness in her life.

She was busily kneading dough on the kitchen table when Waters slipped through the door and put his arms around her. She squealed in fright and grabbed a rolling pin to try to fend off her attacker. Waters released her and cowered in mock terror as she brandished the rolling pin over his head.

"You, you ..." she spluttered. "I think my old heart just about stopped. Now get over here and give me a proper hug before I lay into you with this." She nodded at the rolling pin.

He grabbed her around the waist, his hands barely able to meet, and lifted her about a foot off the floor. He planted a noisy kiss on her forehead and then set her back gently. She resumed kneading the dough as he sat down at the kitchen table.

"I'm just making some bread and scones for your father's breakfast. Have you eaten yet? There's some fresh tea in the pot if you want some."

He said, "Actually, Mrs Mac, I've just come

from the train. I have two weeks leave and I can't wait for one of your home cooked breakfasts. It's all I've been able to think about for the past two days. Mess food all tastes the same. I'll put away my clothes and then I can have breakfast with dad when he gets up." She laughed and brushed an errant grey hair back from her forehead, the floury hand leaving a white trail across her brow.

"Your father was up at five o'clock this morning and off to the river. He's been muttering about a 'big one' for the past few days, but we still haven't had salmon for breakfast."

"Really," he said, not at all surprised. His father's passion for fishing had managed to rub off on his son. "I'll get my rod and join him. Maybe I'll bring back some fish for breakfast."

"Well I won't hold my breath," she laughed. "It's nice to have you home again, John."

"That goes double for me, Mrs Mac," he replied, and set off out the back door. He walked to the small wooden shed behind the garage, where the fishing gear was stored.

This was his father's private kingdom, a place where outsiders were rarely permitted. Waters himself was not granted access to this sanctum sanctorum until he was old enough to realize that its contents were not toys. Scattered around in cigar boxes, old biscuit tins and plastic, airtight containers were the materials used to create a master-

piece. These were the sculptor's marble or the paint-
er's oils.

He ran his hand along the top of the door, his
fingers searching for the spare key to the heavy
padlock. His groping fingers found what they were
looking for and he opened the padlock, turned the
knob, and pushed gently. The door swung back on
well-oiled hinges, almost without a sound, as if noise
would upset the serenity of the interior.

Along one wall, placed neatly in racks like rifles in an armoury, stood his father's collection of
fishing rods, each representing a 'breakthrough' in
technology. At the far end was the oldest rod, made
from split cane, completely hand made, with intricate patterns engraved on the brass reel fittings.
There were a few more of the split-cane variety,
then some fibre-glass and finally, at the other end,
two state-of-the-art carbon-fibre models. One of
the split-cane rods was missing, so he assumed his
father had opted for a traditional pole in order to
catch the salmon.

On the opposite side of the room was his father's workbench, about two feet wide and running
the length of the hut. The focal point of the bench,
which could be bathed in light at the touch of a
switch, was a miniature fly-tyer's vise. Its brand new,
shiny metallic look prompted closer investigation.
Waters smiled when he saw the trademark, Salmo,
the 'Rolls-Royce' of them all. Waters had actually

been planning to give his father one as a Christmas present.

In front of the vise, a well-worn barstool, a souvenir from the local pub, was just the right height for the bench. On the walls around the vise, all within easy reach, stood shelves of boxes, each individually labelled with their contents, feathers from myriad birds: ostriches, peacocks, partridges, grouse, snipe, woodcock, pheasant, and a multitude of others, all stacked alphabetically. Then there were boxes containing different types of fur, and boxes of brightly coloured silk thread and spools of gold and silver wire.

On a shelf within the boxes sat his father's collection of books, each a trove of fly patterns. The books were frayed from use, their bindings held together with pieces of tape or whatever other adhesive was on hand when they fell apart.

To the right of the vise sat a hand-made, wooden box. Waters knew his father had taken it down from the shelf earlier that morning to select a fly. These were his father's prized possessions, each tiny creation the result of hours of work. Each of the flies had a name, splendid names, like the Durham Ranger, Greenwell's Glory, or Thunder and Lightning. What wondrous images those names used to conjure up for him.

Waters opened the box, carefully selected two flies which he recognized, and put them in a matchbox. He then picked up one of the newer carbon-fibre rods, pulled on a pair of rubber boots, and closed the door behind him.

He replaced the padlock, hearing the resounding click when the arm slid into place, tugged the lock a couple of times to make sure it was in place, and then set off down to the river.

Retired Brigadier-General James Waters stood in the middle of the river Wye, waist deep in water. He was wearing a pair of chest waders supported by a pair of bright red braces. Below the suit was his thick green army sweater, a 'woolly-pully', to keep him warm in the chilly morning air.

The river flowed lazily past, creating miniature whirlpools as it swirled around his waist. His eyes were fixed on a spot some thirty feet from where he stood. His cast had been perfectly aimed, and the fly was now floating down past the point where he had last seen the huge salmon rise.

His right hand held the rod firmly, ready to make the final tug to set the barb of the hook into the salmon's mouth. His left hand was winding in the line in the palm of his hand, making a figure eight pattern. This winding motion caused the fly to jerk in the water, like the real thing.

The fly drifted past the spot at which he had aimed, but the salmon did not rise for the bait. However, like all fishermen, James Waters knew the value of patience. He pulled the line back through the air in a great arc to begin the cast once more. The line flew back and forth over the surface of the river until nearly all the line had been paid out. When he was certain the fly would once more float to its target, he allowed the line to settle gently on the surface of the water.

His left hand immediately began the figure eight motion and the fly resumed its jerking motion. Suddenly, the water erupted like a fountain as the huge salmon leapt into the air. The thin, split-cane rod strained against the force of the strike as the salmon tried to free itself. The grey body slammed back into the river, and the line went taut and then slack, again, as it leapt in the air once more, twisting and turning, trying to loosen the hook from its mouth.

The conflict raged on for about thirty minutes, neither side giving an inch. Then, inevitably, the salmon began to tire.

Confident now, James Waters began to reel in the line, the salmon offering only token resistance. As he brought it within reaching distance, he unslung his landing net which he had strapped across his back like an archer's bow. He inched the net slowly towards the fish, which he kept on the surface of the water by the tension of his line. When the landing net slid under the salmon, the side touched one of its fins, prompting it to leap out of the water with a mighty flick of its powerful tail.

At the top of the leap, it flicked its head to one

side and the hook came free. As the salmon fell back into the water, he leapt at it with the landing net, but it was to no avail. The fish was gone. To make matters worse, the lunge had let the top of the fishing suit dip into the water, allowing the chilly waters to flow over the edge and soak his trousers and socks.

"Damnation," he cried, slapping the surface of the river with the net. "Damned fish, I'm going to get you one of these days," he screamed at the empty river, brandishing the empty net over his head like a war club. He turned, hearing laughter coming from the river bank.

John Waters was holding his sides, roaring with laughter.

"Well, I'll be ... What are you doing home son?" asked his father, wading slowly towards the bank.

"I thought I'd come home for the show," Waters replied, motioning towards the river. "It certainly put up a hell of fight. It must weigh at least twenty pounds."

His father beamed, the black mood gone. "Well, I hope you enjoyed it. That damned fish is going to be the death of me. I've almost landed him twice, but at least now I have a witness. That old witch gives me grief every time I come back empty-handed."

His father calling Mrs Mac a witch was no more meant than pigs could fly. His father doted on the old lady and she on him. "Well, dad, I've got leave coming so maybe we can get him between us. Strength in numbers and all that. Anyway, Mrs Mac doesn't think much of your chances on your own. She tells me that she's been waiting for fish for a while."

"That old ..." his father scowled, stopping when he saw the grin on his son's face. "I better get home and out of these wet clothes. Then Mrs Mac can cook us up a fry. Mess food is one thing I will never miss about the army. By now I expect you feel the same."

James Waters grasped his son's outstretched arm and heaved himself out of the river, gasping because of the extra weight of his soggy clothes. He sat on the river bank to regain his breath and then stripped off the fishing suit to get rid of the water. That done, he put his arm around his son's shoulders and the two men squelched off towards the house.

*   *   *   *   *

When Patrick Kelly came awake to the mouth-watering aroma of frying bacon, he climbed out of bed and padded across the small room to the window. It had been dark last night when they landed the chopper on a flat area beside the house, so he had no idea of what Rathlin Island looked like.

He pushed aside the once white lace curtains

and feasted on the view. His room faced the mainland, which was only about half a mile away. The
island itself was no more than a few hundred yards
long, like a blemish in the middle of the bay, a rocky
lump spotted here and there with clumps of red and
white heather. A tiny jetty protruded into the sea,
as if trying to reach its counterpart on the mainland. Two small rowing boats, their paint cracked
and peeling, bobbed at their moorings.

The bay was picture postcard Ireland, guarded
on both sides by the mainland's mighty cliffs, which
formed a perfect U-shape, all that remained from
the passing of an ancient glacier. The top ends of
the U were shrouded in mist, their steep, craggy
sides dotted with tiny white figures: sheep grazing
in almost impossible-to-reach places.

He felt as if he had come home, so vivid were
his grandmother's descriptions. The Emerald Isle.
Everything was green, tiny fields forming a patch-
work quilt of varying shades, their borders sharply
defined by weather-beaten, stone walls. He inhaled
the fresh salt air, all the while delighting in the pano-
rama laid out before him. A sharp pang of hunger
prodded him from his reverie and he turned away
from the window.

A basin of cold water sat on a wooden dresser,
along with a towel, a washcloth and a new bar of
soap, the brand letters still firm and sharp on the
surface. It seemed strangely incongruent with the

dilapidated state of the room. Realizing there was no indoor plumbing, hardly surprising considering the location, he washed his face, the icy water shocking him and removing the last vestiges of sleep. Then he pulled a comb through his hair, which did little to improve his appearance.

The voyage across the Atlantic had been more than a little rough, and he had spent most of the time in his bunk, reading magazines and eating Gravol on a regular basis. His once hearty appetite vanished. He had tried to engage Donnelly in conversation a couple of times but those seeds fell on barren ground and eventually he gave up. The captain had come to the cabin early on the morning following their rendezvous and had taken Donnelly outside for a few minutes. When he returned to the cabin his expression was more sullen then usual, and he did not speak again until it was time to fly to the island.

Now, on dry land again, Kelly's appetite had returned with a vengeance, his stomach grumbling loudly at the enticing aroma. He dressed and opened the bedroom door. Along the narrow hallway, at the end of which was a flight of stairs, were four other rooms.

The stairs creaked as he placed his weight on them. In the kitchen, Tommy Mulholland's attention was directed at a pan of sizzling bacon.

"Good morning Patrick. Could I interest you in

a good Ulster fry? Bacon, eggs, fadge, soda farls, and a strong cup of tea." His voice was bright and cheery. He was obviously happy to be home. It would have been an almost idyllic scene if not for the .38 revolver in his waist-band.

"Sounds good to me," replied Kelly. "I feel as if I haven't eaten for days. I don't like boats."

"You're like me, Patrick. I prefer to keep my feet on solid ground."

"Where are the others?" enquired Kelly.

"The women should be arriving within the next couple of days; I've got to drive down to Larne to meet them off the boat. They had some business to take care of in London. Josie was up about an hour ago and off to the rocks to do some fishing. It's almost high tide so we should be having some fresh fish for dinner."

Since no mention was made of Farrell or McNally, Kelly assumed they were off wreaking havoc in some other part of the province. He sat down at the kitchen table, his stomach now howling for food.

Mulholland shovelled some of the bacon on to a plate, and cracked a couple of eggs into the sizzling fat. As they cooked, he filled a mug with steaming tea and presented the meal to Kelly. The mug and plate had seen better days, their surfaces spidered with tiny cracks and stained from use. It did not affect the flavour of the food, and Kelly tucked in with relish. It was a little greasy, but he ate as if it were his last meal.

Considering the company he was in, that was always a possibility, Kelly mused wryly. It took another helping of bacon and eggs to placate his grumbling insides. "Do you think Josie would mind if I joined him?" he asked, rubbing his stomach. "When I was younger, my grandmother used to take me to the docks, and we'd spend the day fishing. I never really caught anything but she liked to go. She used to take my dad there when he was growing up and I guess it brought back pleasant memories."

"Josie's okay at times," replied Mulholland, "but you didn't exactly get off to a good start with him, did you? Sometimes that black rage comes over him and no one can control him. He almost shot me once, when I tried to stop him from torturing a Brit Intelligence officer. He's a smart kid, that's the shame of it; that those brains have gone to waste. He had a chance to do well for himself and get out of here, but the Brits fucked it all up.

"Me, I couldn't wait to get out of school. My father was a Provo from the early days - fought with Josie's dad, he did, and I didn't need any encouragement to follow in his footsteps. Josie's mother, though, made his father swear never to get the boy involved and he agreed. The mother had high hopes for the lad and made him apply himself to his books. I think she could never reconcile herself to the fact that her husband was a Provo, that's why she pushed Josie so hard."

"So what happened to the brilliant student?" asked Kelly, his curiosity piqued.

"Well, some fuckin' tout informed on Josie's dad, and the Brits went to pick him up one night after everyone was in bed. They like to do that 'cos it upsets the whole fuckin' street. Anyway, his da was always a light sleeper, being on the run all the time does that for you, and he heard the land rovers pull up outside the house. As they smashed in the front door, he was out the back window, down the drainpipe, and away like a rabbit, dressed in his pyjamas and revolver in hand.

"Josie's room was at the back of the house, facing the lane, so the Brits stormed into it, smashed the window and started shooting at his dad. Josie got a rifle butt in the face when he tried to interfere. He was out for a few moments and when he came around, the Brits were congratulating each other on having 'wasted another Mick'.

"Something snapped in him that night. He's killed a lot of Brits since then, trying to avenge his father's death. Now and again I see flashes of the old Josie but they're rare. So you can go and talk to him, but don't expect a warm reception."

Josie Donnelly was sitting on an outcropping. The tide was rising; waves pounded into the rocks, tossing spray like white curtains into the air. He did not hear Kelly approach until the last moment and, startled, immediately reached for his pistol.

"It's only me," he said, holding his hands up.

"Don't sneak up on people, Yank. It's not good for your health." His tone was hostile.

"Tommy told me you were down here," said Kelly. "I wanted to see if you'd caught anything. I did some fishing with my grandmother."

"Oh, did you now?"

"Yeah, she used to take me down to the docks. Same place she used to take my dad when he was a boy."

"Is your da dead?"

"My parents were killed in a car crash when I was seven. My grandmother raised me, said I was the only thing that kept her sane. Her husband, Sean, my grandfather, was caught one night after coming home from a 'job' and hanged by the Black and Tans in his barn. They made her watch the whole thing and then they burned the barn with him and all the animals inside. That's the reason she went to America. She was pregnant with my dad at the time, and my grandfather and her were planning to leave, but the Tans caught him."

A faraway look came to Donnelly's face. "My dad used to bring me here in the summer. We'd go to Larne and dig some bait, then we'd come back and spend the day. We'd fish at high tide and after, we'd go down to the beach for a swim. Me ma would have made us two or three rounds of egg and onion sandwiches and we'd have a flask of tea."

"What kind of bait do you use?" asked Kelly, trying to change the subject of dead fathers.

"I use lugworm. There's some in the tin over there." He pointed over to a biscuit tin, whose lid had been perforated in several places with a nail.

Kelly pried off the lid, curious to see what a lugworm looked like. He poked under the mass of damp seaweed and pulled out one of the worms. It was about eight inches long, about half an inch in diameter, and had tiny legs running down both sides of its body, which rippled at his touch.

"What's this black bit?" he asked, pointing to a small black ribbon which crossed the end of the worm.

"You know, I asked my dad that same question," replied Donnelly, staring out to sea as if willing a fish to take the bait. "He told me to stroke its head and see what happens."

Kelly shrugged his shoulders and, holding the worm gently in one hand, began to stroke its head with his finger. The reflex motion was so fast that he did not realize what had happened until he felt the sharp pain at the end of his finger. The black ribbon, a set of pincers which folded neatly inside the head, had opened and grabbed whatever was upsetting it - in this case, Kelly's finger.

"Jesus Christ!" he exclaimed, flicking his finger to loosen its grip. Eventually it let go, but not before Donnelly had almost fallen in the sea from laughing. Kelly, always one to enjoy a good joke, even one at his expense, laughed too.

The remainder of the morning was spent talking about fishing. Donnelly hooked several large plaice and a couple of cod before turing the rod over to Kelly to 'give it a try'. They were entertained by a huge commorant which flew in lazy circles, dropping like a stone when it spotted a fish. It seemed to have more success than Kelly.

CHAPTER 13
Autopsy

Detective-Inspector Scott Armstrong sat at his desk, poring over the reports which were starting to come in. It was a trickle, but he knew from experience it would soon turn into a flood, threatening to swamp the investigation if not controlled.

At fifty-two years of age, he was alarmed at how quickly his body was deteriorating. Years of poor eating habits, too much coffee and booze had only served to accelerate the aging process. Running his fingers through thinning brown hair, he started to makes notes of people to call, equipment to display the progress of the investigation, additional secretarial help, and urns of coffee from the cafeteria.

Hours ago, he had reluctantly made the requisite call to his wife, feeling badly because she had planned a nice, romantic dinner. Fortunately for him, it was a call she was expecting: the radio and television were full of news about the hijacking of an army helicopter and the attempted hijacking of a jet. Being an officer's wife, she was well aware of what would happen once the investigative machine began to roll. She cautioned him, as always, to get something to eat, to try to get a few minutes sleep, and not to drink too much coffee.

He nodded his head and grunted acknowledgement as if she was in his office, but he was really not listening to what she was saying. His subconscious listened for certain keywords and filled in the appropriate response.

It was now 10:00 p.m., several hours after the discovery of the bodies at the McDonnell Douglas plant and the assault on the jet. He had left the command trailer at the plant and returned to Peel Regional headquarters to brief his detectives. Two had already been sent with the bodies directly to the morgue to observe the autopsies; it was important to know what types of weapons had been used to kill the guards. The body of the American pilot was being stored in one of the stainless-steel refrigerated units until someone from the military was on hand to supervise.

The Ident teams were still at the plant, picking up and bagging any hairs, traces of saliva, body substances, pieces of fabric, and other minutiae. It would be many hours before their task was complete.

As the investigation was expected to range across Toronto, several teams of detectives had been pulled in from other divisions. The police chief wanted results and wanted them quickly. Each team had been given their assignment and told of its priority. The teams then ranged out, like hounds after a fox, hoping to find a trail before it went 'cold'.

At the morgue, Doctor Simon Thompson, a forensic pathologist with the region was examining the first body. The others were being stripped in preparation for their examination. Each piece of clothing was bagged and stored separately, for later inspection. Then the painstaking job of comparing 'notes' would begin.

The doctor's mean, cadaverous look, had earned him the nickname of 'Dracula'. It was often said, though never directly to him, that his clients were often in better shape than himself. A shock of uneven white hair spilled over his threadbare collar, and his skin had a deathly pale tint, evidence that his body was rarely exposed to sunlight.

He was shortsighted and required glasses for

reading or operating, but he steadfastly refused to wear them, instead opting for soft contact lenses. This choice often left him with bloodshot eyes, which only reinforced his nickname.

Complexion and names aside, he was probably the best forensic pathologist in the city, meticulous and thorough, steadfastly refusing to be rushed no matter who was demanding results. He enjoyed his work immensely, becoming visibly animated when presented with new challenges.

It had been a long time since he had been confronted with so much carnage. An open textbook sat on the lip of the stainless steel table, and he referred to it from time to time.

When he pulled the body up on one side to examine the exit wounds, the men on the other side of the table winced. The two detectives were waiting to relay information to the command centre about the types of weapons the assailants may have been using. It was always useful to know what types of weapons the tactical team would be up against.

As he watched, the older of the two, Detective Barry Coates, was reminded of his weekend, examining steaks before throwing them on the barbecue. To the doctor, the body was just another piece of meat to be pulled and prodded. It had long since ceased to be a person.

Coates was a heavyset man with a round, florid face and sagging jowls. A well-nurtured paunch spilled over the top of his belt, consistently forcing the bottom button of his shirt to open. At forty-six, with two failed marriages behind him, he had gone to seed, preferring nowadays the company of a bottle.

He was a footsoldier, intelligent and doggedly persistent when given a task, but not a leader. That fact became painfully clear to him a few years ago when his peers began to outstrip him in rank and promotions. At first it rankled him but then came a gradual acceptance of his station. If being a detective was to be his lot in life then so be it.

As the scalpel twisted, the detective shivered. He offered up a silent prayer that he never land in the morgue at the hands of Dracula. His partner, too, was uneasy, trying to look anywhere except at the body.

"So how are you guys doing?" asked the doctor casually. "I've got some sandwiches outside on a tray if either of you are hungry. It's going to be a long one. Your boss wants all these guys done tonight."

"What kind of sandwiches?"

The doctor finished the Y-incision and peeled back the guard's skin in two large flaps to examine the vital organs. As he lifted up the liver and peered at it intently he said, "I think there are some salmon salad left."

Coates's stomach roiled at the thought. "Oh,

I'll pass, thanks all the same. So what do you think, Simon?" asked Barry Coates. The two men had been acquaintances for many years, but only in a professional capacity.

Dracula responded, "I think we're dealing with sub-machine guns, or machine pistols. Look at the pattern of the bullet holes. "His finger traced an upward arc, from left to right, across the bullet holes in the guard's chest.

"Lucky for us there are only two exit wounds. We might be lucky and get one of the bullets still in the body. Unless, of course, the assailants were using dumdums, in which case all we'll get is fragments. I don't think that's the case, though, the exit wounds are pretty consistent in size.

"We can confirm it if and when we get the bullet out, but I think we're looking at possibly UZI's, MACH-10's or 11's, or Heckler and Koch MP5's. Maybe even a Chech Skorpion. Something of that genre. All of those machine guns have a reputation of pulling up and to the right when they are fired. It takes quite a bit of training to get controlled two- and three-round bursts of fire like the pattern we see here. Did you find any shell casings at the plant, Barry?"

Coates shook his head. "Not a trace. The hitters probably picked them up after killing the guards, which would indicate we're dealing with professionals. And I agree with you about the weapons.

Anyway, if you can get out one of the bullets, that will confirm our suspicions. It will probably be nine millimetre."

The doctor wrapped a long pair of forceps in cotton wool before probing one of the bullet holes. The metal ends of the forceps could damage vital striations, caused by rifling in the gun barrel, which could be matched back to a specific weapon and from there to an individual, if the weapon was re-covered.

He probed for a few moments, then extracted a bloody lump from the hole, dropped the bullet in a stainless steel dish and washed away the blood with a swab soaked in alcohol. Then he turned to the detectives.

"You were right, Barry, nine millimetre. Nasty little thing, isn't it? I'm going to extract the vital organs to determine the exact cause of death. Are you staying?" He smiled, exposing uneven, stained teeth.

"Not on your bloody life, Doc. You know me better than that. We're going back to headquarters now, so if you come up with anything else let us know, especially the trajectory of the bullets."

The two detectives left him to his task. Six bodies, he thought. It was going to be a long night.

At the airport, two policemen were searching through the rubbish bins in the washroom. Several

of the people in the departure lounge and the barman said they saw the two men go into the washroom, a few minutes apart. They also testified the
men pulled guns on the officers. The police had
originally thought the terrorists had overpowered
the officers and taken their guns. Now it looked
like the terrorists had picked up weapons inside a
secure area. All of which pointed to internal collu-
sion.

All the occupants of the departure lounge were
being interviewed before being allowed to board
another plane which had been laid on by the charter
company. It was standard procedure during a homicide investigation to interview all possible witnesses
to the crime. However, these were holidaymakers
who had had their flight delayed by at least one day
already. They were in no mood to be stalled any
further, despite the warm smiles and friendly greet-
ings from the investigating officers.

The two officers were wearing rubber gloves
as they picked their way through the pieces of garbage.

"Yuck," said one of the detectives. "A fucking
condom. And it's been used."

"Maybe they were practising 'safe sex'," said
the other, grinning. "All I've found is about fifty
pieces of well-chewed gum. We should grease the
gloves, then we wouldn't have such a problem.
Seeing as you found the condom, is there a tube of

vaseline in there?"

His partner glared back: "Excuse the pun, but I don't like being the 'butt' of all your jokes."

"Sorry," replied the other. "I couldn't resist. Ahha, what have we got here?" He pulled a torn, tape-covered, brown paper envelope from the bottom of the garbage bag. "Looks like oil stains to me."

He unfolded the envelope and sniffed tentatively at the paper. "Could be gun oil. I think we just struck paydirt. I hope there's some prints on the tape. Maybe we'll get a lead on how the guns got here in the first place."

Up the road, at the McDonnell Douglas plant, the command trailer was a hive of activity. The main gate was closed, all traffic now diverted to the south parking lot. Warehouse One had been sealed off by the ident teams, as they, like their counterparts in the guard hut, combed for evidence.

As part of the investigation, all employees would be interviewed, almost five thousand people. The logistics of scheduling interviews, collecting, and collating the data in some sort of meaningful fashion was going to be a clerical nightmare. The investigating officers, like the media, had connected the attempted hijacking and the theft of the helicopter. The hijackers' mention of the Irish Freedom Fighters immediately cast suspicion on anyone with an Irish background who was in the proximity of the crimes. One puzzling clue, however, were the letters 'R E D' daubed by the helicopter pilot on the dashboard of his car, in his own blood. That information, for the time being, was withheld from the media.

Those three letters could mean anything from being slang for Russian to the colour of someone's hair or jacket. Guessing games. What the detectives needed was some hard evidence.

Across the road from the trailer, at the Red Lobster restaurant, employees were asked if they had noticed anything unusual during the afternoon. Had they noticed any strange accents?

The officers were copying the VISA and Mastercard receipts taken that day, to obtain the names and address of the patrons. An appeal would be broadcast that evening, on television.

More data for the system.

Detective-Sergeant Anthony Boyd peered through the glass case at the envelope which he had just immersed in anhydrin, a chemical which used freon as its liquid base. It reacted with amino acids in the oily residue from a fingerprint, and would disclose the outline of any fingerprints on the paper or tape. He waited the requisite ten minutes, then switched on the extractor fan to vent away the rest of the gas.

Moments later he was holding the object in a pair of tweezers, examining the surface carefully. A smile creased his face as he noted several well-defined purplish prints with their whorls and ridges intact.

He quickly transferred the prints to tape, and then scanned them into the CPIC system where he ran a match on each unique print. The scan came back negative. "Too bad," he said, picking up the phone. He scanned his internal phone list and dialled a number. A gruff voice answered.

"Homicide. Detective Coates speaking."

"Barry, it's Anthony. I managed to lift a few good prints off the tape but there were no hits on CPIC. What else would you like me to do?"

"That's too bad," came the weary reply. "But then again it was a long shot. Airport staff don't usually have criminal records."

"Do you think the envelope was put there by an airport employee?"

"Well the fucking thing didn't get there on its own!"

"Jeez. Testy, testy. I'm only trying to help. The reason I ask is that any airport staff who have access to secure areas have to be vetted by the RCMP."

Coates's voice brightened. "Don't tell me. The mounties take their prints? We couldn't be so fucking lucky."

"Yep. It's standard procedure."

"And you have a contact there so we don't have to go through the proper channels?"

"Right again. I'll give them a call and send over these prints. With a bit of luck it will only take about thirty minutes."

Coates set down the phone and grinned at his partner, Steve Linton. "We've just caught a break on the envelope. Anthony Boyd lifted some prints and is running them past the RCMP; they print all airport staff."

Linton nodded. "Boyd? Is that the guy who has the Tonyland parties every Saturday at Kelseys?"

"One and the same."

"Fuck me. From the stories I've heard I'm glad he's on our side. He is, isn't he?"

"Sometimes I'm not sure!"

Coates was leaning back in his chair, sipping from a mug of fresh coffee when the phone rang. Looking at the clock on the wall he said, "Thirty minutes on the dot." He picked up the phone.

"Homicide ..."

"Barry, it's Anthony. We got a match on a partial." Coates swung his feet out of his bottom drawer and grabbed a pencil. "Give it to me."

"The guy's name is Martin Neeson and he lives at twenty-two Bromsgrove Avenue. He's originally from Belfast, emigrated three years ago and got a job as a janitor at the airport shortly after that. I asked my contact to fax you over his photograph."

"Brilliant, Anthony, fucking brilliant. I owe you a beer for this."

Coates replaced the phone and stood up. He slipped on his jacket and tore the piece of paper from his notebook. "Come on, Steve. Let's go. Anthony came up with the goods. I'll brief you on the way."

"How do you want to handle this?" asked Linton, as Coates pulled the unmarked squad car to the curb opposite Neeson's house.

"Let's just do the routine questioning bit," replied Coates. "It is a bit of a long shot, so we'll deal with search warrants later if necessary."

They made their way across the street to the bungalow where Neeson lived. Light spilled from a living room out on to the grass and both men could see Neeson inside, watching television.

"Looks pretty harmless," offered Linton. Coates grunted in reply.

They walked back to the path and up to the front door. Coates rang the bell. A moment later the door opened and a man looked out. He was in his early thirties, and had a long, thin, stubble-covered face and lank, greasy hair. He wore a black tee-shirt with a Black Sabbath logo on the front, and grubby, denim jeans. He was barefoot. A frown crossed his face when he saw the two men.

"Are you Martin Neeson?" asked Coates.

"As far as I know," came the reply, in a heavy, guttural, accent. "What can I do for ye?"

Coates took out his badge and held it up for Neeson to see. "I'm Detective Coates and this is Detective Linton. We'd like to ask you a few questions about an incident at the airport earlier today."

"I don't know how I can help you," said Neeson, standing to one side to let them in. "This is my day off. Come on in. I was just about to have a cup of tea."

The detectives walked into a narrow hallway which lead into the living room. Music blared from the television as they entered and Neeson grabbed the remote from the sofa and turned the sound down. "Have a seat," he said, and went into the kitchenette adjoining the living room. A tiny counter separated the two rooms. A kettle started to whistle as it came to the boil.

An open pizza box sat on a glass-topped coffee-table, the surface of which was ringed with stains. There were three slices left. Magazines and newspapers lay scattered over all the chairs. Linton looked down at the carpet and winced. Pieces of chips, popcorn, and other unrecognisable debris were embedded in the fibres. "Jesus," he muttered under his breath. "Fucking pig."

"Can I get you a cuppa?" asked Neeson. "I'm just making a tea bag. We can share."

Coates heard water sloshing into a mug followed by the rattle of a teaspoon. "Not for me, thanks," he said.

"I'll pass," said Linton, continuing to survey the room and muttering under his breath. "Fuck knows what you'd catch in here." Coates tried to keep his face straight at the comments, but had to turn away. He was standing about two feet away from Linton.

Two shots rang out in rapid succession, both slamming into the side of Linton's head. Blood splashed against Coates's face as Linton dropped face-down on to the coffee-table, shattering the glass top.

Coates turned and froze. Neeson, a wide grin on his face, was pointing a tiny .22 automatic directly at him. Neeson pulled the trigger and the grin disappeared. There was a clicking sound; a jammed cartridge. His eyes left Coates and dropped to the gun, his fingers working the slide furiously back and forth in an attempt to dislodge the shell.

Coates slid his hand under his jacket and pulled out his .40 calibre revolver in a fluid motion. Reflex had taken over. As the gun slid into view, his other hand came up to grasp his wrist in the classic marksman's stance. He cocked the trigger with his thumb, producing three loud metallic clicks.

Neeson saw the movement and, unable to free the round, dropped the gun on the counter and raised his hands.

"Don't shoot, don't shoot," he cried. "I give up."

"Too late," said Coates, and shot him in the face. The large calibre round tore away the side of Neeson's head, the impact driving him back against the wall. Coates stepped forward and shot him again in the chest. His legs buckled and he pitched forward on to the kitchen floor.

The acrid fumes of cordite filled the room. Coates quickly holstered his gun and lifted his partner out of the ruins of the coffee-table. Blood oozed from a large gash down the side of Linton's face, caused by the shattered glass. A loose flap of bloody skin fell away from his cheek, exposing his teeth, and his hair was matted with fresh blood. His eyes were open, staring. There was no pulse.

Coates, hands bloody and tears in his eyes, laid his partner gently on the ground, took out his radio and called for the emergency services. He then got up and went into the kitchen. An immense pool of blood was gathering under Neeson's lifeless body, and, on the wall, two large blotches, like red carnations, leaked dark streams down to the ground. Using a pencil, he lifted the .22 from the counter and tossed it on the floor.

In the distance he could hear the wail of sirens. He turned to one side and retched violently.

Louise Kennan was a bright-eyed, sixteen year old,

born and raised in Glenarm, a tiny fishing village on the northern coast of Ireland. She was, as with all her peers, interested only in music, boys, and clothes. The village was small and there were not many boys around, so competition was fierce.

Also, she was bright and intelligent, and her teachers were unanimous in predicting a bright future for her. They could not have been more wrong.

Her one older sister, Anne, who worked as a receptionist in the local doctor's office, was forever nagging at her to work hard at school so that one day she might get to university. It was a wish which had not come true for Anne.

When Louise turned sixteen, her classmates threw a birthday party for her at the local hall. There was no boyfriend on the scene at the time, but as most of the locals had been invited, hopefully that situation would be rectified. For her birthday, her mother bought her a new dress and her father gave her some money to buy a new pair of shoes. Didn't he understand that the two always went hand in hand? As well, the usual eleven o'clock curfew imposed by her father was lifted.

At the party set her sights on a tall, brown haired boy who had arrived just after her. He seemed to be a little older than the others and much more attractive. Some discreet inquiries netted her the information that his name was Brendan Mullen, and that he lived in the nearby village of Carnlough. Most important, however, was the fact that he did not have a girlfriend.

He eventually asked her to dance. It turned out to be a slow number and during it her gave her a long, smouldering birthday kiss. She responded eagerly and from then on was never too far from his elbow. When he asked if he could take her home, she was delighted and the envy of all her classmates.

He was nineteen and owned a car, a big advantage over most of the boys in the village. She also found out he was an unemployed lathe operator, laid off when the local factory went bankrupt. When he told her that he might have to go to England to find work, she pouted and he laughed at her.

As it was her birthday, she decided to try a rum and coke, her sister's favourite drink. She liked the taste. By the end of the evening she was laughing and giggling at everything he said. Then everyone seemed to have a haze around them, and the lights and the noise became too much for her. She tugged at his arm.

"Brendan, can we go now?" she asked. "I feel a little funny."

At the car, he opened the door of his shiny, black Escort. "Why don't we go for a drive along the coast?" he asked. "It's a nice night and the fresh air might do you some good."

She agreed and they set off along the coast road to Carnlough.

It was a beautiful moonlit evening, and the salt air blowing off the sea soon revived her. She huddled close to him, smiling as he kissed her on the forehead. As soon as they came to a lay-by, he pulled over and switched off the engine. The sound of waves lapping at the shore surrounded them.

She put her arms around his neck as he reached over to kiss her, pulling her close but broke away suddenly, the gearstick prodding into his stomach. They both laughed, and he suggested that they climb into the back seat before the gearstick damaged him permanently.

Louise clambered over the seat and he followed. He pulled her close to him again and began to kiss her. His lips were soft and warm and she loved the feel of his strong arms around her. What a story she was going to have for her sister. His fingers traced circles on her back, and she trembled at his touch, a little afraid of the feelings she was experiencing for the first time. Her head was spinning a little but she didn't want to stop for fear the mood would disappear.

Then his hand came up under her arm and began to gently fondle her breast through the thin material of her dress. She was confused by her emotions - the tingling sensation in her nipples felt so good, but she had always been told that it was wrong. She broke the embrace and pushed him away.

"Stop it Brendan. None o' that. It's only our first date." She was surprised at the sound of her voice. It was deep and husky.

She wondered if one rum and coke could have such an effect. No wonder her sister had told her to be careful.

But she fell forward into his arms and he began kissing her again, this time a little more aggressively. His hands roamed all over her body, caressing her arms and breasts, ignoring her protests. She could not resist him, her arms had turned to lead. Then, suddenly, he ran his hand up under her dress and began to tug at her panties. It was like an electric shock. She struggled with him but it was to no avail. He slid them off her and began probing between her legs with his finger.

"Please, Brendan, don't do that. It's not right." She said the words, but they were just the opposite of what she was feeling. Her body was on fire, the wetness between her legs betraying her. He ignored her words, opening the back of her dress to unhook her bra. His rough, warm hands caressed her nipples, and their tongues duelled in a passionate embrace. He moved his lips down from her neck and gently took one of her nipples in his mouth, sucking and biting it softly with his teeth. She moaned, grasping his thick, dark hair and pressing his face to her breast. His hand stroked between her thighs.

Involuntarily, she started to thrust up against

his hand, no longer knowing right from wrong. When she heard the sound of his zipper, she realized what he was doing and became frightened. They had gone too far already. She tried to protest, but he pushed her back on the seat and pried her legs open with his knee. She could feel him pressing against her leg, his hardness probing for the entrance to her body. Then he found it, warm and slick with her juices, and he began to force himself inside her.

She started to scream as the pain became more intense, but he covered her mouth with his and began to push even harder. She thought that she would pass out from the pain when something inside her gave way, and he plunged deep inside her. He moaned with pleasure and began to thrust with long painful strokes. All sense of time was gone from her, and she lay back, too weak to resist, until he cried out. His body went tense and he erupted inside her.

She sobbed quietly as he eased himself out of her and pulled up his trousers. She dressed in silence, save for the occasional sob, and they returned to the front seat. Then they drove in silence, until they arrived at her front gate.

"Louise, I ... I'm sorry. I really don't know what got into me. I just ..." He reached to touch her, but she shied away.

"I thought you were ..." she started, but a bitter sting of tears started, and she could not finish. She climbed out of the car but had trouble walking up the path, the pain between her legs almost unbearable. She offered a quiet thank you to God, when her sister opened the door, not her parents. In the darkness of her bedroom, she cried as she related the story to her sister. Then she made her swear to silence.

Two weeks later she missed her period, but she dismissed it as being the after-effects of that evening. When she missed her next period, she knew she was pregnant; she was getting sick in the mornings and could not face breakfast. Her schoolwork began to deteriorate and she started to close herself off from her family and friends. Then one morning her mother confronted her.

"Louise, you've tried to hide it from us, but I'm not stupid. Something is the matter. I'm afraid to ask, but I know the symptoms. Are you pregnant?"

"Yes mum, I am," she blurted out and burst into tears. "Mum, I'm so ashamed."

"Ach love, do you know who the father is?" asked her mother, wrapping her large arms around her daughter to comfort her.

"His name's Brendan Mullen."

"The butcher's son, from Carnlough? I'd didn't know you were seeing him."

"I'm not. It was the night of my birthday and things got out of hand. I haven't seen him since."

Her mother tried to comfort her as the pent-up

feelings she had tried to suppress came to the surface. Her father was called home early from work and the butcher's shop in Carnlough was closed for the day to allow the two families to discuss the situation. They bickered but finally agreed that Brendan and Louise should get married, "for the child's sake," not to mention their own.

Glenarm was a tiny village and an unmarried mother would cause great embarrassment to the family. Louise and Brendan were not consulted. The old axiom "you made your bed, now lie in it" was spouted frequently over the next few days. A wedding day was set and announced in the local paper, amid hasty preparations for the wedding.

Seven months later, Louise delivered, prematurely, a five-pound one-ounce baby boy. The child, named Sean, after her father, was bright and cheerful, and brought back some of the sparkle in Louise.

But when she and Sean came home from the hospital, she found Brendan's attitude had begun to change. He took little or no interest in Sean and would stay out late most evenings at the local pub. Sometimes, he would not return home until the early hours of the morning, glassy-eyed and reeking of alcohol.

Louise was lonely with only Sean for company. The tiny flat became more of a prison than a home until her sister, Anne, started to visit. They would play together with the baby and then talk for hours. Anne would leave before Brendan came home; she did not like the way he undressed her with his eyes. Anne told her that Brendan had fallen in with some bad company and was going to get himself in trouble. When Louise asked what kind of trouble, Anne steered the conversation in a different direction and would say no more on the subject.

One evening, Louise detected a change in Anne. She seemed a little distracted, and when Louise pressed for information, Anne told her that she had met a boy from Scotland while on holiday and had fallen in love with him. They had been writing back and forth for several months and he had asked her to come to Scotland and marry him. The reason that the 'romance' had been kept quiet was that he was a Scottish Presbyterian, a 'proddy', and the local extremists did not take kindly to village girls dating such 'scum'.

Louise was delighted for Anne but sad for herself; she would be losing her only close friend. The novelty of the baby had worn thin for her school mates, and her marriage was a marriage in name only. She wished that she had had the courage to stand up to her parents when they insisted that she go through with the charade.

Unknown to the two girls, Brendan had arrived home early from the pub after getting into a row with one of the locals. When he saw that Anne was visiting, he crept up to the window to eavesdrop.

The next morning Louise's mother opened the door

to get the milk for breakfast. She hoped the milk-man had used the plastic covers she had bought to cover the tops of the bottles. The damned sparrows were always stealing the cream. What she saw made her scream in terror, waking her husband, who came pounding down the stairs in his undershirt. He pulled his wife away from the door.

There, lying in a heap on the front steps, was his daughter, Anne. Her hair had been sheared, with only a few tufts remaining. Her face was battered and bloody, and one eye was puffed up so badly that it was completely closed. What clothes remained were torn to shreds, and she had been daubed with tar. A few filthy white feathers had been stuck on to the patches of tar. Around her neck, tied with string, was a piece of cardboard on which was scrawled the words 'Proddy lover.'.

He picked her up gently in his arms and carried her into the living room. He laid her softly on the couch while his wife ran to the neighbour's house to phone for a doctor.

He knew it was useless to call the police; they would be met with a wall of silence. He clenched his huge calloused hands in rage, wishing there was someone he could lash out at to repay the pain inflicted on his daughter.

Two weeks later, Anne left the tiny village and travelled to Scotland, to start a new life. Louise was heartbroken, but knew Anne had done the right thing by turning her back on the violence and hatred.

Not long after Anne had gone, Brendan announced that he and some of the boys had been offered work for six months in the Middle East. Louise was delighted at the prospect of having Sean to herself in peace and quiet for a few months. She might be able to sneak over to Scotland to visit her sister.

The six months, however, passed all to quickly, and when Brendan returned, deeply tanned and a few pounds lighter, he was flashing a lot of money around. Brendan became extremely defensive when she questioned him about his job. She thought it best to leave the matter well alone.

One evening, returning early from a visit to her mother, she found Brendan at the kitchen table cleaning a machine gun, with gleaming pieces of metal and oily springs strewn about the newspaper-covered table. Suddenly, the truth dawned on her and all the pieces of the jigsaw came together: the late nights, the trip to the Middle East, the money.

"You're a Provo" she exclaimed, shocked and outraged.

"You've caught me girl," he grinned. "That I am, and proud of it. I've got a new set of tools now. You've seen more than is good for you, but it had better go no further. You saw what happened to your sister. The same, or worse could happen to you or the brat if anyone learns of this."

Louise left the kitchen, her mind spinning. Not even eighteen years old, and here she was with a terrorist for a husband and a baby to support. If only she could turn back the clock or make it all go away.

She could not go directly to the police for fear of reprisals. The memories of Anne's battered face still haunted her, and what made it worse was that Brendan had been involved. There was one route: she could contact the police through their confidential telephone. In that way she could remain anonymous and Brendan would get put away before he killed somebody. If he hadn't already killed somebody. It was a horrible thought.

Maybe he might get killed in an ambush and then she and Sean would be rid of him for good. Perhaps then she would meet someone else who would be a good husband and a proper father to Sean.

Perhaps ...

CHAPTER 14
Intelligence

Patrick Kelly's mouth was as dry as dust and his tongue felt as if it had been covered in hair. He opened his eyes a fraction, testing the degree of brightness his retinas would accept. Through the slits he could see his night table and the glass of water he had put there before going out the previous evening.

Fortunately, the night table was not in a direct path from the door to the bed, and so had survived the night. Which was almost more than he could say for himself. In his blurry vision, the water shimmered like a mirage in the desert. A fitting analogy, he thought.

His hand seemed to have a mind of its own as it reached out for the glass, but he finally managed to put the glass to parched lips. It was lukewarm, brackish, and a little cloudy but never had water tasted so sweet.

Just for an instant he was transported back in time to the sweltering jungles of Vietnam. The glass became a filthy, beaten canteen and he was crouching against the trunk of a tree, his rifle leaning against one shoulder. The oppressive heat assaulted his senses as he and the other members of the team swallowed salt tablets and washed them down with water from their canteens. Their sergeant had just given them a welcome 'take five' and they lay sprawled on the ground, thankful for the respite.

He set the empty glass back on the table and experimented with opening his eyes a little more. The previous evening had been spent in a local pub, in the nearby town of Ballycastle. Mulholland had assured him that the pub was 'safe' and had an excellent early warning system. When asked what 'safe' meant, Mulholland smugly explained they had an informant in the police-station, a constable who would let them know of any impending raids. He went on to explain that the sympathizer had been in place for several years and was responsible for passing on a great deal of valuable information.

To help reinforce the informant's cover, he and

Donnelly had 'ambushed' the constable one evening, riddling the man's car with bullets when he was safely out of range. As the informant was admiring their handiwork, Donnelly turned and shot him twice, once in the shoulder and once in the side. They were both through-and-through flesh wounds; painful but not life-threatening.

That was the part which Donnelly had neglected to tell the informer. He hadn't even bothered to inform Mulholland, who almost had a fit when the informer fell to the ground, unconscious from his wounds.

Donnelly's explanation about the shooting made sense to Mulholland, who decided discretion was the better part of valour and let the matter well alone. Donnelly simply stated that the pigs were stupid, but not so stupid as to think that someone could escape unscathed from the hail of bullets which they had pumped into the car. "They'll probably give the cunt a fuckin' medal," was his sarcastic comment about the entire affair.

Prior to going to the pub, Mulholland suggested that Kelly pose as an American tourist. That would satisfy the curiosity of the inquisitive locals, who were a friendly bunch and generous with their drinks. Having an American as a visitor was something of a novelty for them, so they went out of their way to make him feel at home. He was not allowed to pay for single drink during the evening.

As a result, he had drank too many pints of Guinness and a few too many 'wee ones' of Bushmills whiskey. He resolved never to touch the damned stuff again, or at least if he did, it would be in moderation.

There seemed to be a lot of activity downstairs, judging from the noise carrying up to his room. Looking across the room he saw his clothes had been discarded at random. He stood up too quickly, and then had to sit back down as the room swam in circles in front of him. It took two more attempts before the room stopped moving.

After successfully getting to an upright position, he dressed slowly; his limbs belonging to someone else. He went over to the table and splashed his face with the cold, frigid water. Dipping his comb in the water, he attempted to comb his mane of red hair into some semblance of order. He settled for patting the damp strands gently against his head and set off downstairs.

"Bad night Patrick?" enquired Mulholland, knowing full well how badly Kelly was feeling. He had helped Donnelly carry him up the stairs to his room. How Kelly had managed to row across from the mainland was nothing short of a miracle. "I take it you won't be wanting breakfast."

"You got that right," replied Kelly. "I'll just have coffee, strong and black."

"Just the way you like your women!" Tommy

Mulholland al... been very descriptive the... black nurse whom he had...

"Jesus," K... that story, did I?"

"That you... many more. Entertained ... vening. The young barm... r eye on you as well. We... you were just hitting you...

"Well I ... ecause I can't remember ... at was all the commotion I heard...

"The women arrived about six-thirty. I put them in the room beside yours. Seems the crossing from Stranraer was a wee bit rough, so they were a trifle green around the gills."

"Is Josie out fishing?"

"Yes, he's down at the rocks where he was yesterday. You must have made quite an impression; he's stopped saying 'fuckin'' in front of 'Yank'."

"Gee, that's flattering," said Kelly, sarcastically.

"I wouldn't knock it," said Mulholland seriously.

"Fair enough," replied Kelly. "I think I'll join him. The fresh air will do me good. What time should we be back?"

"That's okay, Patrick, I'll come and get you when we're ready to start." Mulholland poured boiling water on to some instant coffee, stirred the liquid, and set the mug on the table.

Kelly clasped both hands around the mug and held it to his forehead. He said, "Oh, and one other thing. What do I have to do to get some hot water for the bath? I'm starting to feel a little grubby."

"I need to put on the water heater for a couple of hours," replied Mulholland. "I'll do it now."

"Maybe one of the women would like to join me?" suggested Kelly and, with a dirty look from Mulholland, added "Or maybe not!"

Kelly's hangover slowly disappeared like an early morning mist, burned away by the sun's rays, and by noon his appetite had returned with a vengeance. His stomach growled with hunger.

Donnelly had managed to catch several large plaice, 'flatties' as he called them, and was going to have Mulholland cook them up for lunch, which sounded just fine to Kelly. They packed up the gear and walked back to the house, and the women were just coming down the stairs when they walked through the door.

"Morning ladies," he beamed, allowing his eyes to savour the tight jeans and tee shirts. Must have something against bras, he thought.

He was a little surprised, when the older of the two replied "Good morning Patrick," her English only slightly accented.

Mulholland busied himself cleaning the fish, and

then frying them in a skillet. With boiled potatoes, peas, and carrots, they all ate heartily. Bottles of ice-cold beer were used to wash down the meal. Conversation was at a minimum.

When they had finished, Mulholland cleared the table, stacking the dishes in the sink. Kelly could not resist commenting. "You're going to make somebody a fine wife, Tommy. You'll have to shave your legs a bit though." He was answered by the standard "fuck you", and the others laughed.

Mulholland disappeared into a back room and returned a few moments later with four cardboard models of what appeared to be military installations. He arranged them on the table and then unfolded a large map of the province. "New hobby, Tommy?" asked Kelly. The look he received spoke volumes.

"Okay," said Mulholland. "These are the targets. We, or rather you and Josie, are going to take out two of them tonight, and the other two tomorrow night."

He pointed to the first two models. "These buildings contain the nerve centres of the military and police computer systems. If we can put them out of commission, we effectively put a stop to the data gathering and cross-checking which goes on all over the Province. The first is the army data centre, and the one behind is the police data centre. If we can destroy them it will be a major setback to their intelligence activities.

"Our source tells us their disaster plan is to use each other as a backup site. That's why we're going to hit them both tomorrow night. The centres are located in different cities, so the timing is critical.

"The next target is the police forensic laboratory in Belvoir, out along the Lisburn road. By destroying it, we can effectively terminate many current cases, which are based on forensic evidence. The final target, requested by Josie here, is less strategic and more of a morale builder for the lads in the movement. It is the headquarters of the Parachute Regiment in Leopold Street. We all know how fond Josie is of the Paras. The rest of the army think they are the elite, although the Royal Marines might dispute that fact. This is going to be a demoralizer for their side if we can pull it off. It will show them that nowhere is safe."

"What sort of defences are we up against?" asked Kelly, "or do you know?"

"Of course we know," replied Mulholland, glaring indignantly, offended his intelligence should be questioned.

"The computer centres are similar in design. They are rectangular in shape, as you can see, and have four towers, one at each corner. Each tower has a spotlight and is manned by two men, each of whom carry an SA-80 assault rifle. As well, there is a 7.62-millimetre General Purpose Machine Gun

(GMPG) positioned in each of the towers. We have reason to believe they have SAM-7 surface-to-air missiles, but we don't know exactly where they are stored. There is a contingent of twenty men on guard at all times, not including the military personnel who run the computers. That's about it."

"Do helicopters patrol the vicinity?" asked Kelly, wondering aloud about possible air-to-air combat.

Mulholland shook his head. "As far as we know there are none. The chopper base in Bessbrook is too far away for regular patrols. Anyway, there seems to be no rhyme or reason to their patrols, at least none we've been able to detect. Ever since we got our hands on those Stinger missiles, they've become a little wary.

"In any case, the army helicopters are not heavily armed. The Apache has more than enough firepower to deal with anything you may meet."

"One last question," said Kelly, impressed with the information Mulholland had just revealed.

"This is the commercial airport for the Province." His finger stabbed at a point on the map. "Aldergrove, I think you called it. I need to know the range of the radar beacon so that we can plot a flight path around it."

"We expected that," answered Mulholland, flicking through a tiny, dog-eared notebook. When he found what he was looking for, he began to read: "Aldergrove airport. Marconi Radar system. Installed 1965, upgraded 1982. Range of beacon twenty miles."

Kelly nodded. "That's all I need to know. I'll check out the chopper. We'll need to assemble the rotors after dark, but that's not a problem. See you later."

When he left the room, the older of the two women turned to Mulholland. "Will he do the job?"

"He'll do our part," snapped Mulholland. "The rest ..." He hesitated for a moment and shrugged his shoulders. "I don't know."

"There will be no problem with our part either," she said, far too confidently for his liking. There was no warmth, just the face of a cat about to swallow a mouse.

She's got something up her sleeve, he thought. And whatever it is, Patrick Kelly is not going to like it.

Mulholland had met both women briefly, a little over a year ago, during a trip to Libya. He and Donnelly were there to secure funds and arms for the IFF. Colonel Quadaffi could afford to be a generous benefactor, what with the billions of petro-dollars flowing into his country's coffers each year. The women were part of the colonel's elite cadre of female bodyguards, his 'green angels' as they were commonly known.

Each member of the cadre was hand-picked and totally devoted to the colonel. During an assassination attempt by members of the Federation for the Salvation of Libya, some guards had thrown themselves on top of the grenades meant for the colonel. The would-be assassins were captured and turned over to the remaining bodyguards for 'interrogation'.

He also knew the two women had been chosen for advanced training in the Raz Hilal camp near Tokra, the most exclusive of all the training camps. The camps at Sirte, Sebha, and Az Zaouiah were normally populated by Westerners, there to learn the craft of terrorism. Only the most eligible were selected for Raz Hilal. He and Donnelly had both spent several weeks there. Their instructors were comprised of Russians, Cubans, and American ex-green Berets, lured there by the high wages offered by the colonel.

Here, they learned about guerilla warfare, explosives, booby-traps, and a miscellany of other deadly skills. On completion of their training, the women had collaborated with a group of Algerian terrorists in carrying out bomb attacks on 'soft' targets in Paris.

What Mulholland originally suspected was that they had been given orders to help the IFF hijack the copter and then use it - and Kelly - for their own target.

Mulholland was told about the alternate arrangements when he picked the girls up at the ferry. He was not, however, privy to any details of their plan. All he knew was that it involved the helicopter and Patrick Kelly. He also knew that Kelly was going to be very pissed off, when they broke the news to him.

He pushed his chair back from the table. "If you say so," he replied. "I would make sure he's not armed when you tell him. He's not exactly slow to anger, if you know what I mean. He didn't get that red hair from eatin' fuckin' carrots."

The women stood up, indicating the conversation was at an end. Mulholland got up also, went to the fridge, and opened another cold beer for himself and Donnelly. He could not shake the feeling that something was going to happen, something that was not part of the plan.

*   *   *   *   *

Major Skinner worked late, not wanting to stray too far from his phone. An ominous silence was felt across the Province, as if everyone were holding their breath, waiting for some cataclysm to occur. It had pervaded the intelligence community for the past few days, but no-one had any answers. Even the 'Freds', former IRA sympathizers who had turned informants, had nothing to tell. But years of police and intelligence work - and intuition - told him something big was going on. And when the terrorists planned something big, high casualty rates usually followed.

Moving over to his terminal while sitting in his chair, like a hermit crab dragging its shell, he jabbed the 'ON' button and began the complex signon procedure. He selected the phone records and began digging through the mass of data, looking for a clue.

No updates had taken place, but a single message from two days ago, one he had high-lighted for a follow-up, re-appeared. The call had been made from a phone box in Glenarm, a tiny village on the north coast. It had been logged in at 3:00 p.m., and it was thought that the caller was female. The message simply stated that there seemed to be a lot of IRA activity going on in the Glenarm area. That was hardly news to Skinner, but the fact that someone actually used the confidential phone to relay the message was intriguing.

He made a note on his memo pad, telling his aide to retrieve a copy of the phone tape. Only keywords or phrases from messages received on the confidential phones were entered into the system. Clerks doing the data entry could miss a significant fact. He wanted to hear the entire message. Sometimes, even background noises could reveal interesting information.

He signed off the system, put his office phone on 'call forward', to his quarters, and then locked his desk. The Queen looked on benevolently from her gilded frame as he shrugged on his jacket and opened his door to leave. He hesitated. Some inner, indefinable sense was making him leery about leaving the office.

He shook his head, as if to get rid of the feeling. He pulled the door closed and heard the resounding metallic click, the heavy metal bolt sliding securely home. It was a familiar, satisfying sound, but he twisted the door handle to make sure. It was an unnecessary action, but it reassured him that his domain would remain sealed until he returned.

Kelly looked again at the luminous watch dial - 10:49, five minutes later than the last time he had looked. He folded his arm behind his head again. He sighed. He was lying in bed in a futile attempt to get some rest before the operation. The sun had gone down behind the twin peaks, and an ominous darkness lay over the island.

The window was open, allowing the off-shore breezes to waft the lace curtains, and he could hear the rhythmic mumuring of the waves as they caressed the shore. It was a hypnotic sound, one which had lulled him to sleep on previous evenings. Tonight his body resisted.

For nearly two hours, he and the others had opted for solitude, each to their own private thoughts. Tommy Mulholland, optimistic as always, remained in the kitchen composing a letter to the press, claiming IFF responsibility for the forthcoming attack.

Kelly could just imagine the words: lots of flowery rhetoric about the sons and daughters of Ireland, about freedom and a nation united once again. Then there would come threats about an endless stream of martyrs and British widows and mourning. And finally, there would be the futile demand for the withdrawal of British troops from the Province. The Irish had a wealth of experience in writing such missives.

He was in the midst of his reverie when his bedroom door opened a fraction, then opened wide, and closed again. He could hear the inside doorhandle being eased up gently. Someone was in his room.

He strained his eyes, but there was no light, no shadow. Floorboards creaked softly as a foot was placed tentatively here and there, testing the wood, the sounds approaching his bed. He feigned sleep. His muscles tensed to pounce on the intruder. Then, much to his surprise, a warm, almost naked, female body climbed onto the bed beside him.

Two warm hands encircled his chest and moist lips touched his face. He allowed his own hands to roam, finding firm, full breasts and smallish, swollen nipples. It was a long time since he had had a woman.

"Thank goodness," he said quietly. "For a

minute there I thought it was Tommy."

He heard a tiny chuckle from behind his left ear, and then those lips returned to his, gently persuading his mouth to open, starting soft and gentle, then becoming more urgent. He responded in kind, caught up in the sea of her emotions, afraid to let go. Her skin smelled of soap, and was silky smooth and firm against his fingers.

In the darkness of the room, he could not see which of the two women had come to him. At that particular moment, however, he did not much care. The lips were now starting to move slowly down his chest, alternately licking and biting. A pair of hands fumbled with his belt, opened it, and pulled down his trousers. Pushing and kicking, he managed to get the trousers and underwear off and fling them into the void of the room.

Her hands grasped his rigid cock, rubbing and stroking, eliciting moans, then gasps as her lips descended, encircling the tip, her tongue probing. His hips thrust upwards, while she sucked him gently, lapping the head of his cock with her tongue before sliding it all the way into her throat. Reaching between her legs, he pulled aside the thin cotton panties which were damp with her juices, afraid all the while to distract her from her ministrations. He found her moist folds, warm and wet, and she thrust herself back against his hand. He slipped one finger, then another into her and felt her muscles contracting.

Just as he was about to explode, she stopped, sensing his climax was near. He whimpered in protest, but it was cut short. She slipped off her panties, climbed on top of him and guided his stiff cock between her legs. She held him there for a moment, just at the entrance, then leaned all the way back, impaling herself on him.

All pretence of secrecy vanished as she rocked back and forth, allowing him to almost slip out before plunging down hard again, driving him deep within her. He matched her stroke for stroke, his hands cupping her full breasts until he felt himself come close to that blissful release. She knew his climax was near and she slowed her rhythm, distracting him, delaying the inevitable.

She allowed him to slip out of her, but continued to rub her moist slit against his cock. His mouth went dry and he grasped her buttocks, lifting her up and slamming his cock into her again and again until he erupted inside of her, feeling her body shudder in response. Her nails dug deeply into his shoulders as he thrust up violently one last time, his back bowed with the effort. She collapsed on top of him and lay there, arms tight about his neck, not moving.

They stayed that way for some time and then she stirred, brushed her lips against his and climbed out of the bed. He managed to utter a throaty

"Why?" The answer floated back from the darkness, bringing him crashing back to reality.

"Tonight you may die."

Then she was gone.

And now I'm going to wake up, he thought. But it was not a dream, and Tommy Mulholland was soon pounding on the bedroom door, telling him it was time to go.

CHAPTER 15
Reverie

The first two days of John Waters's leave passed quickly as he walked, talked, and fished with his father. The afternoons usually involved a long walk followed by a quick pint in the local pub where his father was somewhat of an institution. Waters loved to hear his father's stories about the war and so each evening, following a sumptuous feast prepared by Mrs Mac, they would adjourn to the living room where his father would relate yet another adventure. Waters had often pressed his father to write his memoirs, but the elder man simply shook his head and said, "These stories are for you and me son, not for anyone else."

Sitting in his high-backed leather chair, brandy snifter in hand, and a crackling fire glowing in the hearth, was one of his father's greatest pleasures. He would often be found there asleep, reading a book, or simply gazing into the flames, reliving old memories.

His father, a member of the Office of Strategic Services (OSS) during the war, had parachuted into France shortly after it was occupied by the German forces. His job was to help set up, organize, and train the fledgling resistance movement, then in its infancy. The stories of blowing up arms dumps and train lines and scaling the walls of a Chateau to assassinate a leading German officer was like something out of the movies.

John Waters had come to know the Jeans, Philippes, Marcels, and others as if they were old friends. Each time his father would relate a story, a new facet of one of the men would surface, adding an extra dimension to the picture which he had built up over the years. He often wondered, but had never asked his father what had happened to those old comrades.

He knew only too well from bitter experience that in times of war, friends and acquaintances were bound to be lost. He too had lost friends in the war against terrorism. He remembered in particular his friend Taffy, a lovable little Welshman whose wit and humour he missed so much.

Taffy and he had been dropped one night in a field outside Crossmaglen, known to the military and locals alike as the 'Cross', in South Armagh. Their job was to monitor and report on any movement of individuals across the border, about two miles away from their vantage point. Terrorists had been escalating their campaign of violence in the border areas. The shadowy figures would steal across the border after dark to be picked up by an accomplice on the Northern side. They would then carry out a bombing or an assassination attempt before slinking back to the comparative safety of the South.

Several young soldiers had been killed while on patrol in the Cross, prompting the locals to spraypaint a running total on the side of a white-washed cottage outside the town. It now read 'Provos 7 Brits 0' like the results of a Saturday afternoon soccer match.

Waters's assignment was to locate the terrorists as they crossed the border. Their location would be reported to the QRF (Quick Reaction Force) who would then intercept the terrorists as they made their way north. If not, at least they would cut off their avenue of escape.

Waters and the other members of his regiment would spend days on end, lying in hollowed-out hides under bushes or trees, unwashed, unshaven, watching, and waiting. More often than not, their silent vigil would be fruitless, but there were enough successes to keep their morale high. The word 'CONTACT', the term used when any of the surveillance teams spotted bandits on their way across the border, was enough to send adrenaline pounding through their veins.

Unfortunately, their drop-off was witnessed by a local farmer, an IRA sympathizer who immediately informed 'the boys' about their number and location.

Taffy and he made an old, ruined cottage their base, and had set up their surveillance equipment under what remained of a thatched roof. It was just after midnight and Taffy was scanning the surrounding fields with a Starlite scope, enabling him to literally 'see in the dark'. Waters was opening up some cans of cold C-rats, the army's excuse for food, when he heard Taffy mutter under his breath.

"Jesus, John. We're in for a bit of bother. Have a look over there."

Waters took the proffered scope and pointed it in the direction of Taffy's finger. As night became day, he could see six figures picking their way across the fields towards the cottage. Four of the men were armed with rifles and two carried pistols.

"They've got two Heckler G3's and two AK47's with the clips taped. The others have revolvers.

Fuck!" He knew the taped clips meant at least sixty rounds of ammunition for each AK47.

Taffy and he were not prepared for a heavy firefight. Both of them had Armalite M16 assault rifles with individual weapons sights and the ubiquitous Browning automatics, but no great amount of ammunition. However, they had the element of surprise.

Behind him, he could hear Taffy calling for reinforcements. They both knew, however, that help was needed now, not later. Taffy appeared at his elbow.

"Taffy, I don't think we should run. There's no cover. If the moon comes out from behind the clouds we'd be sitting ducks for those rifles. I think we'd better take them on before they get settled."

"Hardly fair, is it John? There's six of them and only two of us. I think they should go back and get some reinforcements. After all, we do want a fair fight."

Waters smiled, his teeth showing whitely against the black of the camouflage paint. Even in the face of danger, Taffy's irrepressible wit still surfaced.

Waters said, "We better try to take out those guys with the AK's first. That might give us a better chance of holding out until the Cavalry arrives. We'll send up a magnesium flare."

They waited until their attackers were within range and then Taffy fired the flare into the night sky. Immediately the countryside was bathed in an eerie white glow. The terrorists tried to shield their eyes from the brightness. Waters and Taffy leaned into their rifles, sighted on their targets, calmed their breathing and squeezed the triggers. They fired almost simultaneously.

The two terrorists carrying the AK47's seemed to flip backwards, propelled by the heavy slugs slamming into their bodies. The others tried to find cover as soon as they heard the shots. They began firing wildly in the general direction of the muzzle flashes coming from the SAS post. Bright dots, residue from the magnesium flare, still danced in front of their eyes, making it difficult to focus on a target. Bullets zinged off the walls of the cottage, prompting some frightful Welsh curses from Taffy.

Waters and Taffy took their time, selecting their targets and conserving ammunition - one shot, one kill - as they had been trained to do at the Royal Marine Commando sniper school. They managed to pick off another terrorist, who poked his head up a little too far above the clump of rocks where he was hiding.

"Not bad," said Taffy, to no-one in particular as the terrorist's head erupted like an overripe tomato.

The flare, in its miniature parachute, floated slowly towards the ground, rocking back and forth like a feather carried on the wind. When the flare hit the ground, darkness followed, as if someone had turned out the light in a room without windows.

The remaining terrorists seemed anxious to relieve themselves of as much ammunition as possible, and the walls of the cottage resounded to the impact of the bullets.

Suddenly there was silence. John Waters shook his head, his ears ringing from the reports of their rifles. "Look's like they've had enough, Taffy. Maybe they've gone for reinforcements after all. Taffy ..."

He looked over and saw his friend slumped against the wall. He caught Taffy's jacket and pulled him up but the ugly hole in the side of his face told the story. He frantically groped for a pulse, but there was none. He laid his friend's body back on the ground, took the ammunition clip from Taffy's rifle and clambered over the wall of the cottage. Border or no border, those bastards were going to pay.

His training, pounding up and down the Brecon Beacons in Wales stood him in good stead as he chased across the fields, eating up the distance. The three men were not far ahead, running in the general direction of the border, and sanctuary, or so they thought.

He crested a small hill and could see the men, dark shapes moving quickly across the fields, less than half a mile away, and tiring fast. They knew they would be followed and there was no cover available, nowhere for them to hide. But they knew the border was near.

Waters lay down on the ground, switched on his starlite scope, and brought it into focus. He could see the scared faces of the men each time they turned to look over their shoulders.

He sighted on the first man, squeezed the trigger and was sighting on the second before the first hit the ground. It was over in seconds. Three bodies lay sprawled on the ground, apparently lifeless. He crossed the field to where they lay, all the while keeping them covered with his rifle. When he came close he fired again into each body, and, when he turned them over with his foot, the sightless eyes told their story.

Payment for Taffy.

"John?" His father's voice brought him back from his reverie.

"Sorry, dad. I was just remembering an old friend. Someone who didn't beat the clock."

"Son, I know how you feel. I know you love to hear my stories about the war, but each time I tell them I get reminded of all those friends who didn't make it through. Some fell beside me, some died in my arms and some just simply disappeared. The Gestapo had a knack for making resistance members vanish from the face of the earth.

"The pain never goes away. The years may dull

the ache somewhat, but it is always there, a constant reminder of the horrors we endured. But such is the life of a soldier. We were trained to kill the enemy, whoever and whatever they may have been. If some of us died along the way, then that was our tough luck. At least in my day, it was easy to identify the enemy. They wore jackboots and grey uniforms. I don't envy your job, son.

"One thing I will tell you though. No matter what happens, you will always remember the good times you had with your friend. That way they will never die. Anyway, let's get to bed, before I get any more maudlin. I'll be crying in my brandy soon and you know how I feel about people who put water in their liquor."

He patted his son's leg and Waters grinned. "That's a good idea, dad. We must have walked for miles today and the fresh air certainly knocks you out." He stretched and yawned.

"How about we try to get that salmon tomorrow, dad?" he asked, already knowing what the answer would be.

"Sounds good to me, lad. I'll set the alarm for five a.m. and we'll try and get him before he wakes up properly. Goodnight son, sleep well."

*   *   *   *   *

Jim Stewart studied his radar screen in the control

tower at Aldergrove airport, watching the arm swing back and forth like the wiper on a car. As it made an arc across the screen, any current air traffic, small illuminated blips, would flash momentarily and he would note their progress.

Now, at midnight, there were only a few blips, military aircraft or the odd patrol helicopter. There was never any commercial air traffic at night, as pilots from Britain steadfastly refused to stay in the Province overnight.

His eyes were sore from the constant staring at the screen, but his shift was nearly over. He began filling out his logbook. A few moments later, Peter Miles swept into the room, looking fresh and rested, which made Stewart feel even more tired.

A new blip appeared on the edge of the screen, not big enough to be a military transport, but it was travelling much faster than a regular patrol helicopter. The blip went unnoticed.

Miles said, "I've just been down at the pub with the lads, playing some darts. They're still down there, but it's after hours so you'll have to go in the back door. That's if you feel up to it. What about ye? Any action? "

"Ah no, not tonight", Stewart sighed. "I'm too bloody tired."

"You're getting old, Jim," teased Miles, punching him playfully on the arm. "Mairead is taking too much out of you. She really needs a younger man, someone with more stamina."

"And I suppose you're just the ticket?" asked Stewart sarcastically.

"Well, if you really need some help, feel free to call on me any time. I'll try to fit you into my busy social schedule."

The blip traversed the edge of the arc, just within the boundary of the arm, following a course that would bring it across Lough Neagh.

"Anyway, I'm off home" said Stewart, pulling on his jacket. He picked up his flask, which was sitting beside the screen, just as the arm passed over the blip. It pulsed and faded.

"What the hell was that?" he muttered, pointing to the screen at the point where the blip had appeared. He waited for the arm to make its backward pass. The arm touched the bottom of the screen and began its return journey. The screen remained blank. The blip had vanished.

"I think you've been working too hard," laughed Miles.

"Either that or Mairead has. Now you're seeing UFO's. You better have a big drink before you go to bed. Go on, get lost."

Jim Stewart shook his head. He was sure he had seen something on the screen. It was probably a helicopter, or a malfunction or something. The technicians from Marconi had been tinkering with the system, something about extending the range.

The chopper followed its flight plan, keeping well

away from the main routes and residential areas. In the cockpit, Josie Donnelly fidgeted nervously as they approached their target.

Firing systems had been activated, the Hellfire missiles silently awaiting the laser beam to guide them to their targets. The 30-millimetre chain gun in the chopper's nose was switched to automatic. Mounted beside the gun, an infrared camera transmitted pictures of the ground to a miniature screen in front of Donnelly.

For Patrick Kelly, it was like Vietnam revisited. Excitement, commingled with fear, twisted his insides like an anaconda constricting its prey. Adrenaline which gushed through his veins like floodwater through a drain.

Donnelly, having experienced Kelly's nap-of-the-earth flying on the way to meet the freighter was no more comfortable with it now. It was like riding a roller coaster in the dark: his stomach seemed to spend most of the flight in his mouth. And watching his monitor, only served to make him more nauseous. He closed his eyes and prayed it would not be too long before they reached their target.

Their target was illuminated by several concentric rings of lights, at the centre of which lay the computer building. This was the heart of the military's intelligence offensive against terrorism. Millions of pieces of data were stored and retrieved, allowing checkpoints to validate drivers' licenses, license plates, terrorist sightings, last known locations, known associates, and a plethora of other enquiries. Satellite dishes atop the roof connected them to Interpol and the CIA's headquarters in Langley, Virginia. Most of the world's major police forces had access to the data stored here and vice-versa.

The primary central processing unit had two backups, so that if the system failed, another could be switched in with little or no degradation in service. Three shifts, starting at 8:00 a.m., 4:00 p.m., and midnight, included a thirty-minute to facilitate communication between the shift supervisors relating to any incidents or special requests which had occurred during their shift.

It was not a coincidence that Donnelly had planned the attack for midnight. If successful, it would effectively eliminate two shifts of experienced personnel, who would be difficult to replace. The computers themselves would also be extremely costly to replace. The databases were backed up each evening, and the tapes carted to an offsite vault, the location of which still eluded the terrorists. Previous data would still be intact, but it would take months before the appropriate links could be re-established. The biggest reward was the effect the attack would have on the morale of the troops.

At a range of one mile, Donnelly activated the

laser sight and aimed the beam at the larger of the two computer buildings. When he was satisfied, he fired the first set of Hellfire missiles. The missiles, designed to destroy armour-plated tanks, passed easily though the walls of the building into the computer centre. One second later they exploded, scattering bodies and machinery in all directions as the chopper screamed overhead. Kelly flew past the centre for about five hundred yards and then turned to allow Donnelly to fix the laser on the second building. A fraction of a second later the missiles were racing to their target at a speed of eighteen feet per second.

The building exploded in a giant fireball, shattering bricks, metal, machinery, furniture, people, and vehicles. Shards of glass, transformed into deadly daggers, shredded soldiers on the ground who had not taken cover after the first attack.

As Kelly turned the chopper for its final run, surviving soldiers began returning fire. Their light-calibre weapons were ineffectual against the chopper's Kevlar coating, the bullets ricochetting away harmlessly, like angry bees.

Donnelly howled with demonic laughter as the 30-millimetre cannon swept across the compound, tossing soldiers like rag dolls before it. He turned his head from side to side and the cannon followed like an obedient slave, spitting death at any target on his screen.

For good measure, he fired a salvo of 2.75-inch Hydra folding-fin aerial rockets, which exploded in waves of fire across the ground, incinerating anything which lay in their path.

Kelly eased back on the stick and the chopper went screaming off like a demon into the night, leaving behind it the burning building, a funeral pyre for the dead.

He then set his course for the computer centre in Derry. It would take them about twenty minutes to reach that target, their encore for the evening.

The telephone rang shrilly. John Waters was awake in an instant, grabbing the phone off the hook before it could ring again. He didn't want it to annoy his father.

"What is it?" he asked groggily, blinking his eyes, trying to focus on the red, digital numbers on the bedside clock.

"John, it's Major Skinner. We have a crisis. A car is on its way for you and should be there within the hour. I'll brief you when you get back."

Waters heard a click and then the regular dial tone. He placed the phone back in its cradle and switched on the bedside lamp. It was 3:00 a.m. He rubbed the sleep from his eyes, climbed out of bed and began to dress. There was no time to shave or shower. A knock came to the door.

"Come in, dad. It's not locked."

"I heard the phone, son. Bad news, is it?"

Waters smiled to himself. The phone had only rung for a fraction of a second, yet his father still heard it. Old habits die hard, he thought.

"There's a crisis on their hands right now and all leave has been cancelled. A car should be here within the hour."

His father rubbed his chin thoughtfully. "Must be something really bad for them to send a car. I expect I'll hear about it on the news tomorrow.

"Too bad, though. I guess I'll have to get that fish all by myself. I was just getting used to having you around the house too. Ah well, it's all part of the job. Be careful now, and call me as soon as you can."

He put his arms around his son and hugged him hard, a surprising strength in the old limbs. Then he walked out of the room.

Waters said to the retreating back, "So long, dad. Tell Mrs Mac I'll be back soon."

CHAPTER 16
Betrayal

Patrick Kelly lay on his bed, hands behind his head, and mulled over the events of the past two days. Outside his window came the roar of rising tides pounding against the rocks. It was just after lunch time, about thirty minutes from high tide. Josie Donnelly would be off to the rocks shortly as high tide was the time bigger fish came in to the seacoast to feed.

Last evening's attack had been the most violent; the British troops were now on high alert. But the attack on the para barracks was the one which Josie Donnelly had been waiting for. Kelly suspected

Donnelly had used up all the ordnance loaded for that night's attack. He knew that all the Hellfire missiles and Hydra rockets had been fired; the pods were empty when they returned to the island.

The target had been Belfast - the headquarters of the Parachute Regiment in Leopold Street. Donnelly had howled like a banshee as he fired salvo after salvo into the burning barracks.

"That's for my da," he screamed, raking the cannon back and forth across the parade ground, trying to kill everything in sight. The Paras had fired back with anything that came to hand, but they were no match for the heavier armaments of the Apache.

Kelly closed his eyes to the fading images, listening to the rhythmic drumming of the waves. In a few moments he was asleep.

"This will be the last time I will tell this tale, and I must hurry, because my brothers are waiting for me and they say that we must soon be gone. So, if you are listening I shall begin, and I will tell you the tale of the Children of Lir.

"My name is Fionnuala ..."

Kelly sat bolt upright, his hand clutching the tiny gold medallion which hung from a chain around his neck. Four tiny swans were engraved on the medallion, each wearing a necklace.

His heart pounded, streams of sweat rolled

down his face, and his pillow was stained with perspiration. The words were etched in his memory, from a time when his grandmother would read stories to him about Ireland. His favourite, and hers, was the Children of Lir, a tale about a jealous stepmother who put an enchantment on her four stepchildren and turned them into beautiful swans. The spell was so strong that no-one could break the magic.

Unknown to the stepmother, their father's bodyguard, Mechar, had given them each a magic necklace, made from the stones of Truth. Wherever they went, as long as they wore the necklaces, he would be able to find them.

Patrick Kelly's grandmother gave him the chain on his seventh birthday, telling him that wherever in the world he would be, she would always be able to find him.

He carried the medallion from that day on, through school and then off to the hell of Vietnam. Even on the blackest of days, he could clutch the medallion, remember the words of his grandmother, and the gloom would vanish.

It was a sad comment on his life, he thought, that he felt more alive over the past few days than in all the years since Vietnam. There were few friends, perhaps one or two whom he saw on occasion. Those were special friendships, forged in the blood of the battlefield and would never break. And then there was his grandmother, shining like a beacon when his life became dark and tumultuous. She was the one constant in his life, the person he turned to for inspiration when the flashbacks would come. Whenever he was about to complain about his life, he would think about the horrors she had endured and his own would pale in comparison. She was one tough old lady.

Tommy Mulholland, Josie Donnelly, the two women, and Patrick Kelly sat eating their supper in silence, listening intently to the radio. News of the attacks was still the top story. Newspapers, scattered around the room, each gave the headlines to the attacks on the barracks and the forensic lab. It was not only the lead in British and Irish papers, but in all the major foreign papers as well, which pleased Mulholland immensely.

Depending on the paper's political leanings, it was either a major coup for the Irish Freedom Fighters or a dastardly terrorist attack. The British Prime Minister, as always, promised that there would be retaliation against those responsible. He also refused to comment on the growing movement to withdraw troops from Northern Ireland.

Other papers announced that U.S. Army specialists were being sent to advise the military on how best to deal with attacks by the Apache. An emergency session of the cabinet office briefing room (COBRA) committee, chaired by the home secretary, with representatives from each of the security services, had been called to review the situation.

Some enterprising television reporter had gotten his hands on the publicity film of the Apache in action, and was broadcasting it on the news. It had been neatly edited of course, to show the devastating power of the machine's armaments. And there was the salesman stating that with the rapid mask/unmask capabilities of the Apache, there was virtually no way to know an attack was coming; the only way to stop further attacks was to interdict the helicopter after an attack. That meant rapid response. To meet that requirement, the RAF had stationed several Harrier AV-8B jump jets in the Province. The Harriers, better known as V/STOL aircraft (vertical/short take-off and landing), could respond to an attack in minutes.

Mulholland was pleased with Kelly's performance, as were his superiors, the shadowy, well-hidden men who orchestrated the acts of mayhem and destruction. Mulholland's part of the mission was complete, and now he had orders to pass control over to the women. They had one more mission for Kelly to fly.

Passing control was going to be difficult, and Kelly was going to be extremely angry. Mulholland had first-hand exposure to that ire, and did not relish facing it again, so he continued eating, putting off the moment which would arrive all to soon.

Kelly ate heartily, his stomach becoming accustomed to the grease which accompanied each meal. His job was done, and he was looking forward to getting back home to New York, to see his grandmother again. With the funds from the operation, he would be able to pay off his existing loans and buy a new chopper to expand his business.

His grandmother would be pleased. British morale was in pieces, just like the computer centres, forensic lab, and army barracks in Derry, Belfast, and Lisburn. Already the clamour was building to repatriate the troops before any more soldiers lost their lives.

Kelly looked around the table at the long faces. He set down his knife and fork and wiped his face with a tissue. "Why are you all looking so miserable? I'd have thought you'd be jumping for joy after all that we've gone through. The operations have been even more successful than you could have hoped for."

Mulholland put down his knife and fork, wiped away a smear of ketchup from his mouth, and cleared his throat. He turned to face Kelly, his expression almost apologetic.

"I don't know exactly how to tell you this, Patrick, but there is another job which has nothing to do with us. As far as I'm concerned your job here is finished. The ladies however, have other orders. You'll be taking your instructions from them from now on."

"Yes ladies," spat Kelly, the colour rising in his cheeks. "Why don't you tell me what you have in mind?" Kelly was angry and it showed. He could understand why the women had taken part in the Toronto hijacking, but here? Now the pieces of the puzzle were beginning to fit.

At the time, Tommy Mulholland's reason for their involvement had sounded a little hollow, but he had dismissed the doubts. There were too many other things to think about. Now it was perfectly clear. He picked up a bottle of beer, took a long swig. Leia, the older of the two women, spoke up. "There are two things. Please do not speak until I have given you both pieces of information."

As she talked, Kelly noticed Donnelly's hand making an almost imperceptible movement towards his coat pocket, the pocket where he kept his revolver. Whatever it is, Kelly thought, they know I'm not going to like it.

"The final mission will take place in London. President Bush is stopping off there to meet with John Major on his way to the G7 summit meeting in Moscow. A public appearance is scheduled for 10:00 a.m. Friday morning outside Downing Street. Our leader promised revenge for the death of his daughter. We intend to destroy them both."

Kelly gagged on the mouthful of beer, spraying foam over those in close proximity. He spluttered a few times and was about to say something when she held up her hand.

He would never voluntarily carry out the attack, but the expression on her face told him she had something up her sleeve. He struggled to think of what sort of lever she could possibly have. They could threaten his life, but that would accomplish nothing. If they killed him, the attack would never take place. She answered his question for him.

"There is, as I stated, one more thing. Our accomplices in New York have taken your grandmother prisoner to ensure your cooperation. Needless to say, if you refuse to help us she will be executed. In a few minutes you will be allowed to speak to her.

"When the mission is over, she will be set free. You can hardly go to the authorities. Her life is now in your hands."

Kelly stared at her with fire in his eyes, a fire fuelled by the anger within him at being so helpless. He knew with absolute certainty that she would have his grandmother executed if he did not comply. His grandmother's life meant nothing to her; it was merely a bargaining chip to force him to cooperate.

His cheeks rippled as he clenched his jaws together, fighting to remain calm. Under other circumstances he would have reached over the table and snapped her neck like a twig. He said, "Let me speak to her now, please. I want to hear that she is okay. Then I will do what you ask."

He watched as she dialled the numbers, concentrating on the last seven digits. He would have only one chance. Fortunately, she was checking each digit carefully from a piece of paper.

Leia spoke a few words into the phone in her native language and then passed it to him. "You have one minute to speak to her."

He snatched the receiver from her hand and cradled it to the side of his head. There was a crackle of long-distance static, but there was no mistaking the frightened voice of his grandmother.

The frail voice said, "Patrick, is that you? Who are these people? They said I'd have to stay with them for a few days until the business in Ireland was cleared up. They said it would be safer for me here. I don't like them."

He forced himself to be calm and spoke reassuringly into the phone. "Yes grandma, it's me, Patrick. Those people are looking after you just in case anything goes wrong over here. Do exactly what they ask. I'll be home soon. I have one more mission to carry out and then it will be over. So promise me you'll do as I ask."

"Okay Patrick, if you say so. I'd better go now as they're giving me the evil eye again. They're just like the O'Reilly's you used to play with. God bless."

He hung up the phone. "The chopper does not have the capacity to fly to London and back. And we need to get some fuel. The tanks are running low at the moment."

"The fuel is on the way. When the attack is over you will land the chopper on the first piece of waste ground you can find and set the explosives. After that you are free to make your way back to New York.

"When news of the attack is broadcast, our accomplices will release your grandmother. A flight plan has been worked out, with several suggested approaches to Downing Street. You will have to select the most suitable."

Kelly asked, "What happens if we get intercepted? There is going to be heavy security, including air surveillance. Especially since they know about this Apache."

"British surveillance helicopters are no match for the Apache. You will be able to outrun and outshoot them, if necessary. However, if you do get shot down before carrying out the attack, your grandmother will still be executed. Just a little incentive for a successful attack." She stood up from the table, indicating the conversation was over. The others were happy to get away from Patrick Kelly's glare.

Kelly continued sipping his beer, imagining moves

and counter-moves that might extricate him from the snare. Eventually he developed a scenario, but it was extremely risky and could very well backfire. With no other apparent alternative, he began to fine-tune the plan. And he was going to have to act soon. Friday was only three days away.

The others had long since gone to bed, and the fire was beginning to die in the hearth, bringing a chill. He tossed on some more peat logs to stave off the cold. During the evening the others had all deliberately avoided him, leaving him to his intro-spection. If they could only read his mind, he thought.

He sat back in one of the old, overstuffed arm-chairs, his feet resting on the hearth. A bottle of beer sat in one hand, and in the other he held one of the strange nails which were lying about all over the house. Josie was always playing with them, cleaning his finger-nails or scratching his initials on furniture.

He put the nail into his pocket, poured back the last of the beer, and considered going to bed. He was now committed to his plan, which had been reviewed and re-reviewed during the evening. It had been revamped from his original thoughts but it was still extremely dangerous. There was no concern for his own life; God knows how many times he had risked it in Vietnam, but he was now putting his grandmother's life in jeopardy also.

The plan involved a lot of 'ifs', but it was still better than destroying countless civilian lives by simply acquiescing to the Libyans' demands. It would not be long, however, before he found out if the plan had any chance of succeeding.

He put his head back and closed his eyes but sleep eluded him. His mind worked frenziedly, replaying the plan over and over so many times that he could not relax. Eventually he gave up trying to sleep. It was futile. The fire again waned in the hearth and the cold crept into the room like a thief. He pulled himself out of the chair and threw some more peat on to the dying embers. Heat poured out from the hearth and covered him like a blanket. He eased himself back into the chair and sat staring at, but not seeing, the fire.

Slowly, almost imperceptibly, his body began to relax. He always considered himself to be a realist, and the harsh reality was that the plan would probably cost him his life. He was not frightened by that prospect. Since returning from Vietnam his life had not amounted to much: a few dollars here and there from flying tourists around the city. Barroom brawls ate up that money in fines. And there were no steady relationships.

Vietnam had shown him how to destroy, and that urge had clung to him like a leech, bleeding him, not allowing him to get close to anyone.

It was ironic that in trying to exorcise his grandmother's demons he had put her life in jeopardy. Bile rose in his throat and he hurled the bottle across the room in a fit of rage. It shattered against the fireplace, sending pieces rocketing across the floor. Shards of glass winked up from the carpet. He got up from the seat, intending to pick up the fragments, but changed his mind. Perhaps one of the bastards will come down in the morning with no shoes on and step on the glass, he thought. They might even bleed to death.

He carefully navigated his way across the glass minefield on the floor, and went upstairs to bed. Perhaps sleep would come.

CHAPTER 17
Crucifixion

Major Skinner was frowning, deeply engrossed in a daily SITREP report when the knock came to the door. The ever-present cup of tea sat on his blotter, a plate of digestive biscuits within easy reach.

The treasured Parker duo-fold fountain pen had to be refilled from a bottle of ink. Ever a tidy, methodical person, he kept pending reports on his left side, and set the processed reports on his right. In front lay a hand-tooled leather blotter, a gift from an friend who had visited Cuba recently. The Parker had been his own extravagance. He had found something interesting in the reports, and was scribbling notes in the margin for his aide to take further action.

He uttered a gruff "Come in", annoyed at being disturbed. The offending party, a new radio officer unaccustomed to the Major's daily routine, strode across the room until he was almost touching the desk. He came to attention impressively, then did a near perfect salute. He carried a dispatch in his other hand.

Skinner clasped his hands across his stomach, leaned back in his chair, and waited.

"Major, we've been contacted by an Inspector Stevenson from Ballymena. He says that someone claiming to be the pilot of the chopper wants to meet with a representative from the SAS. He has left the phone number of a bar in Ballycastle and will be there until noon."

"Thank you, corporal. That will be all." Skinner took the proffered piece of paper and waited until the door closed. He then turned to his phone. It could be a trap, or it could be for real, in which case he was puzzled.

With twenty-eight men dead and well over fifty injured, the pilot could not expect a deal. But the main priority was to put the chopper out of commission to prevent any more attacks.

He dialled the number and waited.

"Hello, Ship Bar."

He asked for the name written on the piece of paper and could hear the barman shouting "Patrick Kelly." After another pause, a man with an American accent spoke: "Patrick Kelly here."

Skinner was intrigued by the accent and the polite tone. He was accustomed to the profanity uttered by terrorist contacts. This was definitely a horse of a different colour.

"This is Major James Skinner. I understand you want to talk about certain helicopter attacks."

"Before we begin major: if you have put the bar under surveillance, and I do not walk out of here unharmed, you will never lay your hands on the chopper, and the terrorists will continue their plans. Those plans are bigger than you can imagine. Do you understand?"

"I understand perfectly, Patrick, if that is your name. I will make no attempt to have you arrested or followed. You have my word. Now, what do you have in mind?"

"It is eleven o'clock now and I will be back here this afternoon at exactly one. I want to meet you face to face then. If you don't show I will be forced to continue the attacks, something I am loathe to do. You have an opportunity to bring them to an end, so please don't let me down. Goodbye, major."

Skinner stared at the phone, as if it were a foreign object, then replaced it gently in its cradle. He puffed up his cheeks and exhaled slowly, his head spinning. There was more going on than he could get his arms around, and for that reason he felt extremely uneasy. He decided to go ahead and meet with this 'Patrick Kelly'. If Kelly had anything worthwhile to say, then he would listen. If not, there were always his 'wolves'.

Skinner assumed the role, and the dress, of an English tourist for his meeting with Kelly. Sauntering into the bar, a few minutes before one o'clock, he asked for a pint of Guinness and sat down at the bar. He perused the daily specials scribbled almost illegibly on a chalk board behind the bar, and ordered the shepherd's pie.

When the steaming food arrived, he paid the barman, leaving a generous tip, then took the plate and his pint to one of the tables beside the window. Before sitting, he glanced out the window to see if John Waters or Terence Strong were in sight. There was no sign of either man, which was no surprise. They were experts at blending in with their surroundings, becoming almost invisible no matter what their situation.

Having spent several months in special language laboratories in Hereford, his men could mimic any accent. From the harsh guttural dialect of the back streets of Belfast, to the soft, countrified dialect of towns like Antrim or Ballymena, his men could speak as if they had been born there. That was part of the SAS mystique - they always seemed to turn up in the right place at the right time, usually under the noses of their enemies.

A dozen men were sitting, drinking pints at tables, around the room. A few, like himself, were having lunch while the others talked and drank. The latest racing form on the back pages of the newspaper seemed to be getting a lot of attention. Ascot was due to start in half an hour, so there would be several quick visits to the betting shop down the street. The smell of beer hung heavily in the air, but no-one was smoking, and so the atmosphere was bearable.

As he sipped his pint, he surreptitiously scanned the room, his eyes resting a few moments on each face. No warning bells went off.

Bright sunlight suddenly streamed into the gloom, cloaking the latest arrival in darkness. Skinner squinted, but could not make out any features. Then the door slammed shut, forcing the sunlight into exile. The man walked over and leaned on the bar, resting one foot on the brass rail.

By the time he could focus again, the new-comer had a pint in his hand. The man was in his mid-thirties, well-built, with an unruly mop of red hair. Skinner automatically went through the process of memorising height, weight, hair-colour, and distinguishing features. The newcomer and the barman exchanged a few words in greeting, but Skinner was too far out of earshot to hear what they were saying.

Both men glanced in his direction, then the newcomer walked directly towards him, nodding to several of the other patrons on the way.

"I'm told you're a tourist as well," he started. "My name's Patrick Kelly and I'm here on vacation for a few weeks. Perhaps we could compare notes on what's worthwhile to see." He spoke with the same American accent Skinner had heard on the phone. There was a hint of something else in the voice, but it eluded him.

He extended his hand and Skinner rose to shake it. The grip was strong.

Skinner said, "My name's Skinner, James Skinner. Won't you have a seat? I think we may have a lot to talk about." He sat down again and resumed eating his shepherd's pie. He pointed to the pie with his fork. "Are you not eating? The pie is very good."

"Actually, I'm not very hungry," came the reply. "I had the pie yesterday. I think the barman makes a batch of them and then they're the daily special until he runs out. Anyway, we don't have much time. The others are expecting me back before long."

Skinner stared at the tanned face and the blue eyes, glinting in the sunlight streaming through the window. The face had a haunted look. He had seen

it on some of the men who returned from the Falklands. It was the look of someone who was tired
and battle weary.

"Some Libyan terrorists have taken my grandmother hostage. They want me to do a job for them,
or they will kill her. She lives in New York. That's
too far away for me to do anything about it.

"I want to trade the terrorists and the chopper
for my grandmother's life. That's my deal. You have
the necessary contacts in Fort Bragg so what do
you say?"

Skinner stared at Kelly for a moment, trying to
digest all that had been said. He was finding it difficult to imagine that this man, who had just laid waste
to three military installations and killed twenty-eight
soldiers, was concerned about his grandmother's
life. Single-handedly, he had set security forces on
full alert, and now he wanted to make a deal.

"I'm not sure what to say," he replied. He decided to bait the man to see what would happen.
He washed down a forkful of food with a swig of
Guinness. "I think you are trying to make a deal to
save your skin. The security forces are closing in
on you and you're running scared."

Kelly fought to contain his anger, his face suffused with blood. Veins on his necks corded against
his skin and he tensed, ready to spring. Skinner swallowed hard.

"Listen major," Kelly hissed, forcing himself to

keep his voice down. "I was hired to take out some military targets. The men were armed and had the capability of shooting back - they were not unarmed civilians.

"My grandmother is Irish, Connemara born and bred. She left here in 1922, twenty-one years old, pregnant and a widow. Your infamous Black and Tans hanged her husband in front of her, and she has carried that image with her all her life. I had a chance to exact some revenge for her.

"This job for the Libyans came as a surprise. I don't want it. Their crap is none of my business."

Skinner nodded, slowly beginning to understand what was driving Kelly. "Sins of the fathers," he thought to himself. He could recognize the hall-marks of a professional soldier. They find it diffi-cult to return to normal, everyday life. A few make the transition, but most end up in prison, or as mer-cenaries. The need is like that of an addict search-ing for the next fix, inescapable, uncontrollable. The end result is usually a premature death.

Skinner suspected that Patrick Kelly was just such a person. He said, "If you are so concerned about civilians, what about those guards who were murdered in Toronto? They were unarmed but were still executed in cold blood. And the American heli-copter pilot as well. It took him a long time to die. The burst of fire almost cut him in half. He scrawled the letters 'R E D' in his own blood. The police thought he meant the attackers were Russian. I can see that he was possibly referring to you - your hair. Which leads me to suspect that he may have known you. Correct?"

Skinner watched Kelly. He had no idea that his words would have such a devastating effect.

"I didn't know anyone was killed in Toronto," Kelly whispered, trying to regain his composure. "What was the name of the pilot? I have a friend from Vietnam who taught me how to fly the Apache. His name is Bill Crossley. He's the only person who ever called me 'RED'."

"That was his name," answered Skinner. "He must have seen you getting into the chopper and thought you were one of the terrorists." He watched with a flicker of sympathy as Patrick Kelly's eyes misted over.

"Those bastards." Kelly spat the words out with such venom that Skinner winced. "If it wasn't for the fact that they have my grandmother, I'd kill 'em all. Slowly."

Kelly paused, sat forward, and stared into Skinner's face.

"Major, even if you arrest me, they have another pilot who is trained on the Apache. He will carry out the attack and not lose any sleep over it, believe me." He sat back and took a long draught from his beer. "What do you say?"

"I'll be honest with you," replied Skinner. "This

meeting never took place. I can't make the deal you're proposing in my official capacity. However, let me see what I can do unofficially."

"Just to give you some incentive, major, the target they want me to take out is the president of the United States and your prime minister. They are to appear in public in Downing Street this coming Friday. That gives you two days to decide." Kelly pulled his hand from his pocket, where he had been absent-mindedly toying with a small metal object.

Skinner's eyes widened at what he had just heard, but also at the object that Kelly was holding in his hand. "Where did you get that?" he asked, pointing to the nail with the blue flange.

"What, this?" asked Kelly, holding it up for him to see.

"Yes, that. Where did you get it?"

"They're lying all over the place back at the house. One of the Irish boys has a bag full of them, but I've no idea what he uses them for. He doesn't seem to be much of a handyman, except with a gun!"

Skinner reached into his pocket and pulled out an identical nail. Kelly gave him a strange look, wondering what the major was doing with one, too. There was a story here.

"The bastards used them to nail my friend to a plank of wood, in an obscene parody of the crucifixion. He was then set adrift, alive, in a rat-infested river. You can imagine the results. They pulled twenty of these out of his body."

Kelly winced. "That sounds like Josie, all right. Actually..." He paused for a moment, his brow furrowed, as if trying to remember some incident. "Yes, that's it. Mulholland said something about trying to stop Josie from torturing a soldier."

Skinner sighed. "I've been searching for the bastards responsible for his death, and I think you've pointed me to them. I'll tell you what we'll do. Give me the information I need about your grandmother. I also want the names and descriptions of the terrorists whom mentioned."

Kelly spent the next few minutes recalling to Skinner the events which had unfolded since he landed in Ireland. He put particular emphasis on the phone call to New York.

Skinner drained the last dregs of his beer. "You be here tomorrow evening at five o'clock. If I can do anything, it will be done by then, and I will call. If not, well ..."

Kelly said, "There is one more thing. The terrorists have an inside man at the Ballycastle police station. I'd keep them out of it, if I were you. I don't know his name, but he was ambushed about a year ago and shot twice. It was a nice touch to help reinforce his cover. No-one would ever suspect him of passing information to terrorists after that incident."

After Skinner had gone, Kelly ordered another

pint and sat at the bar. He wanted to make the meeting with Skinner seem as natural as possible, in case there were any informants in the bar reporting back to Tommy Mulholland. He paid for a drink for the barman and then engaged him in conversation.

"Nice old guy that," he said, indicating to where Skinner had been sitting. "It seems he comes over here every year and travels around the country. He's a retired teacher and his wife died a few years ago.

"He must be pretty lonely. He invited me to have dinner with him tomorrow evening at the hotel just down the road. He wasn't sure about his schedule, so he said he'd phone here about five o'clock tomorrow to make the arrangements."

"We don't get many Brits over here these days," answered the barman as he wiped and dried a glass. "A British accent is none too welcome in a lot of places. But the oul fella seems pretty harmless. He probably wants some company."

"Anyway, I'd better get on," said Kelly. "I've heard a lot about the Giant's Causeway, so it's about time I went there. Catch you later."

"I hope you like walking," said the barman. "You've got a few miles ahead of you."

When Kelly closed the door, the barman went to the phone, and related exactly what Kelly had told him. Mulholland answered with a gruff "Thanks," and the phone went dead.

CHAPTER 18
Delta

Josie Donnelly sat at the kitchen table, sipping on his tea, waiting for Mulholland to pour himself a cup. A half-smoked cigarette lay in an ashtray full of butts, a thin wisp of smoke rising from it towards the ceiling. Dragging out a chair with his foot, Mullholland sat down.

"So Josie, is the chopper ready for Friday?"

"Yeah. The missiles and rockets have been loaded. The tanks are full as well."

"Grand. The sooner we get rid of the others, the better. Then we can get on with our own business. There's a couple of lads who've been talking to the filth, and need to be taken out for a cup of tea. It has to be done quickly."

Donnelly nodded. "You were a hard on the Yank," he said quietly. "A bit unfair like, springing that on him."

Mulholland's nostrils flared. "Fair! Fuck that. A week ago you wanted to top him. Has he suddenly become your best mate or something? Life's not fucking fair - you of all people should know that."

Donnelly raised his eyes from the table and stared at Mulholland, who shivered, seeing the cold, black rage shimmering there, and instinctively his fingers touched the butt of his pistol.

Donnelly drank the remains of his tea, got up, snatched his rod from the shelf, and strode out of the house, slamming the door behind him. Mulholland watched him go, heading for that spot on the rocks he called sanctuary. It suddenly occurred to him that one of these days he was going to have to shoot Donnelly, to protect himself.

*   *   *   *   *

John Waters and Terence Strong walked into the room, just as Major Skinner slammed down his phone and turned to his window. Outside, a heavy drizzle blew in off the Lough, distorting his view of the city. He shook his head, and returned to his chair.

"Fucking imbeciles. I tell them that Libyan terrorists are planning an attack against Bush and the PM, and they ask me for concrete evidence. Standard terrorist policy to make threats against visiting politicians, they say. Suddenly they've all become fucking experts in terrorist ideology. If I was threatened by a bunch of terrorists who had an anti-tank helicopter in their hands, I would have second thoughts about appearing anywhere in public." He threw up his hands.

Taking a deep breath, he muttered some more and then motioned for the two men to sit down. "Time for a brew," he said, pressing the button on his intercom. "Can you bring in a pot of tea and three mugs, please. Oh, and some digestive biscuits as well."

Turning to Waters and Strong, he said, "I'll bring you up to date on the situation. This pilot, Patrick Kelly, was hired by two of our local hotshots, namely Tommy Mulholland and Josie Donnelly. They are calling themselves the Irish Freedom Fighters. Those are two prize specimens. Ruthless bastards, both, especially Donnelly. We've never managed to connect him with several murders and bombings which we know he did. I have reason to believe he was responsible for the death of Timothy White.

"There are also two Libyans involved, two women from Quadaffi's own personal bodyguard. Kelly wants no part of it, but apparently they have kidnapped his grandmother and are threatening to kill her unless he carries out the attack. That is why he wants to make a deal. We free his grandmother, then he will give us the location of the chopper and the four terrorists."

"Why didn't you just shoot the fooker when you had the chance, Major?" asked Strong, in his thick Geordie accent.

"I thought about it, but he says there is another pilot ready to take over. Anyway, there's no time to go through official channels, so this is going to be a black operation. I'll worry about the particulars later." He paused to let that little detail sink in.

"Either of you have a problem with that?" he asked, knowing full well what the answer would be. Their eyes gleamed like children who had just received a wondrous gift. Both men shook their heads.

"This afternoon I spoke with Charlie Watts, the CO at Fort Bragg. You both know him. He's a man after my own heart. When I explained the situation, he agreed to help, unofficially, of course. He's sending two of his teams to New York to try and free the grandmother. Hopefully they will be seeing action at some stage this evening. He will call me as soon as he knows.

"I want your teams ready at this end; eight men should be sufficient. They should be prepared to move on a moment's notice. Any questions?"

Waters and Strong were excited at the prospects. Too many times they had been shackled by politicians who were unwilling to authorize the elimination of a terrorist cell. Often, they had to sit idly by and watch as bombings were planned, attacks coordinated and executed, and then have the terrorists disappear like wraiths into the night. But now, the gloves were off.

Waters spoke up first. "What do we do about the American?"

As Skinner ruffled through some papers on his desk and produced a single sheet of paper, his aide arrived with their tea. The man set the tray on one corner of Skinner's desk and left. Waters did the honours, and when they were sipping contentedly, Skinner continued. "Fort Bragg faxed me a copy of Kelly's military record: several tours of duty in Vietnam, decorated countless times, trained with the special forces, and specialized in infiltrating and exfiltrating teams deep in enemy territory.

"I really don't know what to do about him. The terrorists killed his friend in Toronto. He didn't know anything about it until I told him. From the look on his face, I imagine they would all be dead if they were not holding his grandmother.

"What about you Terence? Any questions?"

"No major. I think you've covered everything. I take it there will be no survivors."

"I don't think you'll have to worry on that score,

Terence," Skinner replied. "These are the glory boys. They will not let themselves be taken alive. You'll have to be careful because they have nothing to lose. If Kelly gets killed, hopefully in the crossfire, it will tie up that loose end.

"If the mission is successful, there are going to be a hell of a lot of questions to answer. I don't want anyone around who could possibly embarrass us."

Both men nodded their understanding.

"Well then, off you go. I'll see you in the map room later."

*   *   *   *   *

In the Fort Bragg briefing room, Colonel Charlie Watts addressed the two teams from DELTA in his usual no-nonsense tone.

"I've had a call from Major Skinner." He did not have to elaborate; they all knew of the major and the role which he played in Northern Ireland. A call from him coupled with a briefing from the Colonel could mean only one thing. The DELTA force would be seeing action, whether it be training or otherwise.

The colonel continued. "As you are probably aware, the Apache helicopter, which was stolen in Toronto a couple of weeks ago, has turned up in Ireland. A bunch of terrorists calling themselves the

Irish Freedom Fighters got their hands on it and are have managed to knock out several key military bases, especially their two computer centres, and have killed at least twenty-eight men.

"The reason you are here today is that Major Skinner has been contacted by the pilot of the chopper. He's an American, an ex-special forces chopper jockey with several tours of duty in 'Nam. He wants to make a deal.

"It seems some Libyans have gotten into the act and want the pilot to take out a couple of very high-profile political figures, namely our president and the British prime minister when they appear in public in London this coming Friday." The men were literally on the edge of their seats.

"The pilot does not want to carry out the attack, but the Libyans have kidnapped his grandmother and are threatening to kill her unless he agrees to their plan. So he contacted the major who in turn contacted me.

"Apparently the grandmother is being held in an apartment in Queens, in New York. The pilot was allowed to speak to her once, and he managed to get the phone number. I have used our FBI contacts to get the address where the phone is located."

He could see the question on their faces. Could it be they were really going to be sent into action? Ever since the abortive raid on the embassy in Teheran, the DELTA force had maintained a very low profile. Their training had never ceased, and so they were totally prepared to go into action at a moment's notice.

The men were actually jealous when war broke out in the Falklands, knowing their SAS counterparts would be getting to use their specialised training in the field. They had offered their services but were politely but firmly rebuffed.

Major Mitchell, the commander of 'B' squadron, broke the silence. "Colonel, this isn't another of your 'Games', is it? Like that hostage situation you lead us into in Minnesota, when all of us thought we were in Canada."

Mitchell referred to a training exercise in which the men of DELTA thought they were going to release a group of Americans, allegedly taken prisoner by terrorists. When the DELTA force arrived at the site, the actors posing as terrorists were replaced by moving dummies. In a textbook assault, the men destroyed the 'terrorist' dummies, and freed the hostages.

It took a long time for the men to accept the deception, but eventually they understood the reasoning. They had to be able to kill without the slightest hesitation, to carry their training to its ultimate conclusion: destruction of the terrorists without harming the hostages. A moment of hesitation or indecision could cost the life of a hostage or worse still, jeopardize the entire mission.

Charlie Watts responded firmly. "This is for real. It is not an exercise." He went on. "We don't have much time so I'll be brief. The two teams will go to New York and put the apartment under surveillance. I'm playing this one close to the chest: if we call in the FBI or the NYPD, then we'll get into a hostage negotiation which could drag out for days. It would also tip our hand to the terrorists over in Ireland.

"Transport has been arranged for us." He saw the surprise on their faces. "Yes, us. I'm going too. We'll meet at the runway at thirteen hundred hours. Bring whatever equipment you think will be necessary. Dismissed."

The men almost ran from the room. At last they had a chance to put their extraction techniques and their new surveillance equipment to the test in a real hostage situation.

On a rooftop across the road from the old Brownstone building, Sergeant Steven Mallory and Corporal Jim Allen had watched and listened to the terrorists for over four hours. Using high-powered binoculars and a sophisticated parabolic directional microphone, they had determined there were three terrorists, two men and one woman, each outfitted with a shoulder-holster carrying an automatic pistol, type unknown. They seemed to spend most of their time watching television. During the period the two men had been watching, none of the terrorists had checked the street through the window. Obviously they were not expecting trouble.

The old lady was being kept in a bedroom adjacent to the living room. The blinds were pulled but the window was open, and the microphone had picked up her voice asking for a cup of tea. The main door of the apartment opened directly into the living room, which pleased the men from DELTA. It was the ideal situation for a hostage extraction. No time would be wasted sprinting down a corridor after blowing the door. The element of surprise would not be diminished.

The results of the surveillance were relayed back to the colonel, who sat waiting in the back of a mini-van, two blocks from the house. With him, in the van, were the men from DELTA who would perform the extraction. They were all dressed in jeans and denim jackets, under which was Kevlar body-armour. They did not want to arouse the suspicion of any neighbours.

With only three terrorists being identified, Watts decided that silenced pistols would be sufficient for the job. The men were all armed with their standard M-1911A1 .45 pistols, and when the Colonel gave the go-ahead, the men left the van in pairs, slipped into the building from the rear, and four made their way quietly to the top floor. Two remained at the entrance to prevent any civilians from entering during the assault.

Sergeant Soames, leader of the four-man team, and the demolitions expert, carefully placed the lead-cased explosive on the areas of the door locks, the hinges, and the safety-chain. Gone were the good old days of kicking down a door and storming into a room. More often than not, the door wouldn't budge from the first kick, alerting the terrorists, and placing the lives of the hostages in jeopardy.

When the sergeant had finished, he armed a tiny hand-held transmitter and the men cocked their weapons. There was an ominous silence in the hall-way. The men could hear the sounds of the televi-sion through the door as their senses heightened in preparation for the assault. Bugs Bunny was doing something unspeakable to Elmer Fudd. The terror-ists were laughing.

The sergeant held out three fingers, then two, then one, and then snapped his arm down and pressed the detonator.

The men had turned away from the door the instant before the muffled 'Crump' rocked the door in its frame and fell inwards. The men operated on instinct now, as they had been taught during the countless hours of training in the 'House of Hor-rors' at the stockade. The sergeant charged through the opening like a knight across a drawbridge, and the others followed, moving quickly out of each other's line of fire.

The terrorists turned, totally surprised, and then

their heads snapped back as the bullet after bullet slammed into them. The first three men through the door had taken out the terrorists, the fourth made his way to the bedroom.

Mary Kelly was a little bewildered by the noise, but was reassured by the man who was telling her that they had come to take her home. Putting his arm around her, he lead her out past the other men who used their bodies to shield her from the sight of the carnage.

The acrid fumes of cordite made her eyes water, and she accepted the proffered handkerchief, dabbing at her eyes while they helped her down the stairs and into the street. A car pulled quickly up to the sidewalk and a rear door opened for her. Inside was the colonel.

Watts took her hand and helped her into the car. "Good evening, Mrs Kelly, I'm Charlie Watts. Your grandson told us you were in some trouble. I hope they didn't mistreat you."

"I'm fine" she replied, in her soft Irish brogue, dabbing away at her eyes with the handkerchief. "They didn't say much to me. They let me speak to Patrick once, on the phone, but I haven't heard a word from him since."

"Well, I'm sure you'll be hearing from him soon," he said, and, touching her arm in a conspiratorial manner, added, "I'd like you to keep all this quiet. The operation was quite illegal and could get me into all sorts of trouble."

"What operation?" she asked. "I've been off visiting my friend for a couple of days."

Watts smiled. She certainly was a tough old lady, but from what he had learned of her background, he was not at all surprised.

*   *   *   *   *

At 12:30 a.m., Belfast time, Major Skinner listened quietly as his friend Colonel Charlie Watts introduced him to Mary Kelly. She was ready to recount the events of the past two days, culminating in her release. Skinner taped the old lady, smiling when he heard her final words 'May ye die in Ireland' to Kelly.

He turned off the tape recorder and said, "Thanks Charlie, I owe you one. We can get on with the operation at our end now. You'll probably be reading about it in the paper within the next few days."

Watts said, "Can you stay on the line?" Skinner heard him asking Mary Kelly to wait outside his office for a moment, and then a door closed.

"There is one thing, James. I've talked to the old lady several times now. She's as tough as old army boots and she hates the Black and Tans with a passion. I think that some of her doctrine has rubbed off on her grandson. I've taken a closer look at his record and he's a hardy bugger. He was shot down several times behind enemy lines and made his way out without being detected. I'd be careful around him.

"Anyway, I won't keep you any longer. I know you have a lot to do. Good luck, James."

The phone went dead. Skinner pondered his friend's words and then picked up the phone again.

"John. Major Skinner here. The operation in New York was successful. Your guys will be going in tomorrow night. Goodnight." He rubbed his tired eyes, pressed the intercom, and called for his car. Time to get some rest.

*   *   *   *   *

Kelly was sitting at the bar slowly sipping a pint of Guinness. Being a Thursday afternoon, only a few of the regulars had managed to put in an appearance. Kelly was discussing baseball with the barman the finer points of baseball, which the barman called rounders; and how it was to sit at Shea Stadium on a hot summer's day, eating hot dogs and drinking beer. In the middle of Kelly's detailed description of a pitcher's duel, the phone rang. The barman handed it to him. "I think it's your old English pal."

"Patrick Kelly here."

"This is James Skinner. I want you to listen to

something."

Kelly's eyes misted over as he heard the sound of his grandmother's voice, recounting the events of the past two days and the nice men who managed to free her. When the tape stopped, he took a deep breath to try to regain his composure.

Kelly turned his back so that the barman could not overhear his conversation. "Thanks James. Now I'll keep my part of the bargain. The chopper is being kept on Rathlin Island, a few miles from here. The four people I told you about are at the house now. There are sentries posted around the Island, four or five, I think. Also, they are expecting company tonight to take a look at the chopper. The two women are planning to fly from Aldergrove to Amsterdam in the morning, just before the attack. You better take them down sometime tonight."

Skinner replied, "I'm going to put things in motion now, Patrick. I need you to go back to the island. They may get suspicious if you don't show up. My men have all been informed about you and have your description, so unless you point a gun at one of them you will not be harmed."

"Don't worry. I had no intention of skipping out. I have a score to settle with those bastards. They are going to pay for killing my friend. When the shooting starts, I'll do my thing. But there's one other item. My grandmother has an old blessing which goes 'May ye die in Ireland' as I'm sure you heard. I have no intention of dying in Ireland, at least not yet. Do I make myself clear?"

"Perfectly," replied Skinner. "Keep your head down when the shooting starts. We may meet again one day. Goodbye Patrick."

Kelly grinned, a tremendous weight lifted from his shoulders. "I prefer 'au revoir', major. 'Goodbye' has such an air of finality, especially coming from you."

Skinner broke the connection with his finger, waited for a dial tone, and then called John Waters. He checked his watch: 5:15 p.m. When Waters answered, he was told to be in the briefing room by eight along with the other teams.
Next on the list was a phone call to check the weather on the Northern coast for the evening, and finally a visit to the map room to pick up the ordnance surveys of the coast in the general area of Rathlin Island.

Kelly hung up the phone and returned to his pint. "The old bloke can't make it for dinner this evening, Liam," he volunteered to the barman. "He's been out in the sun too long today and doesn't feel well. I suppose I'm going to have to stay and drink some more of this black stuff." He nodded to his pint of Guinness, half-empty on the bar before him.

Liam said, "Well I know one person who'll be

happy to hear that news."

"Oh?" asked Kelly, raising an eyebrow.

"Don't tell me you didn't notice how Mairead has been looking at you these past few days. She's got a thing for you, Patrick, so I'd pursue it, if I were you."

"Fair enough," replied Kelly, taking another sip of his pint. "You tell me that I'll get used to this taste eventually," he said, smiling.

"Aye, Patrick," replied Liam, wiping yet another beer glass. "That you will. Six or seven more gallons and you'll love the taste. Then you can go back to the States and tell them what real beer tastes like."

"I guess I'll have something to eat here," said Patrick. "What's for dinner tonight?"

"I'll go and see what's left," said Liam, and went out through the back of the bar into the kitchen.

Kelly sighed. The die had been cast; there was no going back now. He thought of himself as a realist, and in realistic terms his chances of surviving the night were slim. Despite all the major's assurances, he would not want any survivors. And the others would turn on him like cornered rats if they knew that he had betrayed them.

The barman returned, carrying a huge plate of roast beef, Yorkshire pudding, peas and potatoes. "I'm sorry Patrick, but it was all I could find," he joked, and Kelly's eyes widened at the huge serving.

A hearty meal for a condemned man, thought Kelly, tucking into the food with relish. The daily papers, full of local news, still carried long columns about the attacks on the army bases. A few papers lay scattered around the bar, and after finishing his meal he spent some time poring over them.

After a couple of hours, the bar began to fill up with regular patrons coming in for the evening. Kelly was reluctant to leave; he knew what lay in store. His natural instincts told him to run and keep running, but he had made a deal with Skinner. The major had honoured his side of the deal. Now it was up to him to do the same.

He swallowed the last of his pint, and said goodnight to the barman. The meal lay heavily in his stomach.

"Goodnight, Patrick. See you tomorrow."

I hope so, he thought. I hope so.

The sun, a glowing orb, was setting on the horizon as Kelly made his way to the jetty. When he turned down the lane, he switched off the motorcycle's engine and paused for a moment. There was a small clump of bushes at the side of the road in which he could conceal the bike. If, by some miracle, he managed to get off the island later, he would need to have some means of transport.

It took only a few minutes to camouflage the

bike, and soon he was walking the remaining few yards to the jetty. A second car was parked beside the one used by Tommy Mulholland. It probably belonged to the visitors.

Several small rowing boats bobbed against the supports of the jetty, rocked by the rising tide. He climbed into the nearest boat, unhooked the line, and began to row. It was less than half a mile to the island, but there was a deceptively strong current in the channel, and so it took him almost twenty minutes to complete the crossing.

He was panting from his exertions when he tied the boat to the mooring on the island's jetty. Suddenly, an intensely bright light shone in his face, blinding him.

"Ah, it's only yourself," came a voice from the darkness, and abruptly the light was extinguished. Kelly silently cursed the sentry as he stood on the jetty waiting for his vision to return. When he could discern shapes again, he set off up the narrow, gravelled path towards the house. It was like walking in quicksand, his feet sinking with each step.

Kelly spent a few minutes peering though the window before opening the door to the house. There was much celebrating going on. Several bottles of Bushmills sat on the table, two cases of Harp lager were stacked on the kitchen counter, and several empties lay askew beside them.

The women were in the room, observing but

not participating in the festivities, and there were three new faces: two men and one woman, all well on their way to becoming inebriated.

He eased up on the latch and then pushed the door as hard as he could. It flew inwards on its well-oiled hinges and slammed against the wall. Drinks went flying as the visitors, Mulholland, Donnelly, and the two women dived for cover, their fingers clawing for their weapons.

"Don't shoot, don't shoot. It's only me," he shouted, raising his hands. This must be what it feels like to face a firing squad, he thought, looking down the barrels of five pistols and two machine guns. The women carried their UZI's everywhere. Well, almost everywhere, he thought, remembering the events of the night prior to the first attack.

"Bastard," hissed Tommy Mulholland, making a futile attempt to wipe some whiskey from his trousers. "This is the fuckin' Yank I've been telling you about. He's got a funny sense of humour, as you can see. It's a good job that he's still needed, or ..."

He didn't finish the sentence, but Kelly could imagine how it ended.

"Hi there," beamed Kelly. "Celebrating, are we? Have one for me."

With that, he walked towards the stairs, ignoring the malevolent stares being cast in his direction. No introductions were made nor were any offered.

"Patrick," called Mulholland. "Our visitors

would like to see the chopper. Would you show it to them, please?"

He could see that Mulholland had trouble with the 'Please' part. It was spat out; an order rather than an entreaty.

"Sure," he replied. "I'll show them the bird. Let's go."

Pistols disappeared into holsters, clothes were straightened and they followed him, single file, out to the darkened boathouse where the helicopter was stored. There were no lights so Mulholland brought one of the flashlights, its broad beam serving only to exaggerate the size of the machine.

The visitors were suitably impressed and were all over it, examining the 30-millimetre chain-gun and the Hellfire missiles. "It's a far cry from our home-made mortars," commented one of them. "A pity we couldn't use it some more."

"Can I sit in it?" asked the new woman, turning to face Kelly.

"No problem," he replied, and moved forward to open the door. She stepped up through the hatch and he followed, admiring the curve of her buttocks in the tight jeans. He inserted the keys and illuminated the control panel, which cast a soft glow over her face. She was, by his estimation, in her late twenties and a real looker as well. Such a waste, he thought. He spent several minutes answering 'What's that' and 'What's this' questions for her.

When she was satisfied, he removed the keys and helped her out of the seat. She was wearing a rich, intoxicating perfume. When she passed by, he inhaled deeply, his mind leaping back to the evening before the first attack.

He wondered why the woman, whom he had discovered was called Bibi, had not come back to his room again after that first night. She still treated him with the same indifference as she showed the others.

"All right folks, the show's over. Please pay as you leave," he joked as they returned to the house. His stomach roiled and began to churn as he thought of the coming evening. A quick glance showed him that it was almost ten o'clock. Eight hours to daybreak. He wondered if he would live to see it.

*   *   *   *   *

Skinner, Waters, Strong, and the other members of the assault team stood around the map table, scanning the coastline facing Rathlin Island. Aerial photographs, hurriedly taken and developed, showed the location of the house, the jetty on the shore, and the laneway leading down to the jetty.

Waters pushed the large magnifying glass over the photograph and scanned the island. He was looking for a suitable spot to land his teams. He turned to the others.

"There are only two buildings on the island: the house and the boathouse. The chopper must be in the boathouse."

Strong, an enormous Geordie with an accent that was almost impossible to understand, peered over Waters's shoulder into the magnifying glass. "There isn't a fookin' lot of cover on the island. Is there a full moon tonight by any chance?"

"I checked with the ops room," replied Skinner. "They say it's going to be overcast and cloudy. There's even a chance of showers."

"Marvellous," replied Waters. "If it rains those rocks are going to be slippery. There will be a few sore arses if that happens."

Waters, the leader of the two Sabre teams, decided that it would be best to attack from the seaward side of the island. The teams would launch their Gemini inflatables about two miles up the coast, and then row down to the island under cover of darkness.

One team would land at each end of the island and then make their way to the house, which was located centrally.

From Kelly's information, there were no civilians present, which was a bonus. That meant that anything which moved was a legitimate target. Their first priority, however, was to immobilize the helicopter. If anything did go wrong, the last thing they wanted was for the chopper to be used against them.

Photographs of the Apache's devastation had given them a healthy respect for its firepower.

"How are we going in Boss?" asked Strong. "Fatigues or civvies?"

"This is going to have a high profile; we'll use our uniforms this time," replied Waters. "The police are going to be involved as soon as it's over, and they're not terribly fond of us wearing street clothes at the moment."

Skinner interrupted: "There will be no contact with the local police prior to this operation."

Waters looked up sharply. "Isn't that a little irregular, major?" he asked. "You know how sticky those bastards get on procedure. We're supposed to notify them before any operation takes place in their jurisdiction."

"If you'd let me finish," snorted Skinner, "I know the rules as well as you do. However, it seems the terrorists have a plant in the police station in Ballycastle, and we don't want them to be forewarned. I want these bastards."

"Fair enough," replied Waters. "We'll still need the Quick Reaction Force nearby."

"That's not a problem," replied Skinner. "We'll inform the police when the operation is over - and in such a way as to trap the informer." He paused for a moment, a chess-master re-thinking his strategy. The devil danced in his eyes. "Or maybe I won't."

"I've timed the assault for 3:00 a.m.," stated Waters. "The men are on standby right now to take us to the coast. We'll move into the area after midnight to do some recon, but it should be reasonably straight forward."

"Well, good luck anyway," said Skinner. There was a far-away look in his eyes. He was now planning on how he could make best use of the informer. As far as he was concerned this operation was now history.

CHAPTER 19
Wolves

Patrick Kelly stood at his bedroom window, arms folded over one another, and looked out into the stygian night. He was dressed in a black turtle-neck sweater and black denim jeans. He had forsaken his leather cowboy boots in favour of rubber-soled trainers; they would have a better grip on the slippery rocks.

His bedside lamp cast an angelic glow over him like a golden mantle. He could see nothing in the window save for his reflection, but he knew that, out there in the darkness, the SAS teams would be preparing for their assault. He could sense their presence, almost expecting to hear them like wolves howling on the wind, and he wanted them to be able to identify him on sight.

His stomach began to churn ever so slightly, that old familiar feeling he got before a firefight coming back with the subtlety of a steamroller. He massaged his stomach with the flat of his hand, a futile attempt to soothe the knot building there.

They would come soon. He knew from his experiences in Vietnam that 3:00 a.m. was the optimum time for a night assault. It was the beginning of a period of time when the body's senses were at their lowest ebb; a point when you have to force the brain to override the natural desire to sleep.

He listened to the sounds of the house. All was quiet. The others were passed out in alcohol-induced slumbers, apart from the two Libyan women, of course, who did not drink. They and the sentries stationed around the island posed the biggest threat to his escape.

At first, Mulholland had decided that sentries were not necessary, but an inadvertent visit by a small fishing boat changed his mind. The wayward fishermen had been persuaded to move on, but it was a lesson learned; they had been caught with their guard down. Sentries had been summoned and posted around the small perimeter, the intent being to discourage any other would-be visitors.

Kelly opened his jacket and re-checked some

of the 'toys' he had built late the previous evening in preparation for his escape. He had learned a lot of dirty tricks in Vietnam, and was about to put some of them into practice. A fitting repayment, he thought, for terrorizing his grandmother and killing his friend Bill Mossley.

He had broached the subject of Toronto many times with Mulholland, but each time was firmly rebuffed, being told it was none of his business. He could not determine who had killed his friend, so he was going to exact revenge on them all.

Using a piece of cork he had taken from a wine-bottle, he scorched its bottom with a match, turning it black and sooty. After rubbing the end in long, narrow streaks on his cheeks and forehead, he smeared the black consistently over his face.

He checked the effect in the mirror, switched off the lamp, and paused for a moment to allow his eyes to adjust to the dark. In the narrow hallway, he stopped for a moment outside the room where Mulholland and Donnelly slept, planted his surprise, and then moved on to the women's room where he repeated the process. He regretted only having made two, so the visitors' room he let be, and moved back to the top of the stairs.

Slipping quietly down the stairs was difficult. The risers were old and dilapidated; they creaked and groaned like an old-age pensioner. He had practiced during the week, testing each stair for a place that could hold his weight without protesting. It was easy during the day, but not in blackness.

Three stairs from the bottom, he stepped on the wrong place and the stair squealed. To him, it sounded like a scream. His body tensed, preparing to run if anyone awoke. He held his breath, listening intently for any movement from upstairs. When the silence continued, he stepped carefully down the remaining treads, and then made his way towards the back room where the weapons were stored. He had purloined a few grenades earlier in the week, and wanted now to get his hands on a gun before the fighting started.

He slipped into the room, pulled the door closed, and switched on the light. There were enough AK47 assault rifles for a major assault, so he quickly removed as many firing pins as possible, stuffing them into his jacket pocket. It would have taken him too long to do them all. He would discard them later.

A box, sitting in one corner of the room, contained several pistols. There was a mixture of Ruger .357 magnums, a couple of ancient .38 revolvers, four or five 7.62-millimetre Makarov automatics, and two Czech 7.62-millimetre Skorpion machine-pistols. Another box was filled with sponge-like packing which housed the grenades, some of which he had already stolen. He selected one of the larger pistols, the Ruger, and a box of ammunition.

As he turned to leave, his eyes landed on a wooden crate which had gone unnoticed on his previous visit. Several strange symbols were stencilled on the crate's side. Curiosity got the better of him and he tried to pry off the top, but it was no use. His fingers could not exert sufficient leverage.

His eyes cast about the room for something to use as a lever, and fixed on the folding bayonet of one of the emasculated AK47's. He folded the bayonet down into the 'open' position and jammed it under the lid of the crate. One quick jerk and the lid squeaked open.

Immediately, a familiar odour assailed his nostrils. He tore away the packing material and had his suspicions confirmed: the crate was full of orange blocks of Semtex, a lethal Czech-made plastic explosive. He winced. There was enough explosive material in the box to destroy the house and a good part of the island.

Once more his eyes cast about the room looking for the pieces needed to create a demonic masterpiece. The Semtex was harmless unless paired with a detonator, and for obvious reasons the two were usually stored well apart. The search proved fruitless. There was no sign of the detonators. Probably in some other part of the house, he thought, shaking his head sadly. It was too bad. He switched off the light and crept like a cat through the kitchen to the back door. With a quick glance into the yard

to make sure no-one was about, he pulled the pin
out of a grenade and tossed it back into the living
room.

As the grenade left his hand, he pulled open the
back door and ran for cover of the boathouse, mentally counting off the six seconds. He leapt through
the half-open door, and had just reached six when
his face came into contact with the butt of a rifle,
and his world, like the back of the house, exploded.

The two, four-man SAS teams had landed several
hours before, under cover of darkness, quickly concealing themselves amongst the rocks and sparse
heather. Their first priority was to locate, and eliminate any perimeter guards before the attack commenced.

Using their night-vision binoculars and the
Starlite scopes on their rifles, they quickly identified the guards, a sorry bunch, sitting in pairs, chat-
ting loudly, and smoking cigarettes. The guards were
all armed with AK47's, magazines taped together
for extra firepower. Obviously, they were not expecting trouble.

The house was easily visible. They could clearly
see Patrick Kelly standing at the window, looking
out into the night. They recognized the fact he was
letting them know which room was his, what he
looked like, and how he was dressed, so they would
not fire on him. Their orders, however, were to the

contrary. Patrick Kelly was to become another statistic of terrorist violence.

Which was just what Kelly expected. He bore no ill feelings; Skinner was just another soldier doing his job. If their positions had been reversed, he would probably have done the same.

As 3:00 a.m. approached, the SAS men split up into pairs, gliding from their positions at Waters's signal, and creeping stealthily up on the hapless sentries. A few barely audible gurgles marked their passing as burly forearms clamped across windpipes and razor-sharp commando knives slid between ribs.

One moment the sentries were talking about soccer, or work, or fishing; the next they were dead. The SAS men then took up their positions beside the house. The light in Patrick Kelly's room had gone out. The island was quiet.

Trooper Colin Bowes and Sergeant Steven Lloyd crept up to the boathouse where the chopper was being stored. Their task was to remove the device that would immobilize the chopper, a unit located under the side panel. Lloyd pulled his finger across his throat to indicate he would take out the lone sentry beside the door of the boathouse, whose rifle rested against the side of the shed.

Suddenly, a piece of wood snapped under his foot. The sentry grabbed his rifle and spun around, his finger searching for the trigger. Lloyd cursed silently, kicked the sentry in the balls to silence him, then lunged forward and upwards with his knife. The sentry saw only a blur of movement, tried to back away, but was too slow. Lloyd caught him under the chin, slamming the knife up into his brain.

The sentry's eyes bulged and rolled up into his head until the whites showed. A bloody froth formed on his lips. Lloyd forced the knife deeper, and then twisted the blade. The sentry's body went limp and he pitched forward, dead, into Lloyd's arms.

In that instant Louise Kennan's wish came true. Her husband Brendan died as he had lived - violently.

A quick glance at his watch showed John Waters it was a few seconds to three o'clock. He pulled the velcro cover back over the face of his watch to protect it in case he slipped on the rocks.

Gripping his Heckler and Koch MP5 in black-gloved hands, he touched the transmitter switch on his wrist. He was about to speak, when he saw a black-clad form dash out of the back door of the house, and run directly towards the boathouse. Just as the figure passed through the door, the inside of the house exploded, blowing the front door into the yard. Downstairs windows erupted outwards, throwing glass shards like daggers in every direction.

Waters gave a terse command: "Hold your fire, hold your fire. Take them as they come out of the house. The bang was not ours."

Inside the house there was pandemonium. The deafening roar of the explosion rudely awakened everyone. The two Libyan terrorists were out of bed, and had their weapons cocked and the bedroom window smashed in seconds. Donnelly grabbed his pistol and dived to the floor.

"What the fuck's going on?" asked Mulholland, squirming around on the floor in his sweat-stained vest trying to get into his trousers.

"I think we've got company," replied Donnelly, crawling over and crouching beside the bedroom window. He moved the blinds aside a fraction and peered into the black night. "It's too dark out there to see anything. I'm going downstairs to check the damage. If it was the fuckin' sass, they'd be stomping all over us by now. Maybe one of the grenades went off by accident. Or maybe the Yank topped himself."

He opened the bedroom door and peered down the corridor. Already, heavy smoke was rising up the stairs into the narrow hallway, forming a cloud across the ceiling. Seeing there was no sign of movement, he started to run towards the stairs, but something snagged his ankle. He saw a loop of fishing line caught around his leg. The tug which he felt had just pulled a primed phosphorous grenade out of an empty soup can.

Kelly had removed the firing pin and jammed the grenade into the can to hold the lever in the 'safe' position. When Donnelly pulled the grenade out of the can, he automatically primed the grenade's three-second fuse.

Donnelly was frantically trying to release the line when the grenade exploded beneath him, spreading flaming chunks of his flesh along the hallway. The force of the blast created a gaping hole in the floor, and the phosphorous set fire to the wallpaper.

The visitors, although dazed by the explosions, could smell smoke and decided their best bet would be to get downstairs to where the guns were stored. They hadn't thought to bring their weapons up to bed. Alec Magee, the veteran of the three, volunteered to go first.

The hallway was filled with fumes, and flames licked hungrily at the ceiling. The smoke stung Magee's eyes, making them water as he moved towards the stairs. In his haste and with the reduced visibility, he slipped on a piece of Josie Donnelly's intestines and fell through the hole in the floor.

Fortunately for him, and much to his surprise, he landed on his feet and ran into the back room to find a weapon. He picked up the first rifle he saw, a Kalashnikov AK47, and several extra magazines of ammunition. Braving the flames, he ran back into the living room, smashed the remaining pieces of glass out of one of the windows, and called for the others to come down. They were warned to be "careful of the fuckin' great hole in the floor."

Outside, Waters's earpiece buzzed as he received the same call from each of the teams. "What's going on in there, Boss?"

"I haven't a clue," he replied to all of them. "Somebody ran out the back door a few minutes ago, over towards the shed. I expect that Bowsie will have taken him out. Are you there, Bowsie?"

"Yes, Boss. It was the Yank. He's out cold over in the corner. I think he's the one who started the fireworks."

Waters replied. "Well, he's raised the alarm, that's for sure. We don't know exactly how many are in the house - four maybe - or if the explosion took out any of them. The second explosion has started a fire on the top floor. It won't take long to spread. If there is anyone left, the fire will force them out into the open pretty soon. They will probably come out firing, so keep your heads down. If they try to make it to the boats, they're in for a nasty surprise."

His earpiece crackled again. "Boss, this is Ter. Someone just knocked out what's left of one of the living-room windows, and I can see the barrel of a gun."

"Okay, Ter," he replied. "Take them out whenever you can get a clear shot."

Mulholland crawled away from the bedroom window and peered out into the corridor, which was now a mass of flames. He could hear Alec Magee downstairs, yelling for them to come down. There was no sign of the sentries outside. That left himself, the two Libyans, and the three visitors, all seasoned terrorists. There was no shortage of arms, so they could probably fight their way off the island. At the rate the fire was progressing, however, they would soon be forced out of the house anyway.

He looked down the hall and saw that the Libyans' door was still closed. The flames, however, were starting to blister the paint on their door. At the bottom of the door, just about ankle height, he could see the noose of fishing line in the glow from the fire. The line lead to an empty tin, into which was jammed a grenade. So that's what happened to Josie, he thought. It was the Yank. The bastard sold us out.

He crawled down the corridor on his hands and knees to the booby-trap. When he had set aside the grenade, he reached up and opened the door. He immediately found himself looking down the barrels of two UZI's, a sight which made his flesh crawl.

He coughed, putting his hand to his nose to block the fumes. "We better get out of here. This place is going to go up like a tinderbox." He held up the booby-trap for them to see and then crawled off towards the stairs. The smell of roasting flesh made him retch violently as he passed Donnelly's charred, smoking remains.

The visitors were already downstairs, armed and positioned at different windows. "See anything?" he asked.

"Not a bloody thing," came the reply. "The buggers are well covered. They're waiting for us to come out into the open. They want to shoot us like rats in a barrel."

"Don't worry," replied Mulholland. "I've got a surprise for them." He pulled the old sofa to one side. Underneath, a trapdoor had been set into the floor. "It leads down to that little cove beside the jetty. It was used for smuggling in the old days, but we still use it now and again," he offered. "We," he continued, indicating himself and the two Libyans, "will go down the tunnel and come around behind whoever is out there. When you hear us firing, you come out from the front and hopefully we'll catch them in the crossfire."

Alec Magee did not agree with Mulholland's plan and stated as much. "Not a fuckin' chance, boyo, I'm no fuckin' hero. We've no idea how many of them are out there or what they are armed with. All I know is there used to be sentries, and now they're probably dead. It's probably the bastard SAS, so I don't feel like charging out the door straight at them. Into the valley of death and all that shite is not for me. Why don't we all go down the tunnel and come around behind them. That way there will be less chance of any of us getting shot."

He had mentioned the magic word, SAS. The mystique surrounding them and their methods had elevated them to the status of 'supermen' in the eyes of the terrorists. Hence the reluctance to confront a team of SAS commandos. The others readily agreed, and so all six climbed down into the tunnel.

Mulholland took a small flashlight from his pocket, put his fingers over the lens and switched it on. By blocking the beam, there was just sufficient light to illuminate the underground pathway. Even still, the rocks were slippery which made the going treacherous. The tunnel extended eighty yards to the cove, but in the near-darkness it seemed forever before they could hear the gentle sound of waves.

Waters waited, as did the others, as more and more of the house was consumed by the flames. The light from the flames played havoc with their night-sights, rendering them virtually unusable. There was no longer any movement on the bottom floor, but no-one had escaped from the house, front or back. There must be another way out, he thought. Maybe there's a tunnel. As if in answer, a firefight broke out on the other side of the house where Trooper 'Chalkie' White and Trooper Brian Walker were positioned.

Suddenly, his earpiece crackled into life, and he could hear the anguish in Chalkie's voice. "Watch your backs, watch your backs. They've gotten around behind us. Bri has taken a couple in the leg and we're pinned down. Sounds like UZI's."

Terence Strong and Sergeant Alan Sykes, both veterans of the Falklands, heard Chalkie's message and immediately turned to scan the rocks and crevices behind them. As they did so, two men, armed with automatic rifles stood up in the heather, just a few feet away. Strong recognized Alec Magee and Michael Sullivan immediately as their mugshots were posted prominently on the walls of the barracks.

"Fuck you, Brits," spat Magee, as he and Sullivan squeezed the triggers of their AK47's which had both been set to automatic fire.

The two SAS men were caught. They knew their time had come. They had cheated death on that remote Falklands battleground, on more than one occasion, but the reaper had followed them. They were not going to 'beat the clock', SAS jargon for staying alive.

However, all they heard were resounding clicks. The weapons, which had been emasculated by Patrick Kelly, failed to fire. The moment of triumph faded, and the vicious snarls were replaced by panic as they threw away the useless rifles and ran. The reaper was not to be cheated a second time. Strong and Sykes cut them to pieces with well-placed bursts of fire.

Strong spoke into his walkie-talkie. "Strong here, Boss. Two terrorists are down and out. Am moving to cover Chalkie."

Mulholland and Sheila Morrow had paired up and circled around the perimeter of the island to come up behind the boathouse. Along the way they had stumbled over the bodies of two of the guards, lying in the heather as if in a peaceful slumber. The dark stains on their throats told the tale of their demise.

As they approached the house, now a blazing inferno, they could see the silhouettes of two soldiers staring intently at the back door.

"These two are mine," whispered Morrow, and crawled forward towards the unsuspecting soldiers. She had smeared her face with a piece of coal given to her by Mulholland. Now only the whites of her eyes showed, narrow slits against the black. Inside the house, some of the ammunition had been ignited by the heat and began to explode, bullets flying randomly in all directions.

The two soldiers ducked involuntarily at the sound of the shots, the noise muffling the sound of

Sheila Morrow's approach. As she crawled to within a few feet of them, firing broke out to her left, near the front of the house. She was so close to the two men that she could hear the frantic message from Chalkie White.

Seizing the opportunity, she did not give them time to react. She sprang forward, swinging the assault rifle in a narrow arc, intending to shred the two soldiers. As she pulled the trigger, nothing happened. She looked down in amazement, a fraction of a second before she was slammed back by the bullets pounding into her body.

Both men had heard a sound behind them, and rolled and fired simultaneously, catching her in a murderous crossfire. The impact of the bullets, directed up at her from their prone positions, lifted her off the ground and tossed her lifeless body, like a rag doll, into a clump of heather.

Mulholland, having witnessed some of the contact, decided that discretion was the better part of valour, and retraced his steps to the cove, leaving the others to fend for themselves. He found the rocky shelf he was looking for, stripped off his shoes and eased himself into the sea. He gave an involuntary gasp at the shock of the cold water, and then he started swimming towards the mainland.

Bowes covered the fallen figure while Lloyd picked up the rifle.

"Bloody firing pin's missing," he said. "Lucky for us and all. He had us dead to rights."

"She," corrected Bowes. "It's a she. Can't tell who it is under all that muck, though. We better get over and give Chalkie a hand." He pressed the transmitter switch on his wrist. "Bowes here, Boss. Got a dead one over here. Moving to cover Chalkie. Over."

Kelly came to with the pain of a thousand hangovers pounding in his skull. He touched his forehead gingerly, but it was only bruised; the skin was not broken. He could hear an intense firefight in progress, somewhere across the yard on the other side of the house. He checked his pockets.

Among the things he had found in the weapons room was a cache of money in unmarked bills, and he had stuffed as much would fit into his jacket pockets.

The soldier who had knocked him out was nowhere to be seen, so Kelly slipped quietly away and made for the sea. There was no path to follow, and he had only gone a few yards when he stumbled over a body. From its awkward position, he could tell the person was dead; he had seen enough dead bodies in Vietnam to tell the difference. When he rolled it over, he could see it was the woman he had helped into the chopper, her body almost torn in half by the bullets.

He set off again, this time more carefully. This would be a bad time to twist an ankle, he thought. After a short distance he came to the rocky shelf where he stepped out of his shoes, and tied the laces around his belt. Then, after taking a deep breath to prepare himself for the shock of the icy water, he plunged in and began swimming to the far shore.

John Waters and Trooper Brian 'Spud' Murphy circled around to where the two machine guns were pinning down Chalkie White and Brian Walker. The fire was selective and accurate, not at all what they were accustomed to from Irish terrorists. These two know what they are about, thought Waters. It must be the two Libyan women.

Putting his night glasses to his eyes, he focused on the rocks from where the gunfire was originating. Suddenly, a face popped into view, fired a short burst and then disappeared. As he watched, a second head appeared to the right of the first and another burst of fire was sent in Chalkie's direction.

He passed the glasses to Spud Murphy, indicated where to look and then began to circle around behind the women's position. When he arrived at his vantage point, a clump of rocks about twenty feet away from their position, he signalled to Spud to begin drawing their fire.

Murphy immediately complied and began to fire short, staccato bursts into the terrorists' position.

As the women moved to counter this new threat, they left themselves exposed. Waters stepped out of his cover and felled them with two short, well-aimed bursts of fire.

A hush fell over the island, interrupted by the crackling of timbers from the house as they were consumed by the fire. Waters covered the two bodies with his gun, and Spud Murphy approached and fired again into the prone figures. He then walked over kicked away their machine guns.

"You were right, Boss," he said, shining a penlight on the two faces. "It is the Libyans."

"We'll find out later who they are," said Waters. "For now, put in a call to the Quick Reaction Force. We'd better hang around until they arrive as well. Have the others meet us at the chopper. I want to have a word with this Yank."

The SAS teams gathered at the boathouse, where 'Spud' Murphy was applying field dressings to Walker's leg. Neither of the bullets had hit a major artery, leaving only angry-looking entrance and exit wounds. Walker was in good spirits, despite the pain. Murphy slammed a syrette of morphine into his thigh when he finished dressing the wounds.

Bowes was the first back to the shed and had discovered that Kelly was gone. He was more than a little embarrassed by the incident. He said, "I thought I hit him hard enough to put him out for a few hours. He must have a bloody hard head."

"He's probably off the island by now," replied Waters, shaking his head as he envisioned the major's reaction to the news. Colin Bowes interrupted his thought.

"A strange thing happened, boss. One of the terrorists had us dead to rights and her gun wouldn't fire. We checked - we thought the fuckin' thing had jammed - you know what these AK's are like, especially if you don't keep 'em clean. Anyway, the firing pin had been removed. From the expression on her face, she was just as surprised as we were."

"That happened to us as well," exclaimed Strong. "Exactly the same scenario for us; both AK's had their firing pins removed. We wouldn't be here if those guns had fired. Do you think the Yank might have had something to do with it, boss?"

"I think he had everything to do with it," replied Waters. "The first explosion inside the house was a grenade going off. I think the next explosion, on the second floor, was a booby-trap for the terrorists. He may have suspected what the major had planned for him, and was hot-footing it off the island when he ran into limp-wristed Colin, here."

Some of the men went to the jetty to remove the explosive charges they had planted in the rowing boats. Waters sat beside the chopper to await the arrival of the QRF and the major. In his lap sat the immobilization device. Absent-mindedly, he

picked up a piece of paper lying on the ground beside him. Underneath it lay a well-thumbed, road
map of Ireland. I wonder what the terrorists were
doing with a road map, he mused, and began to
unfold the pages.

CHAPTER 20
Legend

According to Irish legend, a tiny piece of heaven fell to earth one day and was called Connemara. From where he stood, in a tiny cemetery on the hill overlooking the valley, Patrick Kelly could easily understand the sentiment.

The sides of the valley, resplendent in their patchworks of green fields, reached down to the coast where they embraced the cold waters of the Atlantic. Strong breezes blew in from the dark sea creating whitecaps, like feathers, on the tops of the waves.

With the sea air stinging his cheeks, he inhaled

deeply to fill his lungs with the cleansing balm, enchanted by the serenity of the place. It was a far cry from the violence on which he had turned his back, only a few hours drive away.

He had been in the Connemara area for three days, staying in a tiny hotel which catered almost exclusively to American tourists - mostly older Americans who had come to trace their ancestry. "Blue rinsers" was a standing joke with the villagers, because the majority of the ladies had their hair dyed blue, hence the unflattering sobriquet.

On his first day, a clerk in the hotel had pointed him in the direction of the parish priest, Father Michael, as he was commonly known. The priest, he learned, had been born and raised in the area and now lived in a small, thatched cottage on the outskirts of the town. It was easy to locate: there was only one road into the town and one road out.

According to the clerk, the priest was accustomed to having American tourists call on him, asking to peruse the Parish records. They were searching for their 'roots' and were always made welcome, especially so if they donated a 'little something' for the church.

Kelly opened the wrought-iron gate, strode up the gravelled pathway, and pulled on the antiquated brass door-knocker. The brass shone brightly. He heard footsteps down the hallway, then the heavy wooden door creaked open about six inches and jammed. Kelly smiled; obviously the wooden door expanded in damp weather. A flurry of what Kelly thought were Irish curses followed as the priest tugged on the door. Suddenly, and with a loud creak, it sprung open, almost throwing the priest off his feet.

The priest was old, white haired and weather-beaten, the skin on his face looking like well-worn leather. His hair was thinning, receding to form a widow's peak on his forehead, but despite his obvious age the priest's eyes were clear and sparkling, full of warmth and humour.

When he recovered his balance and saw Kelly, a strange look came over his face like a cloud crossing the sun on a summer's day. His eyes widened as if in fright, and an involuntary shiver ran down his spine. It took him a few moments to regain his composure.

"I'm sorry," he offered, putting a hand to his chest and ushering Kelly into his cottage. "You gave me quite a start there, young fellow." His heavy brogue was almost identical to that of Kelly's grandmother. When Patrick teased her about having such a strong accent after all the years in America, she would simply say "you can take the man out of Ireland, but you will never take Ireland out of the man."

He lead Kelly down a narrow hallway into his sitting room where a peat fire burned in the grate. There were three chairs in the room, all in an arc around the hearth. Several small brass ornaments sat atop a mantle beside an antique carriage clock. A bookcase carried many old and new titles.

On a wall hung a painting of Christ with a small red light on its side; this was identical to the one in his grandmother's house, which she referred to as her 'holy' picture. A tall ashtray with a pipe resting in a holder sat beside the chair nearest the fire. On the other side of the chair was a tiny table on which rested a well-worn Bible. The priest eased himself into the chair, crossed his legs, and motioned for Kelly to take one of the others.

He stared into Kelly's face and said, "I'm sorry about that fuss at the front. I thought I'd seen a ghost when I opened the door. An old friend of mine ..." he started.

Kelly interrupted him. "Sean Kelly was killed by the Black and Tans many years ago - 1922 to be exact."

The old man's mouth opened in surprise. "How did you know?"

"My name's Patrick Kelly. Sean Kelly was my grandfather."

"May the Saints preserve us," exclaimed the priest. "And aren't you the image of Sean. I knew my old eyes weren't deceiving me. Tell me, is your grandmother still alive? She suffered so much at the hands of those bastards."

"She always says it's hard to kill a bad thing.

She certainly was well when I left her and that was only a few days ago. I promised myself I would visit my grandfather's grave before I went back to the States. That's why I'm here."

"Well come then, lad," said the priest, propelling himself out of the chair in a manner belying his age. "I'll take you there myself. It's not far from here, only a few minutes walk."

The grave was in one corner of the cemetery, beneath the protective cover of a weeping willow. The priest went directly to the grave, as if it were a familiar place. It was well kept, the grass around it neatly trimmed, and the headstone gleaming like new, without a trace of mould. A simple inscription adorned the greenish marble.

SEAN PATRICK KELLY
JANUARY 16, 1900 - JUNE 17, 1922
MAY HIS SOUL REST IN PEACE

"Who takes care of the grave, Father?" asked Kelly. "It seems to be in better condition than most of the others."

"Why I do," replied the priest. "My name's Michael Kelly. Sean was my brother. Did your grandmother not tell you about me? The very last time I saw her she was standing here, promising that the British would pay dearly for their sins. She turned her back on all of us, and we heard not a word of what happened to her.

"And here you are Patrick, standing in that very spot, and the British army demoralized by those helicopter attacks. Tell me it's a coincidence."

Kelly did not answer the question. Instead he said, "Father, she rarely talked about you and Sean, but I know the stories off by heart. She loved that man so much, and to have him taken away from her in such a horrible fashion hurt her more than we will ever know. His name was given to my father, who was born a few months after she landed in New York." The priest looked up from the headstone in surprise.

Kelly continued. "Yes. She had just told Sean, and they were making plans to emigrate to New York the night the Tans came and strung him up in front of her. She was actually packing her case when the knock came to the door.

"She would never let anyone get close to her again. And then my father and mother were killed in a car crash when I was seven. She took me in and raised me after that and so I owe her a great deal. As for the business in the North ..." He paused, searching for a suitable explanation. "Well, let's just say that my grandmother's words were a prophesy which came true."

The priest gave him a curious look and then changed the subject. He nodded down at the grave.

"It's the nicest spot in the place," he said. "It was the least I could do for him.

"Tell me Patrick, what are your plans? Are you going to be around here for long?"

"No Father, I'm going back to the States in a few days. Is there anything you'd like me to tell my grandmother? I can take a letter, if you like."

The old priest's eyes lit up. "A letter, now there's a thought. I'll sit down and write one tonight. A lot of water has passed under the bridge. Thank you, Patrick. I'll away now and leave you with your grandfather."

"Slain, Father," said Kelly, remembering his grandmother's last farewell, and then sat down beside the headstone.

He visited the grave every morning, bringing a new bunch of flowers each time. The assistant in the shop commented that he must have found a 'special lass'.

His time was his own, and he was quite content to go for long walks in the afternoon. On occasion he would drop by the cottage and have a cup of tea with Father Michael. The letter was getting longer and longer, and Kelly joked that he was going to have to buy a new suitcase just to carry it.

At a small pub down by the harbour wall, he would sit outside each evening, Guinness in hand, to watch the sun go down. The barman, a robust, white-haired ex-sailor knew how to entertain the tourists, and each evening would burst into a rendering of 'Galway Bay', just as the sun began to sink below the horizon. Kelly joined in with him.

It was a song Kelly knew well; his grandmother would rock him to sleep humming the melody. When he was old enough, she had taught him the words, then together, he and his grandmother would sing to his mother and father, their voices drifting out the open windows. By the end of the song practically the entire neighbourhood was singing along with them.

"Enough to bring tears to yer eyes, eh Patrick?" he would say, and then jam his pipe into the corner of his mouth, his eyes twinkling as the tourists lined up at the bar for another drink.

At the end of the third evening, the barman stopped singing and let Kelly continue on his own. His voice rang out clear and true, his eyes closed as he remembered the days of his youth. The barroom burst into spontaneous applause when he finished. He was embarrassed by it all, as he had not realized he was doing a solo. The barman added to his discomfort by demanding another song, holding up a fresh pint of Guinness as a reward. Kelly shook his head, despite the cheers from the crowd, and went outside to enjoy the sunset.

He was starting to feel restless, wanting to get back to New York, back to his stomping grounds. The money he had received in payment for the mission, plus the extra he had taken was sufficient to see him comfortable for a few years. If he was careful.

The main problem was that, for the British, he was the proverbial 'loose end'. They could not afford to let him go free. The potential embarrassment to British and American governments was too great for them to let him live. Especially at a time when covert operations by both governments were being so openly condemned by the public at large.

In a few days, he would to travel to Shannon airport and book a flight home. For the present, he was content.

It was a cold morning, dull and overcast, with the threat of rain heavy in the air. Kelly had just arrived at the cemetery, flowers in hand, when a noise behind him broke the silence. He was not concerned, thinking it might be Father Michael.

"Patrick Kelly." The voice was cold, hard, and full of menace. The man, in his late twenties with tousled brown hair and dark, unforgiving eyes, had one hand in the pocket of his leather jacket. The front jutted out in Kelly's direction. The man either had very stubby fingers or was concealing a weapon; Kelly assumed the latter. His eyes never wavered from Kelly's face as he moved cautiously over the uneven ground towards the grave.

"What if I am?" asked Kelly, knowing full well

this was the man who had been sent to tie up the 'loose end'. "What's it to you?"

"The Major sent me to find you," he said. He certainly didn't mince any words, Kelly thought.

"I thought this is where you'd be. I found your road map in the boathouse, and the area around Connemara was covered in pencil marks. So I took some leave and came down here.

"The major wants you dead, but I want a few words first. That's why I volunteered to come after you. I admire what you did on the island; you probably ... in fact you did save the lives of some of my men, even my own perhaps. I find that rather incongruous. Any of the mercenaries whom I have come across, fall into the category of 'merciless bastards'. You don't strike me as one of those."

"You're standing beside the reason for all of this," replied Kelly, pointing down at the grave. "My grandfather, Sean Kelly, was murdered by the Black and Tans back in 1922. When I say murdered, I mean they held a kangaroo court, sentenced him to death, and then hanged him in front of my grandmother. Afterwards they burned him, the barn, and all the livestock. She has carried the memory of that night and that hatred with her for all these years. I have heard her cry out his name in her sleep, or wake in floods of tears ever since I was old enough to understand.

"The only thing which kept her going this long

was the desire to avenge her husband's death. I may have helped exorcise some of the demons that haunt her nights."

"So killing those young soldiers will compensate for your grandfather's death, will it?" the man asked, his voice dripping with sarcasm.

"My grandfather was young too, and proud to fight for his country. That was not a fitting death for a soldier," replied Kelly quietly. "One day I'll answer for what I have done, but it won't be today."

"You seem very sure of yourself," said the man, a puzzled look on his face.

"I am," replied Kelly, brushing back an errant strand of hair. "Before you do anything rash, you had better read this." He put a hand slowly inside a pocket of his jacket and, with exaggerated slowness, pulled out a single, folded sheet of paper. He extended the paper to the man who caught one corner, flicked it open, and began to read the contents. His eyes alternated between the sheet and Kelly.

A smile crossed his face. "Blackmail. I presume this has been mailed to certain friends who will pass it on to the appropriate media if ... By the way, I like your description of the major."

"You presume correctly."

"Somehow I imagined you would arrange something devious like this," said the man. "I think this lets you off the hook as far as the major is concerned. I'll need to show this to him."

"Fine by me," replied Kelly, breathing a little easier, and turned to leave.

"Well it doesn't let you off my fuckin' hook," came a voice from behind the two men. Kelly shivered. He knew the voice. Tommy Mulholland was standing behind a large, moss-covered tombstone, a wild look in his eyes. In his hand, a Walther PPK automatic pointed directly at them.

"Take your hands out of your fuckin' jacket," he ordered, and the man dropped the sheet of paper and pulled his other hand out of his jacket.

Mulholland hissed at Kelly: "I thought I'd find you here, you fuckin' British tout; all those questions about Connemara and your grandfather. You didn't expect to see me again, that's plain. The Brit here is a bonus for me. SAS, I presume?" Flecks of spittle darted from his mouth.

The man did not respond.

"A wee bit out of your way, aren't you boyo?" Mulholland chuckled. "I can just see the papers now. British soldier kills American tourist on Irish soil. They'll have a field day with that one."

Waters was remembering the words of the Psych instructor in Hereford: 'Fear is a weapon. Your body and mind will react to that fear and can help you deal with the cause. Terror, on the other hand, is uncontrollable fear. If it takes over then you might as well shoot yourself.' His mind worked feverishly, creating moves to disable Mulholland, and rejecting them in the same heartbeat. There was no simple way. Mulholland had approached but was standing just out of reach. He could squeeze the trigger several times before Waters could reach him.

Kelly or himself were going to die if any overt action were made. He hoped that Mulholland would shoot Kelly first, and that way he would have a fraction of a second to act. It might just be enough time to get the gun out of his pocket.

If not ... He found himself wondering if they would put his name on the clock at Stirling Lines barracks, along with the names of all the others who had fallen in action. It was not the most glorious of circumstances.

Mulholland was still ranting on. "You sold us out, Yank, sold us out to the fuckin' Brits. How much did they pay you? It doesn't matter anyway, because you'll never get a chance to spend it."

Kelly saw the wild look in Mulholland's eyes disappear, to be replaced with something dark and evil.

It was killing time.

The pistol was aimed somewhere between them, giving the impression Mulholland couldn't decide which man to kill first. As it wavered, Kelly made his move, pushing Waters to one side and then diving the other way. There was no cover for him, however.

Mulholland's aim pointed towards Waters but then swung back to Kelly. He pulled the trigger at the same instant as Kelly's arm completed its arc.

Waters, now hidden behind a tombstone with his pistol cocked, heard the unmistakable thunk of a bullet hitting flesh. Then he heard a gurgle. He rolled out from behind the tombstone, targeting on Mulholland's head, but then eased back on the trigger. There was no point in firing.

A knife was buried in Mulholland's throat. A trickle of blood ran down his neck and into the collar of his shirt. Mulholland remained upright for a moment, an astonished look on his face, and then the pistol fell from his hand, and his arms moved in slow motion up to his throat. One hand touched the handle of the knife as the light vanished from his eyes. He pitched forward across Sean Kelly's grave.

Waters ran to where Kelly lay face down on the ground. He turned him over and was surprised when he saw, not a dead or dying man, but the grimace on Kelly's face. The bullet had struck him across the shoulder, ploughing a deep furrow which was now awash with blood - painful but not fatal.

Waters inspected the wound carefully, wadded a piece of Kelly's shirt, and pressed it against the torn flesh. "You'll live. If you can walk, I'll take you to the hotel and dress this properly. I don't expect you'll need or want to go to a hospital. A couple of days rest and you'll be ready to move on. Back to the States, I hope.

"By the way, my name's John Waters. And you, Kelly, have saved my life, again.

"No problem," replied Kelly, through clenched teeth. "I have just one favour to ask."

"Ask away."

"Get that bastard off my grandfather's grave!"

CHAPTER 21

Storm

Dark clouds filled the horizon, the scent of rain hung heavy in the air, and distant rumbling heralded the imminent arrival of yet another Atlantic storm. A chill wind was chasing away the last vestiges of sunlight and forcing the men to bury their hands deep in their pockets.

Patrick Kelly and the old priest stood at the side of the new grave. It was almost a year since Kelly had stood in that same spot and looked death straight in the face. Yet it was Mulholland who went to join the grim reaper.

A new headstone, made from the greenish-white

Connemara marble for which the area was famous, was intricately engraved with the names of Sean and Mary Kelly.

The priest dabbed at his eyes with a handkerchief. "It was a fine thing you did, Patrick. They will rest together through eternity."

Kelly smiled. "It seemed that all that kept her going was the thirst for revenge. When that thirst was sated, there was no reason to carry on living. She walked the earth for a few months, but the spark was gone. Perhaps she realised the futility of it all, and finally understood that Ireland would never be united again. All the attacks accomplished was to harden the resolve of the British government. The number of applications to join the army even went up."

"There will be no end to it that I can see," replied the priest, staring out towards the sea. "Not in my lifetime, not in yours either. The British are too firmly entrenched in the ways and the culture of the North to leave now. Besides, if a United Ireland was declared, Protestant extremists would doing exactly what the Provos are doing now. Except they wouldn't be confined to the North any more. Anywhere in Ireland would be a target for them.

"As you have seen in our little corner of the world, this country's economy depends heavily on tourism. If the violence reached down into the

South, the entire country would suffer. Two car bombs went off in Dublin, in 1975. They were supposedly planted by Protestant extremists, but regardless of who left them, the effect was devastating to the economy. God only knows how many people cancelled trips to Ireland in the wake of that disaster.

"It's a shame both sides in this bloody conflict can't sit down and work something out. This country has so much to offer the rest of the world, yet those outside cannot see past the headlines or the pictures in newspapers. They think that all of Ireland is immersed in violence, yet it's only those bastards in the North who are fanning the flames. Decent people speak out but they get shot, or their homes get burned.

"No, Patrick, not in my lifetime."

The old priest shook his head sadly and turned away, making his way slowly across the cemetery, as if he carried the weight of the world.

The horizon was now almost obscured by the sheets of rain blowing in towards land. His heart heavy, Kelly scanned the green fields and the rocky coastline, then returned to the grave for the last time. He knew he would never return.

"Slan libh," he whispered, and the words were carried off on the wind.

John Waters must confront his own mortality when his friend is killed during an operation in Colombia, especially when the man responsible is a former member of his regiment turned mercenary...

TEARS
for a
FRIEND

BY

ROY FRENCH

A Shady Vale book on sale in November 1996

CHAPTER 1

Stoner

"I hate the fucking jungle," muttered Stoner, brushing aside a huge fan-shaped leaf, swarming with tiny red ants. Heat and humidity, combined with the rarefied air at over a mile above sea level, sat on him like the lead weights used to handicap a jockey.

He moved slowly, noiselessly, like a jungle predator, straining to make eye contact with the others. The last golden strands of sunlight were fading into darkness, and around him, creatures of the night were beginning to stir, filling him with a sense of unease. He unpacked his night-vision goggles and slipped them on over his head, securing the rubber eye-patches over his face. Instantly the jungle was transformed into a greenish-tinted tableau, and he could clearly see the others. They had all donned their glasses as well - the jungle was no place to get lost, especially at night.

There were eight men in the group - six Colombians and an ex-Israeli special forces expert named Nathan - the other paid mercenary like himself. This, their first mission together, was the culmination of many weeks of intense training in the mountains of Columbia, and in and around the hacienda of Doctor Pablo Cortez.

The word hacienda hardly did the place justice, given the white-washed, adobe buildings spread out over almost half an acre, and that the seven-car garage was hardly noticeable beside the main house. The walled compound was square in shape, the jungle having been burned away and replanted with lush green grass. In the centre sat the hacienda, the red, barrel-tiled roof visible for several miles in each direction. Stoner thought Buckingham palace would be a fair comparison, in terms of opulence and security.

The place sported the most up-to-date surveillance equipment money could buy: infra-red cameras, which turned night into day; motion detectors buried in the ground at strategic points over the gardens, and lasers mounted on the tops of the walls, whose beams, if broken, would set off six, ear-shattering sirens. The only problem the doctor faced was finding qualified personnel to maintain and understand the exotic hardware.

Cortez, one of the most feared of all the drug barons of Columbia, constantly sought to expand his empire even though he had more cash than he would ever need. For him, it had gone beyond mere monetary gain. He was into power; buying government officials, judges, policemen, military leaders, and the local population. He was hooked, no better off than the unfortunates on the streets of America; the ultimate destination of the white powder he sold. And what he couldn't buy, he took. Stoner and the Israeli were well paid for their skills, with handsome bonuses forthcoming for especially spectacular attacks.

The two mercenaries lived on the hacienda's grounds in a neat, white-walled bungalow. Other guards resided on the grounds as well, but they were not as fortunate in terms of living conditions, having to bunk together in a long, narrow guardhouse near the back entrance.

Outside the walls of the compound, in small, brick houses, lived the peasants who worked the cocoa fields. To them, Cortez was a saint. He had built the houses, a tiny school, and a chapel for them. They cared little for what happened to the white powder once it left their hands. All they knew was that Senor Cortez had lifted them out of abject poverty, provided for their families, and gave their children a chance at an education. They would willingly lay down their lives for him, and in the occasional skirmishes between the drug lords, many of them had already done just that.

Sweat ran down Stoner's soot-blackened face in tiny, irritating rivulets, soaking into his camouflage fatigues and making them cling uncomfortably to his body. He stood a little over six-feet, with a solid, muscular frame, his skin well-tanned from the past months in Columbia. The strain of exercising in the jungle, however, plus the mediocre food caused him to lose a few pounds - not a major problem as yet, but if it continued he would be operating at less than one hundred percent and that, to him, was not acceptable. Dr Cortez paid for, and expected the best money could buy.

Stoner, christened Brian Martin Stoneman, after his father, Martin, was raised in a little town called Cullercoats, a few miles south of Newcastle, in England. His father had worked on the docks all his life, his face and hands scarred from years of dock-fights and bar-fights, and he wanted his son to follow in his footsteps. Young Stoneman however, had other ideas. As soon as he hit sixteen, he left school, much to his father's delight, then immediately joined the army. That did not sit at all well with his father. Some of the biggest thrashings of his father's life came at the hands of squaddies, and were not easily forgotten.

For six years Stoner trained, sweated, and studied, eventually winning his much sought-after Sergeant's stripes. All to give him a chance at the entrance examination for the Special Air Service, the British Army's elite commando unit. He considered himself to be in good shape, but a gruelling forty-mile hike across the wind-swept Brecon Beacons in Wales, dressed in full kit and carrying a twenty-pound rifle was like nothing he had ever faced before. It was doubly tough and disheartening when, on reaching the finish line, the examiner told him the truck which was to carry him back to camp had broken down. He was given the choice - wait for a replacement, which was going to take several hours - or go back the way he came.

Stoneman stoically accepted the breakdown, turned on his heel and set off back down the road. Five miles further on, the truck picked him up. Somehow 'it just started up again'. He was glad, for he did not fancy making the return journey at night, especially in such a desolate place. Several men had perished on the Beacons during such exercises, and he did not wish to be counted among their numbers. The examiner smiled when he saw the look of surprise on Stoneman's face; it was his responsibility to test the resolve of some of the candidates. He did this by applying the 'sickener factor', as he had done by hinting to Stoneman to return to camp the hard way. If Stoneman, as many others did, decided to wait on a replacement truck, when he got back to camp he would have been told, 'Sorry chum, not this time', and sent back to his unit.

It was during the psychological testing that some surprising traits surfaced. In this session, where the applicant is carefully screened to ensure that anyone with a 'Rambo' mentality is rejected, Stoner's answers to some of the questions did not sit well with the interviewer.

In one of the tests, when Stoner was asked several questions to which there were no right or wrong answers, the problem was posed to him; 'A terrorist takes a child hostage, threatening to kill the child if you approach. You cannot shoot without hitting the child. If you do not shoot, the terrorist will escape and detonate a car-bomb which will kill countless civilians. What would you do?'

Stoner replied that he would walk towards the pair, and if the terrorist killed the child, then he would kill the terrorist. His reasoning was that if the terrorist was allowed to escape with the child, the outcome would still be the same; excess baggage slowed you down - the child would be disposed of anyway.

The interviewer, in writing up his findings, expressed some concerns regarding the outcome of the tests, but conceded that Stoneman was not the first soldier to have such behaviour patterns. He stated that Stoneman would obey orders without question, no matter what the order, and was highly self-motivated. He also commented that Stoneman had an almost obsessive desire to be a part of the regiment, and would not take rejection lightly.

The final panel, all veteran SAS campaigners, accepted him into the regiment despite the psych evaluation. They did so because liked the young man's determination. But more so, perhaps, because they saw a little bit of themselves in him. It was the greatest day of his life when he was 'badged', and proudly wore the sand-coloured beret with the famous winged dagger, the insignia of the SAS.

He excelled in the regiment, his natural ability with languages proving to be a tremendous asset. On his first day in Columbia, one of his 'pupils', angry at being singled out for special attention, spent several moments describing in detail the size of Stoner's mother's breasts and genitalia, and what he would do to them given half a chance.

The man's mouth gaped open when Stoner, who had been speaking in English, switched to fluent spanish, explaining to the man how much he loved and respected his mother. He then drew his pistol and shot the man in both knees, a 'Belfast Special'.

The only difference was that there was no Royal Victoria Hospital here, and no doctors who could replace kneecaps with pieces of plastic which were almost as good as the real thing. No, this man was going to be a cripple for the rest of his days, if he did not die from the onset of infection. The lesson was quickly learned; the gringo was not someone to be messed with.

Stoner saw action with the regiment in various parts of the world. Some were covert but others, like the Falklands where he had put his knowledge of Spanish to good use, were well publicised, adding all the while to the mystique surrounding the unit. And then there was Northern Ireland, that melting pot of religious strife and patriotic fervour which proved to be his undoing. His blood pressure skyrocketed each time he thought of the incident which forced him like an outcast from the regiment he loved, and of the shame and embarrassment which followed.

He and his team had staked out a barn in Crossmaglen, the 'Cross' in South Armagh, keeping the place under surveillance for several days from a vantage point overlooking the farm. Technically they were described as a reactive-observation post, military speak for an ambush detail.

The barn belonged to Kevin Hughes, a local IRA volunteer who was thought to have been involved in the murders of at least eight off-duty policemen. Yet the local authorities were unable to catch him; there was always a cast-iron alibi. His reputation was such that it was suggested that he receive 'special attention', hence the covert surveillance.

For days the men watched the barn, taking turns snuggled in warm sleeping bags burrowed into the ground; two men on watch while the other two slept. When their shift was up, the two men on duty would crawl into the comfort of the down-filled bags exited by their comrades, a technique known as 'hotbedding'. Every movement in or out of the farm was meticulously recorded in plastic-backed notebooks, any conversations monitored by a directional microphone.

To the casual observer, Hughes was the epitome of a hard-working farmer. Always up early to milk the cows, then out to the fields, but under that innocent veneer was a cruel, merciless killer. A concrete bunker, laden with weapons and explosives, was concealed in the barn which the team had under surveillance. They had to catch Hughes in the act of moving the weapons, otherwise he would deny knowledge of the cache and plead the innocent victim of a frame by the Brits.

The days dragged by. Just as the men were beginning to get restless, the monotony was broken by a red Ford Granada, unknown to the team, which pulled up outside the house and off-loaded three men. One of them knocked on the front door of the farmhouse while the others waited by the car. Through his night-vision goggles Stoner could easily make out the faces of the men; they were all members of an Active Service Unit known to be operating in the area.

Each time the ASU went out, someone in the security forces died, sometimes more than one person. Their last outing resulted in the death of a bricklayer who had been hired to do some work on the local police station. He was shot to death as he watched television with his four children, the eldest of whom was seven years old.

Hughes appeared at the door, spoke to the men for a few minutes, then walked with them to the barn. Stoner and his team watched as Hughes and the other dressed themselves in navy boiler-suits and black balaclavas, 'standard' provo uniform. They were, according to their conversation, going to take out a local schoolteacher and his wife, whom they suspected of being police informants. Apparently young children in the area were being asked strange questions by the couple regarding the activities of their parents.

A trap had been laid, with one of the children being told to pass on a piece of information about a robbery being planned. That tidbit resulted in a certain bank getting staked out by the security forces, a fact which did not go unnoticed by the locals.

And so the schoolteacher and his wife were slated for execution.

On hearing the discussion, Stoner immediately called control, explained the situation, and asked permission to take out the ASU. The reply came back a few minutes later; do not take any action against the ASU. Maintain surveillance and catch the team when they returned with their weapons. That response was another example of many orders which Stoner had been forced to obey, to stand back and watch as innocent civilians died, all for the greater good.

He could stand it no longer. Here were two ordinary people, taking extraordinary risks to provide security forces with information which could capture terrorists, and they were being tossed to the wolves. Left unprotected, they were now at the mercy of the creatures of the night whom they sought to eradicate.

He paused for a moment, reflecting on his proposed course of action, then flipped the switch on the radio several times, stating that the transmission was breaking up. He left the radio switched on and crawled back to where the team were preparing for a fire-fight. He told them the transmission had been garbled and that there was no definite answer. He would make the decision. They would take the ASU out before they left the farm. There was no argument from the other members of the team as they slunk off into the darkness to take up their ambush positions.

Stoner did not expect the ASU to surrender their weapons and come peacefully. True to form, as soon as he called out to them to drop their weapons, they opened fire immediately, running for cover in the barn. Their fire was erratic, unlike the surgical precision of the men in the bushes. In a matter of seconds all four members of the ASU lay dead or dying. A huge quantity of weapons was recovered from the barn, and forensics tests later proved that some of the guns had been used in recent killings.

The only casualty on the SAS side was the radio transmitter, which somehow had taken a burst of fire from one of the terrorists' weapons. That made it virtually impossible to determine why it had broken down at such a crucial point in the operation.

However, despite the success of the mission, an inquest held at Stirling Lines, the SAS headquarters, disputed the story given to them by Stoner. The verdict was that he should be RTU'd (returned to unit), effectively banishing him from the regiment, the greatest shame which could be accorded a member of the SAS. Stoner listened to the verdict, his ears scarcely believing what he was hearing.

He resigned from the service immediately, rather than facing his former unit; the shame would have been unbearable. Unfortunately for him, a much bigger shock lay in store. Civvy street, the real world, did not really have a place for former soldiers like himself. Jobs were scarce and consisted mostly of part-time assignments as bouncers, minders, or security guards, none of which held any appeal for him. As a result, he drifted from one job to the next, unable to settle in any one place, finding comfort only in the bottom of a glass.

It was in a bar one evening, a little out-of-the-way place called the Hare and Hound, in Isleworth, that he noticed an ad in the newspaper for ex-professional soldiers. Having consumed several pints of best bitter, and being temporarily out of work again, he called the number and arranged for an interview. The mere mention of the SAS opened all sorts of doors for him, and the pay for a mercenary soldier was astronomical, compared to the pittance he had been paid in the regiment.

With each assignment his reputation for 'getting the job done' grew within the netherworld of the mercenary community. His fee also increased and, much to his astonishment, people actually paid what he asked without question. He had set aside a fair nest-egg for his retirement, but the lull after each assignment found him growing restless, and thoughts of retirement were pushed farther and farther away.

He craved action, like an addict searching for a

fix, and it was in the deserts of the middle-east, or the steaming jungles of South America or Central Africa, he found what he needed. He was never more alive than when he was stalking a target, preparing for the kill.

Also available by Roy French:

A SENSE OF HONOUR

WHO DARES WINS

Terrorism, violence, and suspense combine to make this dynamic novel a thrilling page-turner that the reader will be unable to put down. Tension builds as a terrorist group hijacks a Canadian plane carrying 340 passengers en route from London to Toronto. Immediately we plunge into the murky world of secret agents, enigmatic men and women, whose job is to obtain information and kill without mercy.

Available from:
Shady Vale Publishing
527 Brunswick Avenue
Toronto, Ontario M5R 2Z6
(416) 709-1907

PRINTED IN CANADA